LITTLE
ALTAR BOY

John Guzlowski

Kasva Press

Make its bowls, ladles, jars and pitchers with which to offer libations: make them of pure gold.

St. Paul / Alfei Menashe

Kasva Press LLC
Alfei Menashe, Israel
St. Paul, Minnesota

www.kasvapress.com
info@kasvapress.com

Little Altar Boy

ISBN's:
Trade Paperback: 978-1-948403-15-3
Ebook: 978-1-948403-17-7

10 9 8 7 6 5 4 3 2 1

LITTLE
ALTAR BOY

PRAISE FOR *SUITCASE CHARLIE* (HANK & MARVIN—CHICAGO DETECTIVES BOOK 1)

"A tough-as-rusty-nails police procedural set in Chicago in the spring of 1956, terrorized by a series of child killings... Each environment seems spookier than the last in a narrative driven by lyrical anxiety."

— Tom Nolan, *The Wall Street Journal*

"Every detective has a case that haunts him. For the Chicago cops Hank Purcell and Marvin Bondarowicz, that would be the 'dead kid in the suitcase' whose broken body epitomizes 'some kind of evil that was one-of-a-kind, fresh and original down to its buttons.' Guzlowski...lets us know that, back in the day, the city of Chicago was an all-around rough town."

— Marilyn Stasio, *The New York Times*

"James Ellroy fans will appreciate this grim portrayal of the hunt for a serial killer, poet Guzlowski's first novel."

— *Publishers Weekly*

When the first boy was found in the first suitcase, Hank had thought it was the work of a crazy person who had gone off and done one terrible, crazy thing, and he figured the killer's madness would somehow suddenly dissolve and he'd never do such a thing again.

Hank was wrong.

That one terrible thing had happened again...

To Linda — who helped me with every word and more.

PROLOGUE

Nights in the winter in the snow, the old man would kneel in front of the church, weeping until the priest came out and told him to move on.

The old man did as he was told. He was a good Catholic, a good boy, and he always did what the fathers asked him to do.

He struggled off his knees and turned toward home.

And then the priest went back into the dark church and found a pew near the confessionals and prayed for his own soul.

Chapter I

ELEVEN DAYS AFTER Christmas, Hank Purcell was still grumpy, still feeling like Ebenezer Scrooge.

It was 8 PM, and he had been waiting for his daughter Margaret to get home for the last two hours, since supper. And he wasn't getting any less pissed off.

She'd called him from her friend Maureen's house, and she'd said she was coming right home, and maybe she had set out, but the snow coming down probably wasn't helping any. Or maybe she hadn't set out for home. And maybe she hadn't been calling from Maureen's house.

She was always late. Or absent. Or fucked up.

He didn't know why she was like that. He remembered her as a kid, always reading big old novels by Louisa May Alcott and Charles Dickens and drawing pictures of pandas and talking to him and her mom about turtles or sea anemones. Back then, Margaret loved science and the water, and her favorite thing was going down to Fullerton Beach and looking for spiders or ants or any little thing that somehow had managed to survive all the garbage the City of Chicago dumped into Lake Michigan every single day.

But she wasn't like that now. She was nineteen years old, and now she seemed to be more interested in garbage, the shit she and her friends were hearing about love and sex and drugs from the rock and roll records they were listening to. All those Beatles and Rolling Stones and Jefferson Airplanes with their songs about living in yellow submarines and spending the night together and taking pills to get high and then taking other pills to get unhigh.

And it seemed worse since Christmas.

Standing next to the Christmas tree, Hank looked out the window at the falling snow. It was coming down in big wet flakes the size of moths, and he knew the snow would be pretty heavy and deep by the time morning came. He had a funny thought. Maybe work would be cancelled, and he wouldn't have to go down to Shakespeare Substation. That would be nice. It had been a long time since he had a vacation. Even a small one. It would be good not to have to go and try to make sense of the shit that was always going down at the police station.

He remembered when he first made detective. That was seventeen years ago, back in 1950, after five years as a patrolman. He thought making detective was special back then, thought he was special, going down to the station house every day, trying to figure out who the bad guys were and what he was going to do about them. He remembered his first case — the one where the Polack gambler stabbed his wife in the face and gouged her cheek open with a fountain pen. He even remembered the guy's name: Dulik. The guy pleaded not guilty due to temporary insanity. He claimed he had spent four years in the Buchenwald concentration camp and claimed his wife said something to him in German that sounded like something a guard said to him once. It drove him nuts.

Hank knew it was probably all bullshit, but it was the kind of bullshit that made sense. He had been in the war too, seen Buchenwald and some of the other camps, knew what the German guards were like. He wished he could have given Dulik a pass, but he couldn't. His wife's face was a mess, and it would always be a mess because of what Dulik did to it, no matter how many stitches they sewed into her cheek.

The Polack got two years in Joliet for his bad memories of Buchenwald.

Hank shrugged and wondered for a moment if Joliet was anything like Buchenwald. He doubted it, but he wished he could ask Dulik anyway. But he knew he couldn't. The Polack gambler who stabbed his wife in the face was dead, killed by some Simon City gangster in a shower — about a year into his sentence.

Memories. Hank had a boatload of them. More than twenty years a cop. A couple of years busting his ass in the army before that. And twenty years of living in the city before that. A lot of it was shit, the Great Depression, the World War, the killers and thugs he met every day. He could sure use a small vacation and some warm summer wind, the kind of wind Frank Sinatra was always singing about in that song about walking on golden sand.

But Hank bet he wasn't going to get one. Not even a tiny vacation.

Where was his daughter? What the hell was she doing? Listening to some Rolling Stones mumbo jumbo. "Get off of My Cloud"? "19th Nervous Breakdown"? "Mother's Little Helper"? All that shit in those songs about how the kids' fathers and mothers were messing with their minds.

Hank didn't trust any of her friends either, the girls or the guys. Hippies and druggies. Dropouts and boozers. Every one of them. When he asked her about them, she would always say the same thing. "Man, they're cool."

Cool?

He shrugged and shook his head and said, "Fuck." Said it out loud. Said it like he hoped his wife Hazel back in the kitchen could hear him and explain to him where they went wrong in raising their daughter.

The doorbell rang just then, but he knew it wasn't Margaret. She never rang the bell. Mostly she snuck in the back way, hoping to not run into Hank and his smoldering anger.

From the kitchen, Hazel called out, "Hank, could you see who that is?"

"Sure, honey," he said, and went to answer the front door. It had to be a real eagle scout, he thought, to be walking through all that snow flaking and clumping down from the cold, purple evening clouds.

It wasn't.

"Sister Mary Philomena!" he said as he opened the door.

The nun hadn't changed much in the ten years or so since he had worked with her on that Suitcase Charlie business. She was still short and plump and formidable. But now her black coat was white with snow.

"Sister, you're covered with snow. Come on in."

"Thank you," she said, stepping in. "It's snowing quite hard. I was afraid the Diversey Avenue bus wasn't going to be able to make it here. It kept sliding on the snow. At one point, it almost smashed into a parked car. I started praying as fast as I could then."

"I guess those prayers must have worked, Sister," Hank said, smiling.

Hazel came in then. "Sister, you must be freezing. That snow is so wet. Hank, please take her coat. And I'll get the sister something warm to drink. Maybe some tea?"

Hank looked at his wife. He gave her the look he usually saved for impossible situations that made no sense and had no solution he could figure out. Hazel lifted her eyebrows.

Hank took the nun's coat and hung it in the closet near the front door. He smiled. "Sister, I'm surprised anyone's out on a night like this. It's really coming down."

"Detective Purcell, I don't know where to begin, but I must. Is there someplace where we can talk in private?"

Hazel looked confused.

"Sure, Sister, we can talk in the basement. We've got a rec room down there, some nice couches and chairs. It's a good place to talk."

Once downstairs, Hank watched the nun sit down on the couch, and then he sat across from her. He kept thinking this was not going to go well. For a long time, she didn't say anything. She seemed worried, confused. Unsure of herself. She sat there rubbing her chin and running her fingers along the line where her habit met her right cheek.

This wasn't the way she usually looked. Usually she was determined and purposeful, focused. He remembered when she helped him make sense of some of the clues in the Suitcase Charlie murders. Back then, she acted almost like an evidentiary professor, giving a lesson she had given a thousand times before.

He waited for her to be like that again, to compose herself. Pull herself together.

"Detective Purcell, I need your help."

"Sure, Sister, anything, you just name it."

"It's hard to talk about what I have to talk about," she said and paused for a moment, looked around the rec room.

"Take your time, Sister. There's no rush."

"But there is, Detective. There's something terrible happening. I saw it today, for the first time, and it stopped me like a death."

Hank pulled back a bit, and then he leaned forward and listened.

"After the early morning Mass, the six o'clock one, I was measuring the altar for a new altar cloth, and I thought I was alone in the church. It was so silent. Not many people come to those early Masses anymore. Mostly it's just the old widows who live near the church. But even they were gone by then, and the church was empty. I couldn't hear anything. I dropped my tape measure. It was one of the new ones that roll into themselves, and it dropped behind the altar, and I bent down to pick it up, and I looked through the door to the sacristy, and I saw something there."

Sister Mary Philomena stopped then.

Hank had seen this before. He knew she had something to say and what she had to say was going to change everything, change the world as she knew it, and he knew she couldn't bring herself to say it because she was afraid of what this new world would be like.

Hank didn't want to press her. She had to bring it out herself at her own time, her own speed. He waited.

She looked down at her hands. It looked to Hank like she wished she had a rosary in them.

Sister Mary Philomena looked up then, and for a moment made eye contact with Hank.

"I saw one of the parish priests there, and he was doing something. It was something bad."

She said it, and she stopped. She looked back at her hands.

Hank knew what she was feeling. Whatever she had seen the priest do had somehow transferred to her. Women were like that.

They were good at taking on the sins of the world, making them their own. He was surprised Jesus Christ hadn't been a woman. It would have made a whole lot of sense in a hell of a lot of ways.

Then she looked up again, and Hank saw something in her eyes. He knew he was going to hear what it was the priest had been doing, and it was going to come out straight and fast. And it was going to be bad.

She stood up then and said it.

"When I looked, it was sort of dark, and the father's back was to me, and there was an altar boy sitting on his lap, like the father was Santa Claus and this boy was telling him what he wanted for Christmas. I could see his face, the boy's face, and I recognized him. He's one of Sister Patricia's sixth graders, Tommy Sawa. He saw me too, and there was a frightened look on his face. Like he knew he was doing something bad. And he was. I saw the father's hand was near Tommy's right thigh. I don't know if Tommy's zipper was up or down, but I could see the father was doing something with his hand, maybe he was shaking something or rubbing something. I couldn't see what. But I think I know what it was. The boy was so frightened, and he looked so guilty. It had to be bad, really bad. I think the father was doing something, and Tommy knew it was wrong, and I knew it too, and Tommy saw me and he looked frightened and guilty, and he knew I knew, and he knew he was in trouble."

Sister Mary Philomena stopped then. Hank could see she wasn't done, but he knew she had to stop. She was going where she knew she had to go, but she would need more courage than she had ever had before, and it would take her a while to gather that courage together, bring it up from the back kitchens of her soul.

Just then, he heard the back door to the rec room open, the door that led in from the backyard and the garage beyond it.

It was his daughter Margaret.

"Hey, Daddy," she said in a lazy drawl as she stepped into the rec room and stopped when she saw the sister standing in front of the couch.

Margaret was stoned.

Hank knew it by the way she smiled and didn't look at anything at all really.

He turned to Sister Mary Philomena and smiled.

"Hi, honey," he said to his daughter, "I'm talking with the sister about a case right now. You look soaked. You look like you've been walking in the snow for hours. You better go upstairs and change out of those wet clothes. We can talk later."

"All right, Daddy. Sorry for barging in. I'm going to my room. Long day."

Hank watched Margaret carefully climb the stairs pretending she wasn't stoned. She was a bad actor, or maybe he was a good detective, one who had been looking at junkies and seeing through their bullshit for years.

"Sorry, Sister," he said. "My daughter."

Sister Mary Philomena nodded as if she understood the problems he was having with her. And maybe she did.

Hank waited a moment, and then he asked her the question he needed to ask her: "Which priest was it?"

Still standing, she didn't hesitate. "Detective Purcell, it was Father Ted, Father Ted Bachleda."

"Are you sure?"

Sister Mary Philomena didn't say anything for a moment. She just looked at Hank as if he were a clueless third grader. "Yes, I'm sure, and I want you to talk to him, and I want you to tell him you know what he was doing with that poor boy Tommy Sawa, and I want you to tell him to stop."

And then she sat down.

Hank knew the priest, Father Bachleda. He was probably the most popular of the three priests in the parish. There was the pastor, the old priest who ran the show, Father Thomas Plaszek. Then there was Father Anthony, the Polish priest who always seemed a little unsure of himself in English; and there was Father Ted, the youngest of the priests, the cool one, the guy who ran the Teen Club, the parish's club for high-school-aged boys and girls. The guy with all the energy and pizzazz. Good looks and a lot of long black hair too, like one of these recent heartthrobs, Warren Beatty or Bobby Darin. He was always taking the kids to bowling alleys or museums or on field trips to sand dunes in Michigan or Indiana.

"Sister, let me ask you again. This is important. Are you sure about what you saw? Are you sure it was Father Bachleda?"

"I'm sure it was he."

"Sister, I'll talk to him," Hank said, "but I don't think talking to him will work."

"Do you know what I'm trying to say about what he was doing?"

"Yes, I do. I know it's hard for you to say, and I think I understand why you came to me. I'll try to talk to him, but I don't think it will do much good. From what I know about men with this kind of problem, talking to them and asking them to change their ways isn't the way you get them to change. What they're doing has roots that go deep, and those roots aren't going to be changed by having a conversation."

"Maybe it will be different with the father. He's a priest. He knows what's right and what's wrong, and he knows how to stop it or change it. I mean, isn't it his job to tell people how to stop doing things that aren't right in the eyes of God?"

Hank thought about that for a moment. Yes, that's a priest's job, to understand sin and to understand the sinner and show the sinner how he should and could turn from the sin that's making him a sinner. But Hank knew about crime and criminals, and this knowledge told him it wasn't that easy. Understanding sin and stopping it weren't the same thing. A good talking-to would only take you so far.

"Sister," he said finally, "I'll talk to him and see what I can do. Let me drive you home."

"No thank you, you've done enough. I need some time alone. God bless you, Detective. You're a good man."

Hank nodded but didn't say anything. He wished it were true. Both parts. That he was a good man and that God would bless him.

⁂

After he showed the sister out, he went to Margaret's room.

She had changed out of her wet clothes into some dry pajamas, and she sat on her bed with a teen magazine in front of her, *Hullabaloo* or *Rave* or some shit like that.

Standing in the open doorway, he said it slowly, softly. He didn't want to rile her, stir her up the way she sometimes got when they talked. "Honey, please, you got to stop."

"Stop? Stop what?" she said, not looking at him, just turning a page of the magazine, staring at it like she was studying for a test or looking out a window at something strange, unbelievable.

"You got to stop this stuff. You know what I mean. You're high. You've been smoking pot again."

She looked up then and gave him the cold look he knew was coming, and she spoke slowly like he was some kind of idiot and needed to hear each word separately so he could get the point she was trying to make, "No, I haven't. I haven't been smoking. How can you say that?"

"Honey, I'm a cop. I can smell it on your clothes. See it in your eyes, too. As soon as you walked in, I knew it. You've been hanging out with that Maureen again. Hanging out with her and her junkie, loser friends. I told you to stay away from them. They're trouble, and they'll get you into trouble."

She started laughing, but it was a fake laugh. Hank knew it — he had been hearing fake laughs for years. Suddenly she stopped. "I'm not stoned, and Maureen's friends aren't junkies. You don't know anything."

He took a step toward her and pointed his finger at her face. He knew he was losing control, but he couldn't stop himself.

"Look at you! Your eyes — your pupils are the size of quarters. You shuffle around the house with your legs barely moving. The goddamn smell of you. Jesus! You're not stoned? You tell me you're not stoned? What do you think I am — stupid?"

She threw her magazine at him. It hit him in the face before he could brace himself. There was no thought in what he did next. He clenched his fists and took a step toward her, and then he stopped. He knew what he wanted to do, and he knew he couldn't.

She started laughing again, but this time it was a real laugh. There was nothing fake about it this time. She was laughing at him.

His wife Hazel came in then.

"Stop it!" she shouted at Margaret.

Margaret didn't stop. She picked up another magazine from her night stand and threw it at Hank, and then she picked up another and threw that too.

Hank looked at Hazel. "You got to fix this. I can't."

He shook his head, took a breath, and walked out of the room.

CHAPTER 2

SITTING IN THE unmarked Ford cruiser early the next afternoon with his partner Marvin Bondarowicz, Hank took a long drag on his cigarette and let the smoke drift out slowly. He watched the haze fill the car, make everything seem dreamy for a moment. Then he took another drag, deeper this time.

Outside, big flat snowflakes fell the way they had been falling since last night. A soft slow swirl through the gray air.

Hank looked out the window at the ice and snow ruts in the street. The mounds between them must be almost eight inches high. Eight inches high and dirty with oil and coal dust, the sludge that always blew around the Chicago streets.

Marvin snapped him back to the present. "Hey, what the fuck, Hank? We don't have all day with this. What're you stalling for? This is no big deal. We go in, tell the priest he's been caught with his pants around his ankles, and he better cut the shit out or we'll cook his Polack ass, and we're out of there."

"Yeah, a piece of cake," Hank said slowly. "I'm not worried about it. I'm thinking about Margaret."

Marvin screwed the cap off his half-pint bottle of Jack Daniel's and took a pull.

"Margaret?" he said. "That cutie? She doesn't need your worrying, my friend. She's nineteen, a straight-A college freshman at the Circle, and she's got it all figured out. In a couple of years, she'll be going to grad school and dreaming about being a professor."

"She came home stoned yesterday. I could smell the fucking pot all over her. She'd been drinking too. It wasn't the first time."

"Come on, man. That's no big deal. All the kids are smoking now. Grass won't hurt you. Especially this Hoosier shit the kids are smoking. It's 95% Polish oregano. It's LSD you got to watch out for. That's one fucking weird drug, acid. Makes you see mushrooms growing out of your dead daddy's ears. The setting sun turning into a bucket of yellow jello. Or some kid on a merry-go-round yelling at you about the Bay of Pigs. I know what I'm talking about. Yesterday, I saw this guy in the station holding-cell who was high on it. He couldn't even tell you his name or what he had for lunch or whether two and two still made four. He just kept mumbling about Jesus being in the blender and the refrigerator being on fire."

"Have you tried it?" Hank asked.

Marvin took another pull of the Jack Daniel's and shook the bottle. "Say, you want some of this?"

Hank shook his head. "Have you tried it? The acid?"

Marvin smiled. "Yeah, I've had acid. It's tasty in a weird and unpredictable sort of way. But it sure does fuck you up."

Hank rolled down the window and flicked his cigarette butt into the dirty snow in the middle of the street.

"You're not making me feel any better about this, Marv. I'm worried she's hanging out with some bad kids and she can't see what kind of trouble she can get into."

"Hank, come on, take it easy. You and Hazel raised a great kid. She's smart, loves school, dreams about the science stuff she's learning and becoming a teacher. You got a star there, Hank. You been telling me for nineteen fucking years about how great a kid she is and how she loves doing all the right things, and now she comes home a little high, and right away you're making her into a junkie."

"Yeah."

Marvin screwed the cap back on his bottle and slipped it into his overcoat's inside pocket. "Jesus Christ, man. Relax already. You need some fun. Let's get in there and shake up this priest. Really fuck him up!"

"I told you already. That's not what the sister wanted. We're going to take it easy."

Marvin shrugged and laughed. "Whatever you say, daddy-o. I'm cool."

<hr>

The old housekeeper showed them into the main sitting room in the rectory, a big room with a couple of couches and some easy chairs set up in a circle. She pointed to an old brown sofa, nodded and said something in Polish, and then turned away.

"I think she wants us to sit, Hank."

"I guess. I don't know why people always figure cops want to sit down."

"I bet that housekeeper used to be a looker," Marvin said, "but that was probably back in Warsaw before the last war or maybe the one before that. Yeah, a real looker. Like Pola Negri. You remember her? That old silent movie broad? She was a Polack too. You remember? Jesus, where do they find these ancient babes? She's just old raggedy clothes and boobs that stretch down to her knees now. I bet it's pretty tough for her to even wash these floors."

Hank had stopped listening a while ago, but he nodded anyway.

The door to the vestry opened then, and Father Bachleda came in. Smiling and extending his hand, he said, "Gentlemen, please have a seat. The couches are old but still hospitable. Comfy as can be. Can I get you a cup of coffee . . . some tea? Maybe something a little stronger? It's getting late in the day, and it will definitely be cocktail time pretty soon."

Hank sat down on the couch nearest the door and Marvin joined him.

"I wish I could take you up on that drink, Father. But I'm afraid we're here on business."

"Business?" the priest asked, as he sat down in an easy chair opposite Hank and Marvin. "Is it something about that break-in over at the old convent on Washtenaw last week?"

"No, Father," Hank said. "It's something else. There's no easy way to say this so I'm just going to say it. We've heard something about you doing something you shouldn't be doing. Something inappropriate."

Father Bachleda didn't move, didn't stop smiling. "What are you talking about?"

"It looks like someone saw you doing something with one of the altar boys from the school that you shouldn't be doing. It looked like you had your hand in his pants."

The priest's body jerked forward in the easy chair.

"What?" he said. "This is absurd, crazy. I won't listen to this."

He started to stand up.

Marvin gave him a hard look and raised his hands with his palms up, and then he said, "Father, sit down. Relax. You ain't going nowhere, and neither are we."

The priest had stopped smiling. "Who told you this? Who's making these accusations? I want to know."

"The source is unimpeachable, Father," Hank said. "I can't tell you who it is, but it's someone who saw you and got in touch with us."

"And you're going to believe this person over me, a priest?"

"Yes, we are."

"Ridiculous!"

"Father, listen. Our informant saw you with this boy, identified the boy by name. The informant identified you also, and told us what you were doing. And what you were doing will get you arrested in any one of the fifty states."

"Is that what you're saying? Are you arresting me? In that case, I want a lawyer."

"Father, the informant asked us not to arrest you. We were asked to give you a warning. This is it."

"Good God, this is absurd. You accuse me of committing an act that goes against everything I believe, against everything the Holy Catholic Church stands for, and you don't allow me the recourse of confronting the people who made this ugly accusation. How dare you? How dare you!"

Leaning forward, Marvin said, "Listen Father, this is what it is. It's like a warning ticket. This time there's no judge, no jury, no penalty, not even a fine to pay. Next time, we'll come down with the heavy hammers and bust your fucking balls. This here? For now, it's just a friendly warning."

The priest stood up. "I want you two men out of here, along with your accusations and your secret informants. Get out. Dirty, ugly accusations! Get out! Now!"

"Father," Hank said as he stood up, "we're leaving, but the warning stands. Stay away from the boys. Stay clean or you'll be hearing from us, and the next time you see us, we'll be bringing trouble with us."

"Get out, you filth!"

———◆———

Marvin waited for Hank outside the rectory. "What was that all about?"

"What do you mean?" Hank said as he continued walking through the snow toward their car.

"We're talking to an asshole priest who's holding hands with little boys and worse, and all we do is give him a warning?"

"Yeah, that's all we were asked to do."

"Since when did we do just what we're asked to do? You know like I do that now this guy is just going to hide the shit he does. He's not going to stop it."

"Yeah," Hank said, and got into the car.

Marvin got in too, and shut the door. "Guys like him don't take you seriously unless you break off some of their fingers and leave them on the sidewalk for the sparrows to peck at."

"So why didn't you break his fingers? Shove them down his throat? You were there, the same as me."

"Cool it, man. You know you're the boss, and I follow your lead. You don't fuck with him, so I don't fuck with him. But that doesn't mean I can't complain."

"Lighten up, Marvin. I don't need to hear any of this from you today."

Marvin looked at Hank for a moment. Then he said, "Really, you're getting more like your mother every day."

"What the hell are you talking about? You never met my mother."

"You're getting to be an old lady, Hank, that's what I'm talking about. Next thing you know you'll be wearing a skirt and knitting baby blankets."

CHAPTER 3

HAZEL PUT THE two bowls of lentil soup on the kitchen table.

Hank loved soup. He could eat soup every day, but especially in winter. Something about the steam rising on a cold January day brought him back to himself, his family, his home.

He looked at Hazel and asked, "Margaret's not having supper with us tonight?"

"I guess not. I didn't hear from her after school. Before she left this morning, she said she might spend some time with her friend Judy after class. She said she would phone, but she didn't."

Hank watched Hazel dip her spoon into the soup, draw the hot brown liquid toward her lips.

"She was stoned the other night, honey," Hank said. "I smelled the marijuana on her when she came in through the back door to the basement. I think she may have been drinking too."

"I was afraid of that. I tried to talk to her when she finally came upstairs, but she said she was tired and needed to work on something for school. A project about wind turbines, or something like that."

"Wind turbines?" Hank shook his head.

"I hate to see you two arguing, fighting like that."

"Me too."

"It hurt me to see how she threw those magazines at you."

"Yeah, hurt me too," Hank said and smiled. "Do you know who she's hanging out with now?" he asked as he set his spoon down. "Her college friends?"

Hazel gave him a long steady look and then said, "Well, of course I know who *some* of her friends are — the ones from the neighborhood who she's been going to school with since she was in kindergarten. The rest of them? No."

"Isn't it funny she's not dating someone, someone steady?"

"It's not like it was when we were that age. Kids don't get that exclusive anymore. At least that's what Margaret always says when I ask her if there's some special boy."

"So where is she right now? What the heck does she do after classes are over if she doesn't come home? Does she hang out at the library? Go to some malt shop? Why don't we know where she is? I bet she's someplace smoking it up right now. Rolling a joint, lighting it up, dragging the smoke in deep. And we don't have any idea where she's doing this!"

"Hank, we've always trusted her. Since she was a little girl. We trusted her to make the right choices about her friends, make the right choices about what she did and who she did it with. And it's always worked out. I think we need to keep trusting her."

"Trust her? Sure, it always worked out when she was a little girl, but she isn't a little girl anymore — now she's smoking grass and drinking. For Christ's sake, Hazel. She's nineteen."

"Tell me you didn't do stupid things when you were nineteen. I know I did."

"I did stupid things, but I wasn't stoned on marijuana or LSD when I did them. If I had been, I might not have survived to be sitting here talking to you about our daughter."

The phone in the living room rang once and then stopped. Hank looked up. Then it rang again.

"Hank, that's probably her. Let me take it. You're too upset to talk to her right now."

Hazel stood up and walked to the phone, and Hank turned to his soup again. The steam had left, gone away. The soup was barely warm now, its brown surface coagulated into some kind of glutinous mess. This wasn't what he had hoped for when he sat down to eat.

Hazel's voice sounded from the living room.

"Hank, it's for you. It's not Margaret, it's Marvin."

Hank stood up and walked to the living room.

Hazel handed him the phone.

"What's up, Marvin?"

"Hank, you won't believe this. Sister Mary Philomena is dead."

CHAPTER 4

HANK WATCHED THE forensics guys finish up their work.

One of them was packing up his camera. Another took a final look at some coal dust on the floor next to Sister Mary Philomena's body, some kind of configuration near her left foot.

A lot of coal dust littered the basement floor. The boiler furnace measured about the size of a milk truck, and the coal shed that fed it probably came in at 20 feet by 10 feet. Hank knew it would be no trouble to get prints of all kinds, footprints and fingerprints and body prints.

The sister lay on the floor in front of the furnace. The door to the furnace was open and the fire was out now, but Hank could still feel the heat slowly rolling out of it and warming up the basement. Hank looked at Marvin standing by the wall across from the body. He had already taken off his overcoat, and he was fanning himself with his hat.

"What do you think, Chet?" Marvin asked the forensics guy studying the coal dust.

"I think I would be done and out of your hair faster if you didn't ask me stupid questions, Bondarowicz," the forensics guy said without lifting his face from the dust.

Marvin shrugged. "Okay, I just wanted to make sure you weren't nodding off over that coal dust."

Chet called over the fellow with the camera and had him unpack his lenses again and take some close-in shots of the dusty area near the sister's foot.

Hank and Marvin waited.

Sister Mary Philomena's body lay there, outlined in chalk. She looked like she died climbing a series of tall steps: her right leg was raised at a clean right angle, while her left leg was straight, unbent. Blood covered much of the floor around her body, and there was even some on her face and her stiff, square white bib. Hank remembered they didn't call a nun's bib a bib. It probably had some kind of fancy French or Italian name, but if he ever knew what that was, he'd long ago forgotten it; he'd have to find out the right word for it when he started writing up his report. He figured that whoever killed the nun used a knife of some kind, stabbed her in the stomach a bunch of times, perforated her lungs too. She must have died coughing up blood while fighting back. That much was clear from the blood around her mouth, the blood on her hands and black habit, and the blood mixed with the coal dust on the floor — she'd put up some fight. She was tough — he knew that.

Hank watched the forensics guys pack up their gear again.

"So," Marvin said, "you ready to spill it, Chet?"

"The unofficial version?" Chet said, buttoning his overcoat.

Marvin nodded. "Sure, that's my favorite."

"Sister Patricia came down to the basement after dinner to get some textbooks out of a storage locker, and she found Sister Mary Philomena here. The murder took place early this evening, about 7 PM, a couple hours ago. The victim was stabbed a number of times."

"A *number of times?*" Marvin interrupted. "We can see that, Mister Wizard."

"Fuck you. You want to hear this, or not?

"Sure, sure, sorry."

"I'm guessing she died quickly, but it wasn't instantaneous. She struggled with her assailant, struggled hard, but it didn't last long. You can tell because there's a lot of blood where she fell, but not a lot of blood spray patterns. The first cops who showed up said the basement door was open and there were footprints in the snow leading away from the basement door. We checked them, the footprints, but couldn't determine if they were done recently by the perpetrator or earlier. This door leads to the walkway between the convent and the school, and that walkway gets a lot of traffic. It's a pretty regular short cut for the folks in the neighborhood."

"Anything else, Chet?"

"Yeah, it looks like the sister was burning stuff in the furnace just before she was killed."

Hank nodded his head. "What kind of stuff?"

"We pulled some of it out of the furnace — partially burned photos, mostly. Black and whites. Old ones. Small ones. We're going to go through the stuff when we get it to the lab. We might be able to find something, recognize some faces, see if there's anything there that will point us in the right direction. From what I saw, though, there didn't seem to be anything special about them. Some picnic scenes, some nuns in front of churches, some elderly couples, stuff like that. The kind of photos you'd expect. But like I said, we'll give it all the fine-tooth comb, and see if we can find something that will help."

"Where's the patrolman who answered the call?" Hank asked.

"Outside. I'll send him in."

"Thanks, Chet."

Hank watched Sister Mary Philomena's body being lifted onto a stretcher. She seemed shorter now, lighter; the men lifting the nun didn't seem to have any problem with her body. He had always thought of her as solid and strong, but maybe it was just her personality and the habit she wore that gave that impression. He liked her. She always seemed to know what was going on, and even when she didn't know everything, she had a way of making you feel she had a knack for keeping chaos at bay. The perfect kind of nun.

He turned to Marvin. His partner had found a folding chair in the basement's shadows and was sitting there across from the furnace.

"What do you think, Marvin?"

"I think somebody who hated her and wanted to hurt her really bad did this. I bet the forensics guys are going to come back in a couple of days and tell us she was stabbed a bunch of times, maybe twenty-five, thirty times, and the blows were hard and killed her quick — but the killer continued stabbing anyway."

Hank nodded. "I thought the same thing. Crime of hate. We ought to go talk to Father Bachleda after we talk to Sister Patricia and get statements from the other nuns upstairs in the convent."

CHAPTER 5

A YOUNG NUN, a novice, in a mostly white habit led the two detectives to the convent's reception room and asked them to be seated.

Marvin looked around.

"Remember the old convent? That place was okay, but this place is deluxe. Dig the size of this room and these brown leather chairs. Beats those old hard wooden chairs all to hell."

Hank looked at the black hat in his hands. Talking to the people who knew the victim was the part of his job he hated the most. It reminded him of the war, sitting in the company tent and trying to figure out what to say in a letter to the parents or wife of one of the guys in his company who had died. Sorry for your loss? Sorry for my loss? Sorry for telling you the worst news you could hear?

In a lot of ways that had been easier than this. In the war he'd imagine what the loved ones felt, what their trembling was like, what their tears sounded like, but he didn't actually have to see any of it. As a cop he had to see all that and more. One bad thing after another, and then there would be the questions he'd have to ask the person sitting there grieving in front of him — asking, basically, *did you kill him, did you kill her? Was the source of this grief that you're grieving the work of your own hands? Did you bring this mess into the world?*

The door to the reception room opened then, and a tall middle-aged nun with a pale face entered. Her eyes were red and puffy from crying. Hank didn't recognize her, and he stood up and introduced himself. Marvin followed his lead.

"Detectives, please sit down. I'm Sister Rosemary, the Mother Superior of the nuns in this convent." She said that and then she didn't say anything for a while. She just stood there swaying a little, like she had been hit by something and was thinking of dropping to her knees.

And then she spoke. "This is a horrible day, gentlemen. All of us want to do whatever we can to find the person who committed this terrible crime, this murder."

"We were friends of Sister Mary Philomena," Hank said. "We knew her from the days when the sisters were still in the old convent on the corner of Washtenaw and Evergreen. She helped us a lot when we were investigating the Suitcase Charlie killings."

Sister Rosemary nodded her head. Hank could see the tears in her eyes. She pulled a handkerchief from her sleeve and touched it to her cheeks.

"Detectives, I don't know how much I can help."

"I know it's hard. We just need to get some basic information from you. Could you tell us why Sister Mary Philomena would have been in the basement, in the boiler room? Was that something she was responsible for?"

"No, not really. The janitor, Mr. Garbowski, takes care of the boiler and the furnace, everything connected with them both. Here in the convent as well as the other parish buildings, the school, the church, and the rectory."

"Sister," Marvin began, "can you think of a reason Sister Mary Philomena would have been down there in the furnace room?"

"Honestly, Detective, I've been trying to make sense of that since

I heard about this terrible thing. I just can't think of a reason for her being there. Most of the time the sisters don't give the basement much thought at all. We live in the top three floors of this building. I don't think some of the sisters have ever even been to the furnace room. Normally the only time we go down to the basement is when we have to do laundry, usually on Saturday mornings. And the laundry room is at the opposite end of the basement, the west end."

Hank took out a notepad and quickly sketched out the basement's floor plan showing the furnace and coal shed at one end, the laundry room at the other. He wondered what was between them. He asked, "Do the sisters have someplace down in the basement where they keep their personal belongings?"

"Detective Purcell, we take vows of obedience, chastity, and poverty when we become Sisters of St. Joseph. The vow of poverty demands we not own anything. What most of us do have would fit into a single small suitcase. We don't have lockers or anything like that."

"What kinds of things would you put into that suitcase?" Marvin asked.

"You're asking what we own? It's pretty simple. Our habits, our linens, our rosaries, some prayer books and papers, some letters. If the Archdiocese of Chicago asked me to leave Saint Fidelis this minute and join another parish, I would have my suitcase packed in five minutes and be waiting at the door to leave soon after."

"Sister, you have to forgive some of these questions," Hank said, "but we don't know how nuns live. We don't have a lot of experience with them. Would Sister Mary Philomena have had to ask your permission to go down to the basement?"

Sister Rosemary shook her head. "No, the sisters are free to move throughout the convent. The convent is their home. They don't need my permission or anyone's permission to move from one area of the building to another."

"What if a sister wanted to leave the building? Would she have to ask your permission for that?"

"Yes, to leave the building. Part of the sense of obedience under which we live is a sense of order. Each sister is responsible to the mother superior of her convent, and all of the sisters require her permission to leave the convent. If Sister Mary Philomena was planning to leave the building, she would have had to ask my permission."

"So you would've known, then, if she had recently left the building to go visit someone else."

"Yes, undoubtedly. Sister Mary Philomena hadn't asked my permission to go anywhere in the last two weeks. I could easily verify this, if necessary — I keep a record of the sisters' requests for permission to leave the convent for whatever reason. If they need to go to the library on California Avenue or a store downtown or a conference at Loyola University, they would ask my permission and I would make note of it."

"And when they travel, they seldom travel alone?"

"Yes, of course, the custom for the sisters is to travel in pairs or larger groups. When a sister leaves the convent house, she does so in the company of at least one of the other sisters."

"Always?"

"Detective Purcell, I can't imagine a situation where a sister would travel alone."

Hank nodded. He knew that Sister Mary Philomena did travel alone, at least once — when she came to his house a few days ago to tell him about Father Ted and what she'd seen him doing.

"Thank you, Sister Rosemary," Hank said, "you've been very helpful. We've got one more question. The uniformed policeman who interviewed you reported that you said you didn't hear anything from the basement at the time of the murder. Is that correct?"

"Yes, I didn't hear anything from the basement. It was after dinner, and we were all in our rooms on the second and third floors. I don't think any of us could have heard anything happening down in the basement."

"Thank you again, Sister. I think at this point we'd like to talk to the sisters she was closest to, those she would have considered friends. And we'd like to talk to the nun who found Sister Mary Philomena — Sister Patricia, I believe it was."

"Sister Patricia was a very good friend to Sister Mary Philomena, someone she considered her best friend."

"Thank you, Sister. We'd like to see her."

"I'll call her. I've asked all the sisters to be ready to speak to the police. She'll be right down."

When Sister Rosemary stood up and left the reception room, Hank turned to Marvin. "What do you think?"

"She's upset, but she's holding herself together pretty good," Marvin said, flipping back a few pages in his notebook. "One of your co-workers gets murdered not far from where you're standing and you tend to be a little screwed up, hesitant about your answers and such. I know I would be if they fucked you up with a shiv in the basement of my apartment house, Hank. But Sister Rosemary wasn't like that at all."

"Nuns are different from me and you, Marvin. Remember Mary Philomena back when they found the first of the Suitcase Charlie bodies almost outside her front door? I remember you being surprised about how cool she was, not giving up a thing, no tremors, no tears, just business as usual even though there was a butchered kid found in a suitcase a dozen yards away."

"Yeah, I guess. Sure, Sister Rosemary was crying and dabbing her eyes when she came in, but pretty soon she seemed super cool, man. I couldn't even tell if she knew Philomena, liked her or hated her guts. She didn't give a thing away, not a dot, not a crumb."

Hank heard footsteps in the corridor outside the visitor's room. "I think it's them."

"Yeah."

"I think it's getting late, Marvin. Let's talk to Sister Patricia and leave the other nuns to the uniform cops, Rodriguez and Stromski. That'll give us time to see the priests."

"That's a plan, Stan."

The door opened and Sister Patricia came in.

She wept as she walked into the room, tears streaming down her cheeks and onto her jaw and finally onto her white bib or whatever it was called. She seemed young to Hank. She might have been the youngest-looking nun he had ever seen. With her small, round, makeup-free face framed by the thick black cloth of her habit, she looked like a schoolgirl, a child made up in a nun's habit that belonged to someone else, an older relative maybe.

It seemed to Hank like she wasn't even aware of the tears falling from her eyes.

Marvin stood up first and then Hank slowly followed.

"We're sorry for your loss, Sister Patricia," Marvin said hesitatingly and awkwardly. "We know this has been a terrible shock to you. Sister Rosemary told us you were a good friend of Sister Mary Philomena, and that you had a special bond with her. Both Detective Purcell and I knew her. She was an old friend of ours as well."

The young nun sat down, as her tears continued to fall fast and thick. Marvin looked at Hank with a pained, grieved look. It was like nothing else Hank had ever seen on his partner's face in all the years they'd worked together — a face pressed together by an anger that wasn't anger, a softness that wasn't soft. It was the face of an old man unused to crying, a man who didn't know what to do with his face when the tears came. Hank could see Marvin couldn't say anything more, so he stepped in.

"This won't take long, Sister. We know you want to be alone so you can pray for Sister Mary Philomena's soul. We just want to ask you a handful of questions, and then we'll be out of your hair."

Hank paused and looked at the nun to see if she'd reacted. She had been the first one to see Sister Mary Philomena's dead body, and she was taking it hard. He wasn't surprised. She was a kid. Any death was still a shock to her, still a blow as physical as it was emotional, and a death so violent, with her close friend as the victim, must be completely overwhelming. He remembered again his own first sight of the dead nun, her legs trying to climb a stairway that wasn't there, her bib splattered with her own blood, her body suddenly lost to time, without purpose or direction or identity. A moment before, Sister Mary Philomena had been Sister Mary Philomena, and then she wasn't — she was dead, and not even a whisper of her remained behind, not here. Maybe somewhere else there was some piece of her, in some Heaven or almost-Heaven, but not here, not for Hank or Marvin or her students or Sister Patricia.

So Hank let Sister Patricia weep, let her fill her soul with the loss. He let her weep, and she wept.

And then she didn't. Slowly.

When she was ready to go on, Hank was too.

"I'm sorry, detective," she said, wiping her eyes with her handkerchief, trying to wipe the sorrow from her face.

"No need, Sister. I'm Hank Purcell. This is my partner, Detective Marvin Bondarowicz. Like he said, we were friends of Sister Mary Philomena, too. Worked with her over the years. We know how much she meant to you and all the sisters here, and we realize you might not be ready yet to talk about your friend. That's okay. We understand."

"The sister was such a good and holy person," Sister Patricia said, looking straight into Hank's eyes with an intensity he had seen only in the mad and the most devout. "The children loved her. They could feel something in her, something good and selfless. When they were in trouble, they knew she would help without judgment. And when they weren't in trouble, when they were just loving the air and the wind and running in the spring or among the falling leaves of autumn, they knew she was there too, there and loving the joy in them as they loved the joy in the world swirling around them. I know I shouldn't say this, that some of the older nuns might take it as blasphemy or a sin to say it, but I really feel she had the Jesus gift. That the love Jesus passed on to Mary and Peter and the apostles and that they in turn passed on to many others and those others passed on to so many others, that this gift was there in Sister Mary Philomena, a joy and love she shared and passed on to others in turn: the Jesus gift."

"Amen," Marvin said, and Hank looked at him. He had heard his partner say "amen" hundreds of times, in dark places and in light, where evil had been and where evil had been undone; and Hank knew his partner's "amen" this time, maybe for the first time, was as sincere as any word Marvin had ever spoken.

Hank nodded then and said, "Yes, Sister, she had the gift," but he knew he was lying, or maybe just kidding himself, pretending he knew what the hell she was talking about. He didn't know about the Jesus gift or how to talk about it or how to feel it in Sister Mary Philomena or anybody else. She was dead now, and no gift would bring her back or help her. And whether or not the man or woman who killed her knew anything about the Jesus gift or could feel it in her was a mystery as hard and solid as rock.

Hank waited to see if the sister would say anything else. They sat in silence for a couple of minutes, and Hank looked sideways at Marvin and saw his partner looking at Sister Patricia as if she was some miracle as great as God. Hank was ready to keep waiting, to see where this would go on its own.

Finally, Marvin broke through the sister's grief.

"Sister, we've got to ask you some questions. They're not going to be easy, but we need to find the person who did this terrible thing, and maybe these questions will help."

She nodded her head, and Marvin asked her his first question: "When did you last see Sister Mary Philomena alive?"

"The sisters have dinner between 5:30 and 6:30, and Sister Mary Philomena sat across from me. One of the other sisters was talking about a movie she wanted to see. It's called *The Nun's Story*. The sister had read the book some time ago, and she was curious about the film."

"How did Sister Mary Philomena seem?"

"She seemed cheerful, tired but ready to talk. The day had been hard because of the snow. A number of the children weren't able to make it to school, so she'd been busy on the phone all afternoon telling them about their assignments and whether or not their teachers wanted them to do something special to make up for the lost day."

"Did she talk about her plans for the rest of the evening?"

Sister Patricia nodded and looked like she was about to answer his question, but then she paused. Hank could see that talking about Sister Mary Philomena, remembering her, was hard for the young nun.

"That's okay, Sister," Marvin said. "Take your time."

She gave him a slight smile and said, "At the end of dinner, we all usually spend a minute or two talking about the evening. Sister Mary Philomena told me she needed to spend some time on a project Sister Rosemary had assigned her, going through boxes of papers that came with us from the old convent. Nobody had looked at them or asked about them for years, and she was sure that if nobody had needed them for all this time, they must be unimportant — but the Mother Superior wanted them all gone through and sorted and properly filed anyway. Then she was going to do her evening rosary, and then she planned to do some reading. She loved to read Ralph Waldo Emerson's essays, and she talked about how she was going to read the one called 'Nature' again. It was one of her favorites."

"So she didn't indicate in any way what she might have been doing a short time later in the basement?"

"No, she never mentioned the basement. I assumed she would spend some time on those boxes, pray the rosary, and read the essay in her own room. She had a kneeler there, and usually she liked to pray there on her own. She said she appreciated the lack of distractions."

Hank then asked a question. "Did Sister Mary Philomena have any problems with any of the nuns here?"

"Problems?"

"Yes, like disagreements or arguments, anything that would get her blood boiling?"

Sister Patricia suddenly smiled, and the smile made her look even younger. "It's funny you should use the expression 'blood boiling'. Just yesterday, she said Mother Superior, Sister Rosemary, brought her blood to a boil. It seemed slightly ironic when she said it because she didn't look like her blood was boiling. She looked perfectly placid, in fact, just her usual loving self."

"Did she mention what was bothering her?"

"Oh, yes. It was the same thing that had been bothering her since the beginning of the school year in September. Sister Mary Philomena didn't like the idea of Father Ted Bachleda giving the catechism lessons for the fourth graders. She wanted Father Thomas, the pastor, to offer the lessons."

Hank had been hoping the sister would mention Father Ted. He wanted her to begin the discussion of the young priest on her own. "Why didn't the sister want Father Ted?"

Sister Patricia didn't respond at first. She looked down at the handkerchief clutched in her hands. Hank watched her. He didn't want to rush her. There were times when nothing was as important as silence and patient waiting.

Then she lifted her eyes. "She thought Father Ted was overworked. He puts a lot of time in with the Teen Club for the high-school students, and then he also mentors the seventh and eighth graders. Doing the catechism for the fourth graders would involve at least an hour a day with each of the two fourth-grade classes. She didn't feel that would be fair to Father Ted. He also ran the parish carnival this last spring, and plans to do it this year too. And there's one more thing…Sister Mary Philomena never said this, but I felt she liked Father Thomas, the pastor, more than she liked Father Ted. I think she felt that Father Thomas had a warmth and sincerity the younger students respond well to."

"But sister, how did Sister Rosemary figure in with this?"

"Sister Rosemary is a big supporter of Father Ted. She was one of his first advocates in the parish; she made a very strong case for him when he was interviewed for the Assistant Pastor position back in 1962, and that swayed many of the older members of the parish board. She thought his youth and energy would be a nice balance to the age and experience of the older priests in the parish, Father Thomas and Father Anthony."

"Did you agree with Sister Mary Philomena about all this?" Hank asked, looking up from his notepad.

Sister Patricia paused again, and then she spoke slowly. "I really didn't see all that much difference between the two priests, the pastor and Father Ted. I'm sure they both would do a wonderful job, consistent with their talents."

"Did Sister Mary Philomena say anything else about Father Ted or Father Thomas recently?"

"Well, I mentioned to her yesterday that I had seen Father Ted talking to Father Thomas. They were standing on the corner in front of the church, talking about something, and Father Thomas started laughing. He's a tall man, but he has a small laugh. And then after Father Thomas started laughing, Father Ted joined him. I couldn't see his face, but I could see his back and his back seemed to be laughing."

"His back was laughing?"

"Yes, the way a laugh sometimes expresses itself in our whole body, you know, what they call a big laugh, and Father Ted is certainly a man with a big laugh."

"And how did Sister Mary Philomena respond to this?"

"She was cross . . . not the way she normally is — was — at all.

I don't know why, exactly, but I felt she didn't approve of Father Thomas conversing with Father Ted. Or maybe it was that they were standing there laughing right in front of the church. I'm really not sure what caused her to feel that way."

"Did Sister Mary Philomena ever mention a student by the name of Tommy Sawa? I believe he's a sixth grader."

"Yes, I know Tommy — he's in my class. A bright boy, an altar boy too, has been since he was in fourth grade. The way he sings the *Kyrie Eleison* is a pleasure."

"Did Sister Mary Philomena mention him?"

"Oh, Sister Mary Philomena spoke about so many of the children of the parish. She knew them, and knew their names, and where they lived. As I said, she had the Jesus gift. If she stepped out of the convent, even just to walk to the pharmacy across the street, children would stop playing and gather around her, until soon there would be a whole little crowd standing and talking to her. And there would be such joy in their faces, and such joy in her face too."

Sister Patricia suddenly stopped speaking. The memory of the dead nun, her friend, had caught up to her again. Hank could see the shift: One minute Sister Patricia was there with them, telling Hank and Marvin about Sister Mary Philomena, and the next minute she wasn't. Instead she was in the past, where Sister Mary Philomena was still alive, still loving, still loved — and it was clear from the look of sudden terror on Sister Patricia's face that it was a past Sister Patricia did not want to leave, because she knew that leaving the past meant returning to a world where Sister Mary Philomena had just been brutally murdered and left on a basement floor, a world where her friend's Jesus gift had done her as little good, in the end, as it did for Jesus.

Sister Patricia suddenly opened her mouth to say "oh" or "no" or some other word of useless, powerless outrage, but the word never came. Instead, there was the word that was no word and yet every word. It was the first word in the language of grief, the dry mother sob that caught in her throat and gave birth to one painful child after another until her throat and her eyes and her mouth filled with tears and a pain that she could never escape.

It scared Hank. He knew he could not stop it, that no cop could stop it. He was as powerless as she was. A terrible thing had happened and for this nun, this Sister Patricia, this terrible thing would never end. An evil had entered the world, and from the moment it entered it framed every other moment, touched every other moment, and she would never forget it, never shake it off, even if Sister Mary Philomena had managed to slip Sister Patricia some of her Jesus gift before she died.

Here it all was. A hell of a world.

Hank looked at Marvin. His partner looked confused, lost, powerless — just as confused, lost, and powerless as the young nun was. Hank knew Marvin wanted to do just what Hank wanted to do: grab his gun and kill the thing that had entered the world and staked its claim on Sister Patricia's soul. And Hank knew what Marvin also knew: no revolver or automatic, no bullet or handcuff, could ever touch the thing that had touched them and killed some holy place in them.

A hell of a world.

And Sister Patricia's sobs could do nothing to free them from its touch either.

CHAPTER 6

MARVIN STARTED IN right after they left the convent. "You fucked that up, Hank."

Hank stopped at the corner and looked at his partner. "Fuck you. I don't want to hear it now. We got to talk to Father Ted. We don't have time for this shit."

"You fucked it up, man. That nun's a kid, and you should've given her some time, but no. An hour after she saw her best friend dead, a woman like her mother, dead on a basement floor, stabbed to holy shit. Nuts!"

"Marvin, you started the questioning. Remember? You asked her about the last time she saw Philomena."

"Yeah, a softball question. She wasn't crying out her heart and soul when I was asking her the questions."

Hank dug into his overcoat pockets. Somewhere he had a pack of cigarettes. He paused and looked up. Snow was falling again, and it was never going to stop falling. The street lights were a soft yellow blur surrounded by fat dry flakes swirling and rising and falling.

He found the cigarettes finally, and offered one to Marvin. His partner took it, stuck it in his mouth, lit it up with his lighter, and took a deep, deep drag.

Hank waited for him to light his cigarette. "You gonna light my cigarette?"

"Light your own damn cigarette, Hank. I'm through lighting your butts."

"Yeah," Hank said, and reached for the lighter in Marvin's front pocket.

He lit his cigarette and watched the smoke rise into the turning flakes.

Hell of a world.

"Hank, you remember the worst day of your life?"

"Yeah, I remember the worst day of my life, and I remember the worst day of your life. You gonna tell me about it again? You gonna tell me about that day back on Guadalcanal when you killed so many Japs with your bayonet that the blade melted and you had to use a rock to finish those motherfuckers off?"

"Yeah, that's what I was gonna tell you about. That, and that the rock I used was covered with maggots. Don't forget that."

"Yeah, there were maggots thick as vanilla ice cream on the rock, and they got in your hair and your eyes and your ears, and all you could hear was the screaming of the maggots as you beat those Japs to death with that fucking rock."

"Yeah, that was my worst day. Thanks for reminding me. Now, what was your worst day?"

"Mine? I thought you'd never ask. It was just like yours except the Japs were their Aryan cousins the Krauts, and the ice-cream maggots were thick as chocolate ice cream, not vanilla."

"Yeah," Marvin said and drew in the smoke.

Hank did the same.

They dragged down the smoke and then let it out in the swirling snow and the wind that raised everything and then dropped it.

Hank ground his cigarette butt into the snow.

Marvin took another drag and looked at what was left of the butt. "You know another difference between my worst day and your worst day?"

"No. You tell me."

"I killed more of those motherfuckers than you did."

Hank said, "Fat chance," and looked across the street at the church and the rectory. Snow swirled around the two spires of the church, and the whole building looked like a Christmas card. The lights were on in the rectory too, but there was nothing festive about it. Hank started walking across the street. "Let's go see some priests."

Marvin shook his head and flicked his cigarette butt at Hank's back. Then he said, "Why not?"

CHAPTER 7

A YOUNG UNIFORMED cop, a tall skinny kid named Robert Milewski, showed Hank and Marvin into the reception room where they had seen Father Ted the day before.

Hank sat down in one of the easy chairs and said, "Get us the pastor, Father Thomas."

"My name isn't Father Thomas," Milewski answered.

"Don't be a smartass, kid," Marvin said. "Leave it to the pros. Now go get him."

Milewski nodded and left.

Hank looked around the room. He knew what Hazel would say: it needed a woman's touch. The walls were covered with dark wood paneling. Photos of basketball teams and pictures of saints radiant in their martyrdom were scattered on the walls. A glass cabinet held some dusty medals and trophies nobody would ever take a second look at or want to know about.

There was a phone on a bureau next to Hank, and he thought about calling home. Only a few hours ago, when Sister Mary Philomena was probably already dead but he didn't know about it, he and Hazel had been sitting waiting for their daughter to come back, hoping she'd come home from wherever she had dragged herself. It felt like a lot longer.

Murder, like combat, plays havoc with time. Maybe only a couple of hours had gone by, maybe a couple of days. Shit like this slows time down, speeds it up, makes it run and crawl at the same time. Hank wanted to know if his kid Margaret had gotten home after what seemed like forever.

He picked up the phone next to him and did what he wasn't supposed to do from someone's private phone, without asking permission, in the middle of an investigation: he called home.

Hazel picked up on the second ring.

"I'm on a case, honey, and I can't talk," Hank said. "Is she there yet?"

"No."

"Shit. I'll try to call back later," Hank said, and hung up the phone.

Marvin looked at him. "Margaret still not home?"

"What do you think?"

"Jesus, Hank, she's probably just stuck in the snow somewhere waiting for a ride home."

Hank shook his head.

———

Father Thomas, the pastor, opened the door to the room and paused at the threshold. "Did you gentlemen ask to see me?"

"We did, Father," Hank said. "We've got some questions for you about Sister Mary Philomena. Please have a seat with us here."

The priest moved slowly into the room. A cane helped him some. He seemed unsteady, weak on his pins. Hank remembered the first time he'd met Father Thomas, back about ten years ago. He was all fire and ambition then, the new pastor bent on transforming Saint Fidelis into the best parish this side of Humboldt Park.

Finally, Father Thomas stood across from the detectives and let himself drop into the seat.

"We're sorry about what happened, Father," Hank said.

The pastor shook his head. "A terrible business, a terrible business. It makes me groan to see the things happening in this parish, this neighborhood. A nun killed, right here, just across the street from the church and the rectory, next door to a school building where children sit and learn their prayers. It makes me weep as I pray."

"Father, yes, it's a terrible thing," Hank said. "We know it's been tough on you, but we've got to ask you some questions. Can you tell us something about the working relationship between Sister Mary Philomena and yourself?"

"A good nun, did her job, dedicated and devout. A good school principal too. She started a couple years before I came to the parish, about ten years ago, and now she's gone. Dead."

He shook his head slowly for a moment, and then he went on. "And she was never tired, never less than fully engaged in the running of the school, not the old one or the new one she and I built together. It was always such a fulfilling task...but the neighborhood's changed. When we started, it was mainly Poles, the old ones from the early immigrations of sixty or seventy years ago and the new ones from after the war, the Second World War. We worked for them, and now they're leaving and the ones that are coming in...I don't understand them. They're Hispanics, Mexicans and Puerto Ricans, almost all Catholics, but many of them won't set foot in our church or send their children to our school. I don't understand it. Isn't our Church their Church? Isn't our Jesus their Jesus? The schoolchildren learn from the Baltimore Catechism that the Catholic Church is One and Holy, but these new Spanish-speaking immigrants seem to think it's not One. And if it's not One, then I don't know what it is. If Jesus didn't die the same for a little boy who speaks Polish as He did for a little boy who speaks Spanish, then I'm not sure who He died for or what the point was in His dying.... But I don't think I should have said that. It's not charitable or pastoral to say such a terrible thing."

The old priest stopped again, and he didn't seem to have anything else to say.

Marvin picked up the slack. "Father, you think the sister had any enemies? I know it's hard to imagine, but we got to ask it. Was it possible that someone had it in for her?"

"I can't imagine such a thing. She was a good and holy woman. Everybody loved her. You knew her, knew her concern for everyone. Why would someone want to kill such a good person?"

Hank thought a moment, weighed the irony of Father Thomas's statement, thought about how Jesus was a good and holy person too, and how they hung him up on a cross, pounded thick spikes into his hands and feet, bled him to death.

"Can you tell us how you spent your evening, the time leading up to your hearing about the sister's death?"

Father Thomas leaned forward. "Yes, I was having dinner."

"And the other priest, Father Bachleda?"

"Father Ted was over at the hospital with Father Anthony. They may even still be there. This kind of weather is hard on the older people in the parish. They try to do too much, shoveling snow, pushing their cars out of ruts. You know what it's like. They end up in the hospital, Norwegian American, the hospital right next to Humboldt Park."

"Were you alone here in the rectory?" Hank asked.

"No, not alone. Mrs. Popowski, our housekeeper, was here too. She serves us our dinner every night."

Hank nodded and looked at the old pastor. He seemed tired and shaken, and maybe a little confused, too. Hank felt like the interview was done. He closed up his notepad and looked up at the priest again. Father Thomas had changed a lot since he'd come to Saint Fidelis. Getting a new school and a new convent built, plus all the other work of tending to the souls of the parish, had drained the energy out of him. Hank felt like he should step over to the old priest and help him stand up. But he didn't.

The pastor lifted himself slowly up off the couch and stood there, propping himself up with his cane.

Hank and Marvin both shook his hand.

"Thanks, Father, for talking to us," Hank said. "We'll probably be back tomorrow with some more questions after we get the forensics report on Sister Mary Philomena."

Father Thomas took a step away toward the door, then turned and said, "Why would somebody do such a terrible thing to such a good woman?"

"We'll find out, Father," Marvin answered.

"I suppose that in the end it doesn't matter," Father Thomas sighed. "She's gone. Gone to her grave before her time. There was so much for her still to do for the children of the parish."

CHAPTER 8

HANK SAT ALONE in his car in front of his house and watched the snow fall. He knew he should go in and get some sleep, but he didn't. He wanted to watch the snow for a while and think about the day.

The snow had been coming down slowly for the last couple hours, even before he and Marvin left the rectory after talking to Father Thomas. New snow always made the city pretty, like someplace you'd want to live. The bare tree branches white with snow. The parked cars like miniature mountains. Everything quiet, every sound muffled by the whiteness. Almost like all the bad shit suddenly was buried in the snow.

But he knew it wasn't.

This wasn't the kind of case Hank liked.

He liked them simple. A fight over a card game in one of the bars on Division Street that ends in some mope getting shot. Two Puerto-Rican waiters at Joe Pierce's Deli getting into a knife fight over some Polish girl that neither of them had a chance with. A husband and a wife scrapping over a check or a bottle of Cutty Sark till one of them was dead and the other was weeping. Simple crimes that you could close as easily as a book.

He knew this one wasn't going to be like that. He had a priest who was doing it to a schoolboy. He had a dead nun who might be dead because she turned the priest in. Or maybe not.

He wished he could have seen the priest Sister Mary Philomena had fingered again, Father Ted. Looking him in the eye, talking to him, would have been good. Hank might have been able to spot something in him that would make this case a little simpler than it was looking now. But the detectives hadn't gone looking for him. When Marvin called the hospital from the convent, the receptionist said he was in one of the Intensive Care units, had been there and on other floors since late afternoon.

So the pervert priest had a nice solid alibi.

The other priest, Father Anthony, the old Polish priest, was there at Norwegian American too. Everybody had an alibi. Everybody except the killer, and Hank and Marvin still didn't have a clue who that was.

Hank didn't want to go home, didn't want to walk the twenty paces between his car and the front door of his bungalow. He didn't want to know his daughter Margaret wasn't home yet.

Sometimes he wished he was Marvin, a guy without a family and the kind of worries that a family brings up. But then he realized that this was stupid. Marvin was a guy with so many problems and so many worries that nobody wanted to be like him, maybe not even Marvin himself.

Hank got out of the car and started fishing for his key.

CHAPTER 9

WHEN HANK OPENED the front door, Hazel was just stepping out of the kitchen.

"I haven't heard from her," she said.

"You're kidding," Hank said.

"No. I tried reaching her at her friend Judy's number a little after eight o'clock, but Judy's mom said the girls weren't there and hadn't been there."

"She said she was going to Judy's. Isn't that what she said?"

"Well, she wasn't there."

Hank sat down in his easy chair in the living room, and Hazel sat down on the couch across from him. He didn't say anything for a while, but when he did he was still angry.

"Jesus Christ," Hank said. "She's been gone since early this morning. Now it's almost midnight and where the hell is she? Did she even go to classes today? Jesus!"

"Hank, we got to take it easy with this."

"She's a kid — nineteen. What about that guy from her math class? The guy she was spending time with, tutoring him, I guess...Steve?"

"I tried calling him and some of the other kids she's friends with, but it was no good. No one's seen her all evening. But the good news was that a couple of the kids said they saw her in class today. So we know she was there, at least."

Hank shook his head and took a pack of cigarettes out of his pocket. He lit one and reached for an ashtray.

"I wish you wouldn't do that," Hazel said.

"What?"

"You know. Smoke."

Hank shrugged, and Hazel looked at him and shook her head. "Then at least give me one."

They smoked their cigarettes, and as Hank started to light another, Hazel stood up and moved toward the kitchen.

"It looks like it's going to be a long night," she said. "I think I'll make some coffee."

CHAPTER 10

NEXT MORNING, HANK pulled the unmarked Ford slowly to the curb. There was still snow mounded up everywhere, and he didn't want to rip his undercarriage apart. Marvin didn't seem to notice.

He was smoking and yakking just the way he had been since the two detectives had left Shakespeare Substation. "You know Dick Muder, a street cop out of Wood Street Station? He got shot in the face last night. He was sitting in his squad car with his partner, that mick Stu O'Brien, over there by Edward Street and Chicago Avenue, and some asshole put a couple bullets into his car."

"Was he hurt?"

"I'm telling you, he was shot in the face. The bullets shattered the glass, and it sprayed his face."

"I know Dick. Is he okay?"

"You're not hearing me. He was shot in the face."

"Is he okay?"

"Yeah, he's okay. The bullets missed him, and all he got was a bunch of scratches from the glass. It didn't blind him or cut his ears off, but he's still as stupid and homely as ever.... So how's Margaret? You get all that stuff with her straightened out?"

Hank turned to Marvin. "Nothing's straightened out. She didn't come home last night. She's been gone for 24 hours now. More."

"Holy shit!"

"Yeah, holy shit."

"What're you gonna do?"

"We don't know. Check around, talk to her friends, see if anybody knows anything."

"If you need me for backup, Hank, you know I'm ready. Jesus, 24 hours, that ain't no joke."

"Yeah, no joke. Let's go talk to Father Ted."

Entering the church, Hank felt what he always felt in these old immigrant churches any day but Sunday: the silence and the emptiness. Maybe it was because on Sundays they were so full of life and the noise of life, old people breathing and coughing and clearing their throats, babies crying, and young kids getting yelled at by their moms. But it wasn't like that today. The silence and the emptiness were there now, waiting to hear an old lady's Tuesday prayer or some drunk's millionth confession. Hank wasn't much of a churchgoer, not much of a believer at all anymore, and this kind of silence and emptiness spooked him. It was like God wasn't here today, and maybe He wouldn't be here tomorrow either. Hank wondered if people who had some kind of faith felt that way too. He couldn't remember.

Walking toward a rack of candles at the back of the church, Hank saw the young priest, Father Ted, and he motioned to Marvin. The priest was sitting in the first pew in front of the crèche, just a little to the right of the altar. There was a metal stand with rows of unlighted candles in front of him. His head was down, and it looked like he was praying in the empty, quiet church. Taking off their hats, the two detectives started walking toward him. The sound of their shoes in the church startled Father Ted; he lifted his head for a moment, and then he put it back down and continued to pray.

When Hank and Marvin finally reached the front of the church, the priest stood up and said, "I was just praying for the soul of Sister Mary Philomena. Such a good woman, and such a brutal death."

"We wanted to talk to you about it, Father," Marvin said.

"Yes, of course. Most of what I know is from the morning papers. The *Tribune* had a long piece and a cover story. But I would be happy to help in any way I can. Please sit down."

The detectives sat in a pew next to the priest, and he began talking immediately.

"The papers said she was stabbed repeatedly, more than a dozen times. How can that be?"

Marvin said, "Different people kill differently. I figure this killer was maybe not used to killing. Maybe he couldn't tell when the sister was dead, so he just kept stabbing. Or maybe he hated her so much that he wanted to stab her and keep stabbing her so he could get some of that hatred out of his system. I think what we can be sure of is that the killer here wasn't a pro. This was no mob hit, in clean, out clean, no evidence."

Hank gave Marvin a *clam up and don't give away the show!* look.

Marvin saw it, gave a tiny nod, and added, "Or it could be a pro who doesn't want to look like a pro."

"We've got some questions for you, Father," Hank said. "First, when was the last time you saw the sister?"

"I was just thinking about that. I saw her at the eight o'clock Mass Sunday morning, just a couple of days ago. She was there as usual."

"Did you talk to her?"

"Yes, sort of. She took Holy Communion from me during the service, and as she knelt at the altar railing, I said, 'Body of Christ,' and she replied, 'Amen,' just before I put the Holy Eucharist on her tongue."

"Did you notice anything 'off' or different about her at that time?"

"Well…now that you ask, there was something a bit strange." The priest looked first at Marvin and then at Hank. "I gather you're not an actively practicing Catholic, Detective Purcell, but I'm sure you remember that traditionally after one receives communion, one's eyes are cast down. Sister Mary Philomena's eyes weren't turned downward, however, after I gave her the Eucharist. She looked first at me and then at the altar boy who was standing behind me."

"Who was the altar boy, Father?"

"Tommy Sawa."

"Did she do anything else? Say anything? To you or to the boy?

"No, nothing else unusual. I just turned to the next communicant and placed the Holy Eucharist on his tongue."

Hank suddenly felt cold in the big empty church. He wished the interview with Father Ted were done with. He didn't like this priest, didn't like what Sister Mary Philomena said he had done with the altar boy, didn't like the fact that he didn't seem to feel guilty about anything. A fucking priest…. And Hank wanted to go out and look for his daughter.

"A couple more questions, Father," Hank said. "Where were you between 6:00 and 7:00 yesterday evening?"

"I thought Father Thomas explained all that to you already."

"He did, but we need to hear it again from you."

"All right, no problem, Detective Purcell. I was at Norwegian American Hospital with Father Anthony, the other senior priest here at

Saint Fidelis. You know, we try to have at least one of the parish priests there every day, going through the wards, visiting the sick, consoling and comforting them and their families. Because of the cold and the snow this last week, of course, there have been more of our parishioners in the hospital than usual. So Father Thomas sent me there, and he asked Father Anthony to help as well — especially since many of the sick right now are elderly and he believes they find it more comfortable to speak with someone who's actually from the old country instead of an American like me, even though I speak fluent Polish."

"What time did you get to the hospital?"

"I guess it was a little before five. We like to get there before the patients begin eating dinner, but the snow slowed us down. And then we left a bit after nine. We left the hospital and went to get a little late supper at Ricky's Restaurant — you know, over on Division and California. I think we left there around 10:30, maybe a little later, just before they closed down for the night."

"That's kind of a long time for a late snack, Father," Hank said.

"Yes... we were talking, too. Father Anthony had some questions. One of our Polish parishioners is thinking of trying to bring his young nephew, just a boy, here from Poland. Father Anthony thought I might be able to help."

Marvin had been studying the crèche just across the aisle from them. He suddenly turned and looked at the priest. It wasn't a soft look. "You think you're the guy to be giving another priest pointers about bringing a little kid over here from Poland? That's some shit."

"Is this more of those absurd accusations?"

"You mean the ones about you being a pervert?"

Hank turned to Marvin. "Cut it out. Let's stick to the business at hand."

Marvin looked at Hank, stood up, walked over to the crèche, and knelt down in front of it. Hank had never seen Marvin kneel except when he was injured. It was an odd sight. He wondered what Marvin made of the crèche — his people, long-ago Jews, gathered around the manger where the baby doll Jesus was supposed to be.

Hank turned to Father Ted. The priest was watching Marvin.

"He's Jewish, isn't he?" the priest said to Hank. "He's not like his people usually are — he seems to have an attitude problem. You ought to try to give him some advice sometime, Detective Purcell, some pointers on how to be a decent cop."

"Come on, Marvin, we're done here," Hank said. "And thank you for your time, Father Ted. If we have any other questions, we'll get in touch with you."

"Is that it? You aren't going to say anything? Your partner called me a pedophilic pervert."

Hank shuffled his way out of the pew toward the aisle. He paused for a moment, looked back at the priest, and said, "Fuck you, Father."

Chapter 11

HANK DIALED HIS home and pressed himself into the phone booth in front of the Walgreens Drug Store on North and California. The wind had picked up while they were talking to Father Ted, and now it was whirling around Hank, whipping the snow up, darkening the day. He could barely see across the wide street in front of him to the city bus moving slowly through the snowdrifts.

Hazel finally picked up the phone.

"Have you heard from Margaret yet?" Hank asked.

"Nothing. This is crazy. We haven't heard from her since yesterday morning when she left the house. We got to do something, Hank. She's never done this before. She's always phoned, made excuses when she was going to be late, let us know where she was and who she was with."

Hank pulled his fedora down hard against the snow and blowing wind and leaned harder into the phone booth.

"I know, honey, I know. Yesterday you said that Margaret told you about some guy that Maureen was seeing, a guy with his own place. You said that the two girls had stopped by his place last week, somewhere near the lake, and she was very impressed that Maureen knew someone in that neighborhood. Maybe she's there. Or maybe that guy knows where Margaret is."

"Hank, I talked to Maureen at her mom's house. She didn't know anything about Margaret. She said that the last time she saw Margaret was Saturday. They went to see some movie downtown."

"Shit. Maureen ought to be home from classes sometime this afternoon. Give her a call and try to find out the name and address of this friend of hers. I'll go over and check him out when I can — maybe he knows something. I think you told me that Margaret said he lived somewhere near Clark and Diversey. I'll drive down there and call you from a pay phone when I get there."

"Hank, this is crazy."

"Crazy is all we got."

CHAPTER 12

HAZEL HAD COME through with the guy's name and address, and Hank stood in front of the two-story townhouse on Wrightwood Avenue that belonged to a fellow named Frankie Jones. The snow was still falling, and the gray afternoon was pretty much gone.

Hank was glad he'd left Marvin at the station, waiting for the forensics on Sister Mary Philomena's death. He needed to be alone with this, no matter what happened.

Standing in the wash of slowly falling flakes, Hank looked around and remembered when he had first seen this street. He was a kid, maybe twelve. He and his brother walked from their house near Logan Square all the way up here, three miles or more, but it felt like twenty. It was probably 1932, the Great Depression going on at full strength, his father and mom both trying to make a nickel to bring some potatoes home, and he and his younger brother Carl were alone in the house and hungry. Hunger makes you do stupid things, and they decided to walk to Lake Michigan to take a swim. A couple hours later, they finally got there all right, but what he remembered now was how beautiful this area seemed, as beautiful as the lake itself.

This was where the rich folks lived, close to the lake and a couple buses away from the working men and women in their cobbled-up twenty-unit apartment houses around Wicker Park and Humboldt Park and Jefferson Park. There, Hank knew families that shared four rooms with a couple of other families, families that rented sheds in the basements of those big apartment buildings for a nickel a day just so they wouldn't have to sleep outside in the park. It wasn't all like that back then, but enough of it was — and yet, even as a kid, when he looked at these swell two- and three-story single-family homes Hank knew that not everybody in America was living in the Great Depression. Not everyone was hungry.

And this neighborhood hadn't changed much since then.

Looking around him now, Hank — even two weeks after Christmas — could see the Christmas trees still up in almost every window, lighted up and sending their joy and warmth into the street, and he could also see the money behind the Christmas trees, the plush couches and chairs, the golden chandeliers giving off golden light like heaven, the paintings on the walls, Picassos and Thomas Hart Bentons and Georgia O'Keeffes.

How the hell did Margaret's friend Maureen ever get tied up with a guy in this neighborhood? Or maybe the question was, what the hell was a guy like that doing in a neighborhood like this? Either way, the only way to find out was to ring the bell.

The door opened and a young skinny guy in jeans and a t-shirt stood in front of Hank. His dark soft-brown hair came down to his shoulders.

"Frankie Jones?" Hank said. "Sorry to be bothering you, but I'm looking for someone, my daughter."

The guy took a step back and tightened his hold on the door.

"What?" he said.

"My daughter, Margaret Purcell. Maybe you met her. She's a friend of your friend Maureen Banks. Maureen said you might have some information about Margaret."

"That's crazy, man. I know Maureen, but I wouldn't say she's any friend of mine. She's the fat redhead, right? Lives on the west side, over by Austin Boulevard?"

"Yeah, that's her. Can I come in? It's snowing pretty bad."

"What the fuck you talking about? Let you in? I wouldn't let in any of Maureen's friends. She's a fucking thief. She stole my wallet last week. Her and her skinny friend."

"What did the skinny friend look like?"

"What did she look like? Fuck, I told you. Skinny. Now get the fuck away from my door, man."

Hank knew what was coming next. He braced himself.

The wooden door came smashing toward him, and he threw himself against it, smashing back, smashing the skinny kid in the chest with the door and knocking him on his ass and down on the floor.

Hank quickly stepped into the foyer of the townhouse and extended his hand to help the kid up.

Frankie Jones ignored him and clutched his chest and rocked back and forth howling. "You killed me, man, you fucking killed me."

"You'll be okay, son," Hank said and sat down in one of the easy chairs across from the Christmas tree. In the background he could hear a radio or a record player, Elvis singing a carol. It was faint but Hank recognized it. Elvis was singing about having yourself a merry little Christmas. Kind of syrupy — what ever happened to rock-n-roll, Hank wondered.

"You alone here?"

The guy rubbed his chest. He looked dazed.

"Are you stoned, Mr. Jones?"

"Why the fuck should I tell you?" Jones said, then after a few seconds he nodded.

"Okay, you sit there. This will just take a minute. I'm looking for my daughter, see. Like I said before, her name is Margaret, and we heard she came here with Maureen some time last week. I don't mean you any trouble. I'm just a father looking for his daughter who's disappeared. Any kind of help would be appreciated."

Frankie Jones coughed and slowly got up on one knee. He seemed wobbly, and Hank wasn't surprised. The kid took a powerful blow to the chest from that door.

"Yeah, I know Maggie. She was with that bitch Maureen when Maureen stole my wallet. I hope they have fun with it — there was only a five-spot in it. I was broke as Jesus that day."

The kid finally got himself off the floor and sat down on the couch.

"Any idea where they were planning to go? Anybody else with them?"

"I don't know where they were going, but there was a dude with them too. Older guy named Willy. Not that much older, but older — you know what I mean. I figured they had some kind of plan with him, how they were going to use my money."

"Can you tell me anything about this Willy?"

"He's just a dickhead Maureen hangs out with sometimes. He's got a bad scar on his left cheek. He pencils in a beard so it looks like he doesn't have a scar, the beard shades it. A real jerk, that guy. He says he's a dealer, but I sure as hell wouldn't buy anything he was selling."

"You know where I can find him?"

"He's just a guy Maureen knows. Like I said. I don't know where he lives or works or if he goes to school. He's just an asshole friend of hers."

"Thanks," Hank said. "I'll show myself out."

CHAPTER 13

LIEUTENANT O'HERLIHY SAT behind his desk and asked it plainly: "What do you got?"

"Not much." Hank wished he had something more to tell his boss, but he didn't. "The coroner's report came in with pretty much what we expected. They estimated 35 stab wounds, and figured by the clotting that she was dead before the killer left her there."

"And the forensics?"

"Forensics went through the convent and the school building and the rectory and the church, basically all the parish property including the garages, and didn't find anything. We figured with all that stabbing and all that blood — and the fact that blood shows up bright as anything on snow — that there would have been some kind of trail of blood, something that would give us some direction, but there's nothing."

"How about your interviews with the other nuns and the parish priests?"

"We got nothing, and Rodriguez and Stromski, the patrolmen helping us, got nothing. Same thing with the neighborhood canvas. We had a dozen cops going door to door and searching alleys from California to Western, and from Division to North Avenue."

Marvin leaned forward in his chair and turned to Hank. "You going to tell the lieutenant about Father Ted?"

"What about him?" O'Herlihy asked.

"Sister Mary Philomena came to see me a couple of days before she died. She wanted to tell me something about Father Ted Bachleda."

"And how long were you going to wait before you told me?"

Hank shrugged. "She didn't want to press charges against Bachleda. She just wanted us to give him a warning."

"Come on, already. What did she say about him?"

Hank knew he should have brought this up earlier. He'd been stupid not to.

"She said she saw Bachleda doing something inappropriate with one of the school kids."

Marvin turned to his partner. "*Inappropriate?* You sound like a little girl, Hank. I'll tell the lieutenant if you won't. The padre had his hands down a schoolboy's pants. Sister Mary Philomena said she saw it, and she had us go talk to the guy to straighten him out."

"And this is the first I'm hearing about this? *Talk* to him? *Straighten him out?* What did he say when you 'talked' to him?"

Hank said, "He said that he didn't do it."

"And you believed him?" O'Herlihy asked.

"No, but we did a follow-up interview with him after the murder, and it didn't give us anything that would connect him to the killing."

O'Herlihy wanted more. "Where was he the evening the sister was stabbed?"

"He was at the Norwegian American Hospital, visiting parishioners there. We checked it out."

O'Herlihy glared at Hank, "Is that it?"

"Yes," Hank said. "We warned the priest, Father Bachleda, like the sister wanted. He's got a beautiful alibi for the murder, and we left it at that."

"You got the name of the kid?"

"Yes. Tommy Sawa, a sixth-grader over at Saint Fidelis."

"I'm not sure why I need to be telling you guys this. You've been cops long enough that you ought to know your jobs by now. Here's what you better do. Go talk to Tommy Sawa and see what you can get. Then go talk to that priest again. Pronto."

CHAPTER 14

SITTING IN THE unmarked car outside the Wood Street Station, Hank waited for Marvin to say what he was going to say.

"Hank, you've been playing this stupid. Not talking to the kid, not talking to the priest again. I don't get it."

"We talked to the asshole, Marvin. He denied it. The sister didn't want to take it beyond a warning. End of story."

Marvin took a pint of Jack Daniel's out of the glove compartment, unscrewed the cap, and took a long pull on the bottle.

"But Sister Mary Philomena, who just happened to be the person who told you about that asshole, is now dead, man," he said and passed the bottle to Hank.

Hank raised it to his lips and took down a couple of big swallows. It burned plenty, but it was a good burn. So he took another hit.

"Marvin, you telling me that you think this priest snuck out of the hospital, into the convent, either knew the sister would be in the basement or else somehow got her to follow him down there, and then stuck a knife into her thirty-five times?"

"Why not?"

"Why not? I'll tell you why not. First, he didn't know it was Sister Mary Philomena who talked. I didn't tell him, and you didn't tell him, and you can bet the sister didn't tell him. Second, even if he did know she was the one who squealed on him, he knew very well that he didn't really have anything to fear from her. He knew it and so did she, probably. People don't take that kind of accusation against priests seriously. Never have, never will. Priests are always getting this shit. Maybe it's true, maybe it's false, but regardless, the people on top, the monsignors, the bishops and the cardinals, even the popes won't do shit about it, because they figure it's going on and will probably continue to go on and why the hell should they rock the boat?"

"I don't get it."

"You heard accusations like this before, right?"

"Sure."

"And what happened?"

"...Nothing."

"Why?"

"It's like with corrupt cops. You don't want to press charges on them because it might get back to you or somebody you know."

"Yeah, exactly," Hank said, and reached again for Marvin's bottle of Jack Daniel's.

"I don't know..." Marvin said. "We need a break here. Maybe the kid is the answer."

Chapter 15

THE STAIRWAY OF the apartment house was dirty. Hank could smell cat piss and cat shit, plus maybe some other kinds. Above him, a low-watt yellow light bulb hung down from a cord, giving out just enough light so nobody healthy and sober would trip down the stairs. Someplace above them in one of the apartments, a dog barked and then growled for a moment. Then it shut up.

Behind him, Marvin said, "Somebody knows we're coming, and they're breaking out the tea and biscuits."

Hank ignored him and continued climbing the stairs to the second-floor landing.

He checked the name card on the door and made sure the name Sawa was penciled in there, and then he rang the bell.

They waited for a couple minutes, and then Hank knocked on the door.

The barking picked right up again, and it quickly turned to growling, low and gravelly. It sounded like the dog was on a leash pressing toward the door.

"Well, we found the mutt," Marvin smiled.

"Yeah, we're good at that."

A minute later the door opened, and the growling got louder and lower.

A tall, wide guy, beefy as a wrestler, stood there in the doorway looking at them. He didn't look like he was preparing to say anything. He had a belt in his left hand. Behind him, over the growl of the dog, Hank could hear some weeping. He figured that was what the belt was about. Hank tried to look over the wrestler's shoulder to see what was going on. No dice.

Hank turned to the wrestler again. "We're Chicago Police detectives."

"Yeah, so what?" the wrestler said.

Hank's eyes tightened, his lips parted like he was planning on saying something else, but then he didn't. He didn't say anything. He just stood there looking at the big guy with the belt in his left hand. Behind him the growling stopped and the barking started up again.

Marvin stepped onto the landing. "You got one noisy pooch there, cowboy. Anybody ever told you that? Huh?"

"No," the wrestler said as he put his right hand on the doorknob.

"You planning to close the door on us and leave us out here on this dark landing while you go back in and give that pooch some Purina Dog Chow?"

"What the fuck are you talking about?"

"I'm talking about your dog, mister. We're getting complaints night and day about your fucking mutt. Your neighbors are telling us he's hungry, and you ain't feeding him. Haven't fed him in a coon's age, not that I know how long a coon's age is. But that's what we've heard. Heard you've been a mean daddy to this Purina Dog Chow chewing mutt you got growling its pants off there behind you."

"You look like a Jew but you sound like a spic."

Marvin stared at him.

Hank knew where this was going. Just as he started forward to get between the two men, he stopped.

Marvin was laughing. A real laugh, not some bullshit laugh that you laugh to show you are not a guy to mess around with. A real belly laugh.

The wrestler looked at Marvin. His hand tightened around the belt and for a second it looked like he was going to do something with it — and then it didn't. He took a step back and said, "Come on in, the house is a shithole, but that's not my fault. Blame my wife and my stupid kid."

Hank and Marvin walked in, and Hank could see right away that the wrestler wasn't kidding about what the place was. Except for a beautifully shaped and decorated Christmas tree near the front window, it was a shithole.

Socks, shirts, belts, shoes, schoolbooks, empty cans, old rolled-up newspapers, crushed cigarette packs, some busted-up Christmas gift boxes, even a couple of bibles — everything was scattered around the floor of the front room. The coffee table in the center of the room had magazines and cups filled with cigarette butts stacked in no particular order.

"What happened here?" Marvin asked. "You empty out your pockets?"

The wrestler grimaced. "Now you sound like a Jew."

Marvin shrugged. "At least I'm going to leave this shit behind when I leave. You're not."

Hank moved toward a clear space near the front windows of the apartment. "We need to ask your son some questions, Mr. Sawa. It's in connection with the recent murder at the convent."

"Jesus, what's my kid got to do with that?"

"Just some routine questions, Mr. Sawa."

The kid looked beaten, scared, worked over.

Hank knew it as soon as he saw him coming down the hall from the kitchen. His eyes were swollen and so was his face. Snot on his left cheek, and the cheek was bruised, blood rising to the skin, filmy and greasy. Hank wanted to say *Jesus* but he knew the kid's dad would take it out on the kid, beat him again, work him over with the belt coiled in his hand. And the kid had already had more than enough.

Hank shot a quick look at Marvin. His partner looked pissed, angry as hell, but Hank knew he wouldn't do anything to make it harder on the kid either.

Hank spoke gently. "Tommy, come over here and take a seat on the couch. I'm Detective Purcell and this is my partner Detective Bondarowicz, and we've got some questions to ask you. We're not here to give you a hard time or accuse you of anything. We've just got some questions."

Tommy sat down on the sofa his dad was already sitting on. But he sat as far as he could from his old man. The kid's eyes were fighting not to make eye contact with anybody.

"Okay, Tommy," Hank said. "First, we got to know if you heard about the sister, Sister Mary Philomena, what happened to her?"

The kid looked at the red flowers in the carpet on the floor in front of him. He didn't answer right away. It was like he was lost in the dark lines of the roses.

Then he wasn't.

His eyes popped big and open on Hank. "I know what happened to the sister. The kids have been talking about . . . a lot of stuff."

Hank nodded. He wasn't surprised. He would have been surprised if the kid hadn't heard.

The wrestler growled something at his son, but Hank couldn't hear it. Then he turned to Hank and said, "Tell the detective what he came for."

The kid didn't say anything for a moment. Sweat was starting to bead on his forehead. Then he said it.

"Sister Mary Philomena got stabbed. Fifty times, they said. Even when she was dead, the killer kept stabbing her. It happened in the basement of the convent."

Nobody said anything for a couple of moments. Then Marvin asked, "Where did you hear all this, son? And when?"

"In school, Tuesday, the day after it happened. All the kids were talking about it, soon as they got there. I was late and a lot of the boys and girls were already sitting in the classroom talking about it. I don't know who told me first. Maybe it was Barbara Slater. She sits across from me."

The kid stopped talking. He looked down at the floor, the red roses darkening as they spiraled away from the center of the carpet.

Hank didn't say anything either. He just waited for the kid to find himself again. Maybe he'd remember something more from what he heard at school. Hank looked at Tommy's dad. He was waiting too. Staring at the kid. It looked like he was getting ready to jump up, maybe poke the kid, get him talking.

The kid must have felt it too. He brushed some of the snot off his face and pressed even tighter against the armrest of the sofa. He didn't look at his dad, didn't look at Hank or Marvin. His eyes were digging into the rug, its dark red flowers. Hunched forward, his arms wrapped around his stomach, the kid started weeping. It started with a series of quiet, forced breaths that raised his back over and over, and then found release in tears.

The boy's father snarled, "You fucking fairy, don't be such a baby. Always bawling like a girl—Jesus!" And he stood up and grabbed the kid by his right arm and jerked him off the couch and slammed him onto the floor. "Come on, stop it, stop it already!"

The kid lay there. His snotty cheek was pressed against the roses, his tears nourishing them, his hands digging into the flowers for comfort, for whatever safety and protection they could give.

"You gonna let these cops see you like this? Come on, get up!" The wrestler started unrolling the belt he still held in his hand.

Hank stood up. "We'll take it from here, Mr. Sawa."

Sawa turned away from the weeping boy and faced Hank. "What're you talking about?"

"Your son's had some kind of trauma. He needs air. Needs to get away from here. We're taking him outside. Don't worry."

Hank bent over and put his hands on the boy's shoulders, gently lifted him up, helped him to get to his feet.

The wrestler stood by the couch, looking stunned, and then started moving toward the boy.

Marvin extended his hand, palm up. "Don't!" was all he said, and the wrestler stopped.

"Don't worry, Mr. Sawa," Hank said. "We'll take good care of your son."

CHAPTER 16

A HARD WIND off Lake Michigan swirled the falling snow. Each flake, white and large as a quarter, turned gray once it hit the gray street. It was quiet, and beautiful too — sort of — if you liked gray mounds of dirty snow along rutted sidewalks. Hank couldn't remember the last time it snowed so much. Not since he was a kid, he figured.

He turned to the boy then, Tommy Sawa. Hank could see he was cold in his short-sleeve shirt. He and Marvin had wanted the kid out of his house so fast that they'd left without grabbing a jacket or a hat for him.

"What are we going to do with you, Tommy?" Hank said.

The kid shrugged. He was trying to stop crying, but he couldn't. He wiped the tears out of his eyes instead.

"When's your mom come home?" Marvin asked.

"About 4:30. She works the day shift."

Hank looked at his watch. It was four o'clock.

Marvin took his fedora off then and put it on the kid's head. "Where do you usually go when your dad gets this way?"

The kid stood there in the snow watching a billion flakes swimming around his head.

After a moment Tommy finally stopped crying, and he started talking again. "Donald Walton's house. That's where I go. He's my best friend. He lives a couple houses down. That's where I usually go when I've got troubles at home. His mom's home during the day, too. I can wait there till my mom comes home. She walks past Donald's house from the bus stop, and I'll see her. My mom knows how to handle my dad when he gets like this. I'll be okay there."

Hank thought about that for a minute. He figured that like most kids, Tommy had a lot of grit when it came down to it.

Hank said, "Fine, we'll take you there, drop you off. Before we go, is there anything else you want to say about Sister Mary Philomena and what the kids were saying about her?"

Tommy thought for a moment. "She was a nice lady. Always helping kids. She never got angry or mean like some of the nuns. I liked her. I hated that she was killed."

Marvin pulled his collar up. "Yeah, kid, she liked you too. She was worried about you."

"Worried?"

"Yeah," Hank said, "She told me a while ago that maybe Father Ted was giving you a hard time."

The kid didn't say anything at first. He stood there wearing Marvin's oversized fedora and seemed to study the snow falling around him. The hat made him seem younger, seven or eight rather than eleven.

"Father Ted?" Tommy said. "I serve six o'clock morning Mass for him sometimes if one of the older boys can't make it. He's okay."

"He ever give you a hard time, Tommy?" Marvin asked. "Rag you out?"

The kid watched the snow fall for a moment longer. Then he said, "He doesn't like the way I say some of the Latin stuff during the Mass, but that's about the only thing he complains about. He says my Latin sounds like Spanish."

"He ever hit you?"

Tommy didn't answer right away. He looked at the two detectives and said, "Like my dad?"

"Yeah."

"No...he once gave me a hug."

Hank said, "When was that?"

"After confession, once. I usually go to confession to Father Anthony — he's easy to talk to, somehow — but one time I had to go when Father Anthony wasn't there and Father Ted was the only priest taking confession."

"How come he hugged you?"

"I told him I hated my father and I wanted to kill him. I told him I knew this was a sin, but I couldn't help it."

Hank nodded.

"He told me to say five Our Fathers and five Hail Marys. The next day when he saw me he gave me a hug."

"Father Ted seems to be a good guy," Hank said.

"Yes, he is," Tommy said. "He went to my dad after that and told him not to be so rough on me, and for a while it really helped. My dad wasn't as mean. But then he started up again. Around Thanksgiving."

"Have you talked to Father Ted about how your dad is being mean again?"

"No, I don't like to bring it up. I don't like people knowing about what's going on at home, and my father *really* doesn't like it."

The kid was done. He didn't say anything more, and Hank stood there looking at him, giving him the chance to add anything he felt he needed to add. But there was nothing. Hank looked at Marvin. Marvin gave him a nod and said, "Kid, you're getting cold. Let's take you to your pal's house."

"Yeah," Hank said. "Let's go to Donald's house."

CHAPTER 17

HANK AND MARVIN sat in Larry's Diner, a couple blocks from the convent at Saint Fidelis. It was dark outside now, and there wasn't much traffic moving. Too much snow for too long — people were just happy to sit in one place and wait it out. That was certainly the way Hank felt.

Marvin put some sugar in his cup, stirred it with a spoon, tapped the spoon on the side of the cup.

"How long has it been since you heard from Margaret?" he asked.

Hank looked up from his cup and didn't say anything.

He didn't want to say anything. Didn't want to talk or even think about his problem. It had been almost three days since he and Hazel had seen their daughter, when she had left for school Monday morning. She was excited about something that was going on at school, some kind of project that she and some of the other girls were working on. She'd seemed like her old self, the Margaret she was when she was five and eight and twelve and sixteen. The Margaret that loved books and learning and projects.

Hazel gave her a kiss and a hug that morning, and Hank gave her a hug, and then she was gone. Gone into the gray morning, the snow-filled streets.

And she was still gone.

"About sixty hours," Hank finally said. "Since Monday morning."

"What are you going to do about it, Hank?"

"I think I need to talk to her friend Maureen. I spoke with this guy that Margaret and Maureen met with around a week ago. He said the girls were going around with some dealer named Willy, a guy with a scar on his face who pencils in a beard to try to hide it. The guy didn't seem to have a very high opinion of this Willy clown. Maybe you can help — ask around, see if you can find out about this Willy, get an address or something."

Chapter 18

HANK KNOCKED ON the door of the basement apartment again and waited. Maybe Willy the Dealer was stoned, or maybe he was a late riser. Or maybe he wasn't there at all. Marvin hadn't come up with anything, but Maureen had. She told Hank she hadn't seen Margaret since they went to the movies together on Saturday, before Margaret went wherever she was now. Maureen gave him Willy the Dealer's address, this shithole at the end of a long basement corridor in a fifty-unit apartment house on the far North Side. That had been enough to get him here, and fast.

Hank knocked again, harder this time, and waited for another long minute. Nothing.

He put his ear to the door and listened. Still nothing.

Then he pressed his shoulder against the fucking door and pushed as hard as he could.

The lock burst through the rotten wood of the door, and he was in.

He very soon wished he wasn't.

The room was dark, and it smelled of shit. A lot of shit. Hank pulled back quickly and started gagging. He covered his mouth and nose with his hand. This was bad. He searched for a light switch by the door, found it, and flicked it on.

He saw immediately where the smell was coming from. The floor was covered with piles of shit, maybe a couple dozen turds altogether.

"Jesus Christ," he said. "What the fuck?"

Trying not to breathe, he walked slowly and carefully across the living room toward the hallway and the kitchen. The smell was bad; he thought at first it might get better as he moved further into the room, but it didn't. And there was another smell here that was worse than the smell of shit, and he was moving toward it.

Hank pulled his revolver out of his shoulder holster and took the safety off. He moved into the hallway that he knew had to lead to a bedroom or two in the back. There were two doors off the hallway, both closed. He opened the first one and looked in. Beatles posters on two of the walls, John, Paul, George, and Ringo staring at him through psychedelic glasses, kaleidoscope eyes. On the third wall, Marlene Dietrich in some kind of black and white sparkly dancer's outfit stood holding a gorilla's head under her arm, wearing some kind of weird crown on her head. The room was empty of furniture. There were a couple of sleeping bags spread on the floor and some dirty pillows stacked in a corner.

But there was nothing that smelled worse than stale sweat in here, certainly not whatever it was that smelled worse than the shit in the living room.

That smell was coming from further down the hallway.

He walked to the next bedroom and shoved the door open with his shoulder.

The first thing he saw was a dog, a golden retriever. It was dead. Somebody had killed it and nailed it to the closet door. There was blood on its face. Blood on its fur. Somebody had nailed the pooch with its back to the wall and cut its chest and stomach open. Guts and blood and all that stuff nobody should ever see had poured out of it and settled on the floor, and was rotting there.

The dog looked like it had been dead for at least a day.

This was what he had been smelling. The smell of death and corruption. The smell that was worse than the smell of shit.

Hank pulled his handkerchief out and put it over his mouth. He wanted to puke, but instead he bent down and reached for something resting in the pile of intestines and shit and blood that had rolled out of the golden retriever when it had been crucified and sliced open.

It was a small black and white photograph.

He recognized one of the people in the photo. It was his daughter Margaret. She was standing there in front of some dark car. Next to her was a skinny guy, probably in his mid-twenties, with a stupid fake beard. The guy was standing with his arm draped over her shoulder.

Hank still wanted to puke, but he knew this wasn't the time for it. Instead he went into the kitchen and called the police.

CHAPTER 19

STANDING OUTSIDE ONE of the interrogation rooms at the Rogers Park police station, Hank watched two detectives questioning Margaret's friend Maureen through the one-way glass. They weren't giving her a hard time, but still she seemed nervous, worried. She had a light-blue handkerchief in her left hand, and she kept pressing it into the table. The detectives wanted to know what she knew about Willy the Dealer and his dead dog, and they weren't getting much.

The door opened behind Hank. It was his partner.

Marvin took a toothpick out of his mouth and walked up to the mirrored glass. "What's up, Doc? The fat girl singing?"

"Nothing much going on here. Maureen told these guys the same story a half a dozen times. She said she met Willy at a friend's house a few weeks ago. Her friends had been calling around looking to score some grass, and somebody called up Willy, and he came over — Mister Knight in Shining Armor. That was it. She met him that first time when he brought the dope, and after that, over the space of a couple of weeks, she went to a few coffee houses with him, listened to some blues together at the Quiet Knight a couple times. It was all pretty casual. There was no sex, no drugs other than the grass, no kissing even, except just once when they were both really high."

"It doesn't sound like she's having a very exciting love life."

Hank turned to face his partner. "Don't fuck around."

Marvin smiled an apologetic smile and shrugged. "Sorry. This girl Maureen say anything about Margaret yet?"

Turning back to the one-way mirror that separated them from the interrogation room, Hank said, "Yeah, she mentioned Margaret. She was with Maureen when they first met Willy Reichard, and Margaret was with them both when they ripped off that guy I spoke to, Frankie Jones down on Wrightwood. Turns out he deals too — for some reason he didn't mention that to me when we had our little talk."

"So she doesn't know anything about where Margaret's at now?"

"Doesn't sound like it."

"Shit."

"Yeah, shit."

Just then, one of the two detectives in the interrogation room stood up. It was McGruder. He was an old cop, tall and beefy, an Irish guy who liked his doughnuts Polish style, stuffed with jelly. He filled the interrogation room like a fat shadow.

He loomed over Maureen — it looked like looming was a specialty of his — and slapped his fist down hard on the table.

The kid's eyes jerked up. She looked frightened.

"You're telling us, miss, that you were just a 'casual friend' of this Willy Reichard. That you didn't know much about him or any of his dealings?"

"I'm sorry. I told you everything. I didn't know him that well. I didn't know his friends either, any of them."

"So how come you helped him rip off that other dealer, this guy Frankie Jones? You steal things for people you don't know? Rip off somebody because a stranger asks you?"

Maureen was weeping now, rubbing her eyes with her light-blue handkerchief. "Willy said it was just a goof. He said we'd get Frankie's wallet and drive him crazy looking for it, mess with his head a little. It was all supposed to be fun."

"Stealing ain't no joke, miss!"

Marvin turned to Hank. "This kid doesn't know shit."

"Yeah. I wish she did. I wish she knew something about Margaret."

"Yeah."

CHAPTER 20

HANK STOOD ON his porch and looked out at his backyard and the garage beyond it. In the summer there would be tomato plants in their cages and oleander plants, but right now there wasn't much to see. The snow had stopped falling, but it wasn't going anywhere. The roof of the garage had about a six-inch layer of the stuff on it. There was more on the bushes and on the ground, a white cold pillow of snow. The temperature had stayed just below freezing for the last week, and the snow was accumulating faster than it was melting.

He thought about last winter, when Margaret was still in high school. Margaret and her friends from school went caroling in the neighborhood. It wasn't something that you saw much anymore, people caroling, but there they were, Margaret and Maureen and about ten of their girlfriends caroling up and down the street. They'd stop in front of one house after another and sing, mostly the old carols like "Hark! The Herald Angels Sing" or "O Little Town of Bethlehem", and sometimes they would jazz it up with something like "Rudolph, the Red Nosed Reindeer" or even "Jingle Bell Rock". The girls would sing and laugh and sometimes start throwing snowballs at each other, not throwing hard, but just for fun. And then they'd sing some more, and then afterwards, all of them stopped by at Hank's house and Hazel brewed up hot chocolate. The kids were so happy and excited — some were still singing and laughing as they unwrapped their scarves, and some were talking about their favorite Christmas gift ever, the yellow, pillowy bear they got when they were four years old or the pink hat and matching coat Grandma had given them when they were ten.

While Hazel carried more hot chocolate out to them, Hank just stood there in the living room thinking about how these girls, with their laughter and singing and stories of Christmas gifts past, were their own special kind of Christmas miracle. They were grownups, soon to be in college or working or married — and kids, all in the same breath.

A tap on the kitchen door behind him jostled Hank out of his memories, and he turned around. It was Hazel, waving for him to come in. Dinner must be ready. He didn't feel much like eating, but Hazel insisted. She was right, of course.

Hank put his bowl of vegetable soup on the kitchen table across from Hazel and sat down.

"I thought you'd like some soup," she said.

"You're right about that. Nothing like soup on a cold night."

Hazel took a piece of rye bread and spread some butter on it. "Is there anything new about who killed Sister Mary Philomena, honey?"

He shook his head and looked back at his soup, stirred it some, and then looked at her again.

"What a terrible thing," Hazel said. "She was so kind, so giving. I just don't know how someone could kill her. I only met her a few times, but she always made me remember that the world was capable of goodness, maybe even holiness."

"Yes, she was someone special. Sister Patricia, one of the other nuns at Saint Fidelis, said Sister Mary Philomena had the Jesus gift, something that was passed down from Jesus to the apostles and from there down the years to a few people here today. I think I know what Sister Patricia was talking about."

"I just don't understand how someone would kill her, and do it so violently."

"I know. The way she was killed...I don't understand it either, and I'm supposed to be an expert. It makes me think about the Suitcase Charlie killings. Back more than ten years ago now.... I sometimes think those killings opened the door to something terrible and the door stayed open all this time, but I know that's ridiculous. That's not how murders work, inspiring other murders that different, that many years later."

"But something does seem different," Hazel said. "What happened to those children in the Suitcase Charlie case, and what happened to Sister Mary Philomena...these killings seem so different from the crimes we knew in the old days, before the war. These killings seem angrier, crazier, like they were done by people who had completely lost control of themselves."

"Maybe it was the war. All those people killed in the concentration camps, for the craziest of reasons or no reason at all. Six million Jews dead, and so many others dead too. 50 million? 60 million? All kinds of people, mostly not soldiers, just people, moms and dads and children. Maybe the war opened the door to some kind of evil, and we haven't figured out a way to close that door again, and if we can't close the door these crazy murders will keep happening, keep reminding us that the evil is here."

Hank looked at Hazel, who was staring down at her soup. He expected her to say something. She was good about that. Sometimes, when he has overcome by some terrible thing at work, she would talk him away from it, free him, at least for a time, from the terrible stuff; but today wasn't one of those times, and he knew why she couldn't do it. Like him, she was thinking about Margaret, praying for their daughter's life.

Chapter 21

LIEUTENANT O'HERLIHY LIT his cigarette and blew out the match. Then he looked at it for a second and dropped it in the silver ashtray on his desk.

Hank knew what was coming. The pep talk. Half scolding and half chumming up. He had heard it from his dad, and he'd heard it from all his commanding officers during the war, and he'd heard it from O'Herlihy down all the years the older detective had been his boss. Hank leaned back and waited for it all to roll over him.

"Purcell, I think I know what's bugging you, and I don't blame you. Your daughter disappeared, and one of the last times she was seen she was in the company of a pot-head, that drug dealer Willy Reichard."

O'Herlihy paused and looked at Hank, probably looking for a nod or a shake of his head, but the detective didn't give his boss any acknowledgment.

"What I'm saying is that I know you and Hazel are having a heck of a bad time, and I want you to know we're ready to take some of the pressure off you. According to regs, we can't help you look for Margaret because she's over eighteen and there's no evidence of foul play, but at least we can free up some of your time so you can look for her yourself."

"Lieutenant, you can't take me off Sister Mary Philomena's murder. She was a friend, someone I worked with, a good person. I've got to finish what I started."

"I hate to say this, Hank, but to me and Captain Feltt, it doesn't look like you and Bondarowicz are getting anywhere with the investigation. We know all the people at the rectory and the convent have been interviewed, but it's led nowhere. You're at a dead end."

"Lieutenant, like you said, we've interviewed everybody we were supposed to interview. I've looked at the reports from the two patrolmen backing me and Bondarowicz up, and I've talked to them about their reports. We've done everything by the book. We're not slacking on the job here, sir."

O'Herlihy shrugged and took another drag on his cigarette. "I'm not saying that, Hank. I'm just wondering if all of this bad business with Margaret isn't putting too much on you, on top of a case like this. I know you and Hazel have been trying to find her, following leads about where she might be, tracking down her friends, talking to them. It's like you're leading two investigations at the same time. It's not good for you, not good for either one of the investigations, not good for the department. You're wearing yourself out."

"Yeah, I'm just working in a coal mine, going down, down, down."

O'Herlihy put out his cigarette in the ashtray on his desk and looked up. "Huh?"

"Sorry, sir, it's just something from a song the kids are listening to. I admit I've been distracted some, trying to find Margaret. But I've never cut back on what I was doing to find Sister Mary Philomena's killer."

"You think you can do it? Solve the case?"

Hank didn't say anything for a minute. He knew if he said he couldn't, O'Herlihy would get somebody else to pick it up, and maybe they'd do better on it than he was doing, and maybe not, but for sure he wouldn't be the one who found Sister Mary Philomena's killer. So Hank lied, or at least tried to sound more confident than he felt.

"We can do it, sir."

O'Herlihy stared at Hank for a long time and then nodded. "Okay, you stick with finding out who killed the sister. See if you've missed anything. Talk to the people you already talked to, talk to the friends of the people you already talked to. You got to find this one. The papers are saying we're getting sloppy and stupid. They're starting to look at all the cold cases they haven't thought about or talked about in decades. Just yesterday, there was a piece in the *Sun-Times* about the Suitcase Charlie murders. That case has been hanging around our necks like an albatross for ten years already. Can you believe that? We need the newspapers to start talking about our successes, not our failures."

CHAPTER 22

"MARVIN, PASS ME the bottle," Hank said as he pulled the car over to the curb in front of the rectory at Saint Fidelis.

"You already want a drink? I know it's almost three o'clock, but we haven't even started the fun part of the day yet. Haven't talked to a single pedophile priest. Haven't looked into the possibly lying eyes of any of those Sisters of St. Joseph. Haven't even rescued any kids from their own delightful fathers. Why don't you wait until after we talk to those bastards in the rectory again before you start knocking back shots?"

Hank turned to his partner. "Give me the bottle."

"All right. My pleasure. Cutty Sark or Smirnoff's? You finished my bourbon."

Hank gave him a look and took the Cutty Sark. It burned as it went down, and Hank thought that was the way it should be. Burning to remind him he was a sinner and he was going to hell, but not today. He let the burn fade to ashes, and then he took another swallow, and then he said, "Now, let's go in and nail those fuckers."

Mrs. Popowski, the rectory's housekeeper, let them in and led them past the front desk toward the sitting room.

Hank recognized her, of course. She was dressed the same way she'd been dressed every time he'd seen her before — a faded, loose-fitting green wrap-around dress, the same kind of thing a lot of the Polish cleaning ladies in the neighborhood wore. It must have been some kind of uniform they brought from the old country. Like all the other times, she didn't say much, just told them that Father Anthony was the only one of the fathers present. The others were downtown for a fundraiser, something to do with hungry children in China.

Marvin gave a laugh and said, "I bet."

Mrs. Popowski paused and gave Marvin a hard look. "You shouldn't make fun of the priests, mister. God doesn't like it." There was a trace of an accent, but her English was perfect.

Marvin laughed some more. "Honey, if He don't like it, He shouldn't be making so many wacky guys crazy for little kids and then calling them to the priesthood."

She looked at him like he was crazy and said in Polish, *"Strasznie głupi,"* then shrugged and led them into the reception room.

"Please sit, detectives, I'll tell Father Anthony you're here and you want to talk to him."

Hank and Marvin sat on the old couch.

"What did she say?" Marvin asked.

"I've got no idea. Probably something about you being the second coming of King Sobieski."

"That'll be the day."

They didn't have to wait long for the priest.

Father Anthony came in, shook their hands, and nodded his head as he greeted each of the detectives.

There wasn't much to him — he was short and bald and a little on the pudgy side. But there was also something old-world about the priest, some kind of gravity, a formality in the way he held himself as he shook their hands, almost like he was a soldier and he was giving them a salute. Hank wondered if Father Anthony had been in the war. He was about the right age, and the war had been pretty hard to avoid for a Polack. Hank wondered what the guy had done in the war — fought, hid, maybe just kept his head down and prayed for Poland and for the Americans to come. He wanted to ask, but he knew he wouldn't.

Hank saw that the priest was going to stand until his guests said otherwise, so he gestured for him to sit and said, "Please, Father."

"Yes, of course. Thank you."

Father Anthony had an accent and spoke carefully, but his English was good enough. Hank was glad of that. He didn't want to drag this interview out with a translator.

"Father, we want to ask you some questions about the night Sister Mary Philomena was killed."

"Yes, I already talked to the other policemen."

"We know. This is just a follow up, routine in fact."

"Yes, that is fine. I'll be happy to answer your questions. Terrible, this killing. The sister was a good nun, a good teacher, and a good person. I wish I could help your investigation, but there's not very much I can tell you, I'm afraid. I wasn't here that evening. Father Ted and I were at the Norwegian American Hospital that night, seeing to our parishioners who were in need."

Marvin leaned forward. He seemed more impatient than usual. "Yeah, yeah, we know the two of you were there. We got the basic info from the patrolmen who interviewed you. We know when you got to the hospital, how long you stayed. We know all that. That's not what we want."

The Polish priest looked at Marvin. Hank could tell his partner's approach was getting the man nervous, and he didn't want that, at least not yet. He stepped in, giving his fellow detective a quick look that Marvin had plenty of practice understanding. "Like my partner says, we've got the basic information, but if you could repeat it again for us, we'd appreciate it."

The priest didn't say anything for a moment, and then he responded, "Yes, of course. I understand. We got to the hospital at about five o'clock and left around nine, or perhaps a few minutes later. That's what we usually do, although most of the time only one of us visits each evening. We arrive just when they are serving dinner to the patients and leave just before the nurses chase all visitors out for the night."

"Thanks, Father," Hank said. "I guess what we want now is just your general impressions of that evening, maybe some odd little detail that you forgot to mention before, maybe something that's come to mind since then. Or maybe something you noticed in the day or two before the murder, or after it."

"Honestly, gentlemen, I would love to help, but I can't think of any way that I can. Sister Mary Philomena was a great woman. Her death leaves the parish diminished. I'll tell you the kind of thing she did: One time there was a poor Polish family, refugees, what they called DP's back then, Displaced Persons. This was not long after the war. They were living in a shed in the basement of one of the big apartment buildings on Washtenaw Avenue. A family of six living in a little shed underground, a mother and father and four children."

The priest paused and looked down at his hands. His voice was starting to break. Father Anthony made a visible effort to pull himself together and go on with his story.

After a moment, he looked up at Hank again. "Those refugees had it hard, living in darkness, sleeping on flattened cardboard boxes, eating cold food when they could get it. I don't know how the sister found out about them, but she did, and she went to the landlord of this building and asked him if there was a vacant apartment there. He said there was, and she asked him to let this family live in the vacant apartment. The landlord laughed and asked who would pay the rent. The family had barely enough money to pay for their shed in the basement, a dollar a week, and the rent for the vacant apartment would be six times as much. So Sister Mary Philomena said she would pay. The landlord laughed again — I suppose he knew that the sisters take vows of poverty, that they have no money. Anyway, he said that of course he would rent the apartment to the family in the shed, he would rent it out to anyone who had the money. And do you know what Sister Mary Philomena did?"

Marvin shrugged, and Hank said he didn't know.

"Well, this building had thirty or forty apartments. She went immediately to the first apartment on the first floor and knocked on the door, and asked the people there — a Polish refugee family that had been here in America for perhaps two years — if they could spare some change to help another family living in a shed in the basement, and the mother of that family said '*Mój Boże*' — 'My God' — and went and got her change purse and took out two quarters and gave it to the sister, and the sister thanked her and went to the next door, and there she asked the next Polish family, one that had been here for thirty years, if they could help the children sleeping in the basement, and the father gave a dollar and his daughter gave the sister a nickel. It went like this until Sister Mary Philomena had visited every apartment in the building, and then she went to the landlord and gave him his $30 for the first month's rent. Then she went down to the basement and told the family there that they could move to their new apartment on the second floor, and the mother wept, and the father kissed the sister's hands, and she helped them move their cardboard boxes up to the apartment. Then the next day, she and another sister called up Fish's Furniture Store over on North Avenue and asked them if they had some furniture that was damaged or broken. She offered to fix it so she could give it to the family of refugees."

Hank hadn't heard this story before, but he wasn't surprised by Sister Mary Philomena's resourcefulness and determination.

"Father, Detective Bondarowicz and I both knew the sister. She was a fine person. Did you have a lot of contact with her?"

"I didn't have very frequent contact with her, but then I don't have all that much contact with either of the other priests or most of the nuns. They are all of a different generation, in effect — Father Thomas and Father Ted and many of the nuns are of Polish background, but they were born here and they think and act like Americans. My normal contact with Sister Mary Philomena was limited to the work she did on the altar preparations or the decorations she arranged for the holy days. She did very good work, very conscientious."

"Was she the sister responsible for coordinating the altar boys?"

"I'm sorry. What do you mean 'coordinating'?"

"Was she responsible for scheduling which boys would serve at which Masses, things like that?"

"No, I think that would have been Sister Rosemary, the Mother Superior. She scheduled the Masses, made sure the boys knew their prayers, made sure the boys did a good job as altar boys."

"Did Sister Rosemary have much trouble with the boys?"

"Well, boys are boys. They like the idea of serving at Mass, but they don't always like the work that comes along with it. Memorizing the prayers, getting up early in the morning to be at a 6 AM Mass...that is difficult for some of the boys. Then there's a certain level of spiritual devotion you need to be a server. You know it's God's work in many ways, but it's difficult for a young boy to remain focused on that at all times. Not every boy has the necessary level of faith and discipline."

"Do you lose a lot of altar boys each year?"

"About seven or eight boys volunteer each year. Maybe two stay with it. So yes, I suppose you can say that we 'lose' a lot — not every boy, not even every good, devout boy, is meant to be an altar boy. As our Lord says, 'Many are called, but few are chosen.'"

Marvin took a toothpick out of his pocket and stuck it between his teeth. "Tell me, Father, what's the relationship between the boys and the priests like?"

"Well, I think it depends on which boys and which priests. I would say that I've seen a wide range of relations. Some are casual and some are profound, almost like the connection between a father and his son. The boys that stay on as altar boys are the ones who feel this closeness."

"And what are the relations between the boys and the sisters like?"

"It's different, of course. The sisters often see themselves as mothers to the boys, and the boys may see themselves as sons. But the relations between the sisters and the boys are also relationships between classroom teachers and students — there is always an element of discipline involved. With the priests and the boys there is, I think, more of an element of the spiritual sometimes. The priest serving at the altar is not just a man; he is the living embodiment of Jesus Christ. The boys, the best of them, feel this, see themselves as disciples, sometimes almost as apostles. I've seen boys who started by serving at Mass become good priests, even pastors. As I said, the connection between priest and altar boy is a profound relationship, with many levels, much depth."

The priest stopped then. He seemed puzzled for a moment, and he looked at Marvin. Hank knew where this was going and leaned back on the couch.

Marvin said, "Father, you got to understand, I wasn't brought up Catholic. I'm a Jewish boy from the other side of Humboldt Park. I went to a synagogue, you know. Had a rabbi for a teacher. Sometimes we'd hear stories, when I was a kid, about the priests and the altar boys. We didn't hear these from the rabbi, you understand, but we heard them just the same, and sometimes we'd even hear stories about the priests and the nuns."

"Yes?" Father Anthony said, softly but directly.

Hank figured the priest also knew where this was heading, and would want to get it over with as soon as he could.

"Well, what I want to say is that sometimes when I was a kid we heard stories about the priests and the sisters fooling around, and sometimes we heard stories about the priests and the altar boys fooling around. You know what I mean — doing stuff they shouldn't. Dirty stuff, you know? I guess these stories all had their origins in the fact that priests and nuns are supposed to be celibate, so any kind of sexual contact is a big deal. You understand?"

Father Anthony nodded, and then he shrugged. "Yes, of course I understand. I wish I could say there is never any truth to such stories, but that would be a lie. Priests are men. And even the best men sometimes fall into sin."

"How about nuns, Father?"

A look of disbelief appeared on the priest's lined face. "Are you suggesting that Sister Mary Philomena was having sexual relations with an altar boy? That is absurd!"

"Father, we're cops. We got to look at all the angles," Marvin said, and added after a short pause, "Did you ever hear any rumors at all about Sister Mary Philomena and any of the altar boys?"

"Never. She was an excellent woman. A holy woman. She would never consider such a thing."

"Well, Father, how about the sister and one of the other priests? What kind of relationships did she have with your fellow priests at Saint Fidelis?"

"She respected all three of us, respected us and the work we do. I don't know what you are trying to imply here."

Hank leaned forward. "Father, most murders are committed by people who know their victims intimately. Men kill their wives and girlfriends, women kill their husbands and lovers and sometimes even their children, aunts kill uncles, uncles kill nephews, children kill their parents. I hate to say it, but most people who kill, kill their friends or the people they love. It's not like in the movies where random strangers kill random strangers in a shootout on a dusty street in some cowboy town. We're figuring that Sister Mary Philomena was killed by someone she knew, maybe someone she knew and loved. Or maybe she was killed by someone who wanted her love but knew she wasn't going to give it to him. Or her."

The Polish priest shook his head and stared at his hands.

"I guess," Hank continued, "that's why my partner Detective Bond-arowicz is asking these questions that are so hard to answer, so hard to even think about. Sister Mary Philomena lived in a very small, very tightly contained community. She shared that community with about twenty other people, the priests and the other sisters. It's a good possibility that one of that small group killed her."

Father Anthony's head was shaking. "You want me to tell you if she was in love with one of the other priests, Father Ted or the pastor, or even one of the other nuns? Are you asking whether I loved her and killed her?"

"Yes," Hank said.

"Gentlemen, you are not subtle."

"Subtle is for Sherlock Holmes and the detectives on TV, Father," Marvin said. "We ain't got the time to play those kinds of games."

"Are you sure? Sister Mary Philomena was killed several days ago. In all that time you haven't come to see me, talk to me. You sent a couple of foot soldiers."

"Patrolmen," Hank corrected him. "Qualified, trained patrolmen who know their jobs."

"Yes, patrolmen," Father Anthony said. "I told them what I knew about the sister, told them about when I saw her last, told them about my friendship and my infrequent contacts with her. There wasn't much else I could tell them. I knew of her goodness, but nothing of her personal life."

Hank leaned back. "How long have you been here, Father Anthony?"

"In this parish?"

"No, in the country, the United States."

Father Anthony didn't hesitate. "Just over twenty years now. I came soon after the war. The Soviets who took over Poland in 1945 were not very friendly toward the few priests who had managed to survive the Germans. I was able to escape, first to the British side, then to the American sector, then to America. Saint Fidelis was almost completely a Polish parish then, just after the war. They needed a priest who could speak and read Polish, who could understand how people who grew up in Poland thought and believed and felt in this new country."

"So you were here when Sister Mary Philomena first came to the parish?"

"Yes, I'm sure I was, but I don't recall what exact year it was that she came. I didn't have much contact with the nuns or the school back then — and, as I said, I still don't."

"How come?"

"I'm pretty much an *isolato*, a recluse. In Poland before the war, I was a professor of English literature in Warsaw. I loved reading, loved lecturing, but contact with people — even my students — wasn't something I sought out. I'm still that way somewhat. I am no longer a teacher by profession, but I still spend most of my free time reading."

"A professor of literature?" Marvin said. "So how come you're not teaching anymore?"

"The archdiocese sends me where I am needed. This is where they needed me when I came to Chicago, and it seems that this is still where they need me."

"When you were a prof, I bet you saw a lot of hanky-panky between the other teachers and their students."

"There was some. Not much, really. In my experience, some students tend to become infatuated with their teachers, assume that they are gods — or at least herald angels. Yes, I've seen this. It begins in dreams of joy, and ends in grief and sorrow."

"How about here in Saint Fidelis Parish?"

"You're referring to Father Ted, I believe?"

While Marvin let that question hang in the air, Hank looked at the priest. His expression seemed unchanged. His face looked attentive. There was no fear in his eyes, no sweat on his forehead, no shaking. He didn't look like a guy hiding anything. He didn't look like a guy who would fear any kind of question, so Hank asked him one more.

"Did you know that Father Ted was sexually intimate with a student?"

Father Anthony didn't say anything for a moment. He was looking at something behind Hank. Hank wanted to turn around, but he didn't. He knew the older priest was thinking about the young priest who was so popular with the young people of the parish. Then Father Anthony looked again at Hank.

"Father Ted is popular with the children. They see him as young, vibrant, speaking their language. He knows the world they live in — the songs they like, the heroes they worship, the dreams they dream. These children are more emotional than we were in my generation in Poland, and probably more emotional than you were in your generation here. They hold hands, they kiss, they embrace. Father Ted understands this. I've seen him put his arms around young people, mess up the hair of the boys, blow kisses at the girls. For a priest of my generation, such things would be unthinkable, but for Father Ted? Not so much."

Father Anthony paused and looked at Hank again, nodded his head and spread his hands. "This is what you want to know. Yes?"

Marvin answered before Hank could. "Well, it's a start, Father. Did the intimacy get any more intimate than messing with their hair and blowing them kisses?"

"Excuse me, but what does this have to do with the death of Sister Mary Philomena?"

Marvin took the toothpick out of his mouth and looked at its chewed tip. "Death weaves a tangled, mangled web, Father Anthony."

"I suppose so. And you want to link this death to something Sister Mary Philomena knew about Father Ted, something about him and his relationship to some young parishioner?"

Marvin smiled. "Who sounds like Sherlock Holmes now, Father?"

"Honestly, I've known Father Ted from the day he started here at Saint Fidelis five years ago; and although I can't say I have ever been extremely close to him, I have had many conversations with him, and I've spent time with him, and I've seen him interacting with students. Sometimes he knew I was watching him, and sometimes he didn't."

"What do you mean, sometimes he didn't know?" Hank asked.

"The church, for all its size, doesn't have a lot of room where one can be alone, be private. There's the sacristy behind the altar, and there is a supply room beneath the altar, and of course there is the rectory that we are in right now. These are the only places where you can perhaps feel that you can find some privacy."

Hank nodded.

"But even these private places really aren't private. People always are entering and leaving, moving through passages to get to this place or that, seeing who goes where. There's almost no true privacy here, even in our own rooms."

"What are you saying, Father?"

"I'm saying that over the years I came into rooms where Father

Ted was alone with boys and with girls, and never did I come into such a room where Father Ted was doing anything that might be considered inappropriate."

"Like what, Father?" Marvin asked.

The old Polish priest did not hesitate.

"Like touching them between their legs, like hugging them fiercely and sinfully, like taking their clothes off or putting them back on. Nothing like that, nothing at all."

CHAPTER 23

AS MARVIN TURNED up his collar against the wind and snow, he asked Hank, "Do you believe that old goat? You think he was on the level about Bachleda?"

Hank didn't say anything for a moment. He stood on the corner of Hirsch and Washtenaw and looked at the church. It was lit up against the darkness and the cold and the wind, and the snow swirled across its gray facade.

Hank thought about that last winter of the war in the Ardennes. So long ago now, but he could still feel the snow and the wind there wrapping themselves in darkness. It was the winter that would never end. The shivering that would never stop. He'd never thought that people could die that way...some men died shivering and some died not shivering, slipping into their frozen selves like children falling asleep anywhere they could. He remembered his pal Frank Miller. They had been together since boot camp in the summer of 1943, in the South Carolina swamplands. Frank was a joker, and Hank remembered how he was joking about the cold in the Ardennes that night, joking how it wasn't as bad as one cold night he remembered in Alaska, and then his eyes closed and his lips stopped moving, and everything was still about him, and he never finished the joke. Maybe that was the punchline: to die just before the punchline.

Hank pulled his coat tighter against the Chicago cold, turned around, and looked back at the rectory. He suddenly wondered what the priest they had just interviewed was doing and thinking now. Was he in his room, on his knees, praying for forgiveness? Or praying that Hank and his partner would catch the son of a bitch that killed Sister Mary Philomena? Or maybe he was just saying a little prayer of thankfulness that they'd finally left him alone and stepped outside into this cold that would not stop.

"Wake up, Hank! What the hell you thinking about?"

Hank looked at Marvin. His partner didn't usually bring up the past, but Hank knew that Marvin's years held as much bad crap as his own — a lot of it was crap they'd gone through together. And even if Marvin would never admit that all the crap got to him, Hank could see the heavy years in his partner's eyes. "I'm just thinking about the war and the cold that last winter in Belgium. You didn't know the cold."

"Yeah, not much thirty-below weather out there in the South Pacific. Just the fucking heat. Maybe the cold would kill you, but the heat drove you nuts and left you alive. Nobody talks about it now, but it drove everybody crazy. Some guys got so hot they headed for the beach and never turned around. Got in, started swimming, and drowned out there or got themselves eaten by fucking sharks. And let me tell you, Hank, they don't give you a medal for getting chewed up and shit out by a shark."

"So you don't mind the cold?" Hank said.

"Not a bit."

"Me neither, I guess, except that it brings me back there.... So what about what Father Anthony said?"

"Well, it's pretty clear we got a difference of opinion. Sister Mary Philomena, may her memory be a blessing, called Father Ted a bad man. Father Anthony says he didn't see a thing going on with Father Ted and the kids in the five years since he came to the parish. So who you gonna believe?"

"And what's any of that got to do with who killed Sister Mary Philomena?"

"Nothing, or maybe nothing, or maybe something. It's a puzzle."

Hank turned his collar up against the wind and the spinning, twisting snow. "Yeah, I'm going home and sleep on it. Maybe by the time I get up, some joker will have turned himself in for this mess."

Chapter 24

BUT HANK DIDN'T sleep on it.

After dinner and some time talking and worrying together, he and Hazel got into bed, but he couldn't fall asleep. He twisted, turned, pulled the covers up, pushed the covers down, listened to the neighbor's big mutt growling about something in the backyard, and then he gave up on sleep, got dressed, kissed Hazel goodnight again, grabbed a 2 x 3 color photo of Margaret, and drove east on Diversey through the falling snow toward Lake Michigan and Broadway.

That's where Chicago's hippies hung out, and the beatniks too, the ones who hadn't heard that their time was done and they needed to go back to wherever and whenever they came from.

So Hank drove slowly up Broadway, past Melrose, past Addison. There weren't many people out. There was too much snow, too much cold. But he saw a few — some old folks coming home from a late factory shift somewhere, and a couple of young people rushing somewhere. He couldn't see any faces, much less recognize them; it was too dark and cold and windy, and everyone's head was tucked down into their chest. But Hank watched the way they moved, the way they hunched into the wind, the way they held on to their babushkas or hats. After all these years, little things could tell him a lot.

And as he drove slowly up Broadway, he watched especially for his daughter Margaret. He knew he would recognize her if he saw her walking past him, even in the dark, even in the snow. Even if he couldn't see her face or her hair.

He took a left on Irving Park Road. He could see the wall that separated the street from Graceland Cemetery. He could feel the darkness even more there, and the cold. He bet there was nobody hanging out among the gravestones and mausoleums tonight, not like in the summer when the hippies went there to smoke marijuana and drink cheap Italian red wine. He wondered if that was where they were going to bury Sister Mary Philomena, there alongside the dead governors and senators, army officers and ball players. Alongside the brother of Charles Dickens and the heavyweight champion who they wouldn't allow to sail home on the Titanic because his skin was the wrong color. Some things, Hank figured, even a heavyweight champ couldn't fight against. Guy probably wasn't too unhappy he lost that one.

At Clark Street he took another left, heading south down to Diversey and the long drive home.

But he didn't go home, not just yet.

He stopped at a bar. He didn't know what he hoped to find there. Maybe he just figured he had to do something about something, even if the something was nothing.

He got out of his car and locked it up. He looked south, down Clark toward Fullerton. The block looked like shit. On both sides of the street there was a mix of bars and crappy little grocery stores and greasy-spoon diners and coffee houses and empty storefronts that used to be something but were nothing now. Most of the stores and diners were locked up. The bars and coffee houses weren't. The abandoned stores that were nothing were just nothing — maybe some had locks, but anything there was to steal was long gone now.

Hank walked through the falling snow into the Bear and Bull Tap and took a seat at the bar.

The bartender walked over to Hank and put a cardboard Schlitz coaster in front of him. "What can I get you?"

That was an easy question. "A double Jack Daniel's on the rocks."

The bartender nodded and turned his back.

Hank waited for his drink and checked out the action in this place. A short aluminum Christmas tree with a half dozen dim blue lights stood on a table at the back of the tavern, just between the doors to the men's john and the lady's john. The tree looked like crap, like it had been knocked over one too many times by drunks crawling their way to the toilets.

On the jukebox, some rock and roll guy with a high, nasal voice was singing about how there was a time for everything, a time to be born, a time to die, a time to plant, a time to reap, a time to kill, a time to heal, a time to laugh, a time to weep.

Hank knew where the lyrics were from — he was a Catholic-school boy after all, even if he never saw the inside of a church now unless someone had been murdered there. They were right out of Ecclesiastes, and he'd always liked this bit more than most of the Bible. He nodded his head and listened as the song told him how there was a time and a season for everything. David's son, whoever he was, got that right.

There were some guys sitting along the bar. They were alone, smoking and not smoking, looking at their drinks or looking at the mirror in front of them. They didn't look like hippies or beatniks. No long hair, no fringed leather jackets, no funny cowboy hats, no dayglo rainbow colored t-shirts, no bell-bottom trousers, and no beards or goatees or beads. They seemed like the kind of guys you'd expect to find in any bar in Chicago any time in the last fifty years at two in the morning. Bored losers, lonely guys looking for something they couldn't name, or maybe looking for something they could name but didn't want to.

Hank swiveled his barstool. Along the wall, there was a scattering of small tables. Three couples there, and one of the couples was two guys. They were holding hands, dreaming into each other's eyes. They looked happy, looked good together.

The bartender set the Jack on ice in front of Hank and said, "That'll be a buck fifty."

Hank paid him, and before the bartender could turn away, Hank stopped him. "Let me ask you a question."

The bartender looked at him for a moment. Hank could see the guy was sizing him up — just like any halfway smart bartender knew to do with a stranger who asked questions. Then the bartender said, "Sure, as long as it's nothing personal."

"Personal to me or personal to you?"

"Either way. Nothing personal."

"Huh," Hank grunted. "What if I said I was a cop? Does that change the rules?"

"Yeah, that changes the rules," the bartender said and put the $1.50 back on the bar.

"No, you keep that. I just want to ask some questions."

The bartender looked at the money, then looked at Hank, and then shook his head. "Okay, shoot."

"Where are the hippies?"

"What the fuck? Seriously? Hippies?"

"Sure, I'm serious. I read in the *Tribune* just this last Sunday about how the hippies hang out in these bars and clubs on Clark, between Fullerton and Belmont, give or take. And that's why I'm here. I'm looking for hippies."

"In this place? They don't come here. Yeah, I mean sometimes I see a couple in here, but that's only sometimes. Anyways, I think this whole hippie thing is shit, a few kids and a lot of hype. You know what I mean — something the papers build up to sell papers. Like with the beatniks. Remember how big a deal they were supposed to be? I've been here for twenty years, ever since the end of the war, and I don't think I've ever seen a single live beatnik walk in."

"You get runaways?"

"Yeah, sure, they do show up sometimes. Especially in the winter with the snow and all, the cold nights. They come in here to get warm. They stick around sitting at a table for a while. They usually don't hang around for long — I roust them out. Bad for business. I tell them they got to buy or leave, so they leave."

"How do you know they're runaways?"

"You tend bar, you know," the bartender said, nodding his head slowly.

Hank dug into the pocket of his jacket and pulled out the 2 x 3 photo, the one of Margaret. He handed it to the bartender.

The bartender looked at the picture, turned it a bit to get some light on it so he could see it better.

"She a runaway?" Hank asked.

"Yeah, she's a runaway."

"How can you tell?"

"You're asking me about her. That's a tell."

Hank drank some of his whiskey and reached his hand out to retrieve the photo.

"She's my daughter," Hank said.

"Oh, Jeez, I'm sorry. I didn't mean any offense."

"She's been gone for four, going on five days. Where would you start looking?"

The bartender reached over to the draft beer spigot and filled himself a tall glass. "I don't know. Maybe I would start walking up and down the street and showing the photo to kids passing by."

"Yeah, that's what I was figuring to do."

"Good luck."

"Yeah," Hank said as he finished the Jack Daniel's and stood up.

It was still snowing outside, still dark out there too.

As he reached for the door, he remembered something he had heard or read years ago: *When you open a door into a dark room, you never know what you'll find.*

He felt that way right now.

Outside the snow fell soft and slow into the dark street, and Hank stood there and wondered what he should do next. There were no cars, no buses, just the dim street lights giving off some of their yellow light and the dim neon lights of the bar behind him, the Bear and Bull Tap, coloring the sidewalk red.

About twenty feet in front of him, a woman walked toward him out of the snow and darkness. She wasn't in any kind of rush. He could tell that by the way she walked and the way she looked straight at him. As she got closer, he knew too that she had no intention of just walking past him.

"Hi," she said as she stopped a foot away from Hank. "You got a cigarette?"

He nodded and dug one out of the chest pocket of his trench coat.

"It's a Chesterfield," Hank said. "Is that okay with you?"

The woman smiled a little and nodded.

"You need a match?"

"Yes, I need a match. And a warm drink by a fire."

"I can help you with the match, but not with the fire."

"That's okay. I can handle that. I live right up the street here. No fireplace, but I've got heat."

Hank lit her cigarette, and she said, "Come on, follow me."

And he did.

CHAPTER 25

HANK PICKED THE clear plastic evidence bag up off Marvin's desk and held it up to the long fluorescent light above his head.

The knife in the bag was unusual, but he had seen its kind before. It had a thin black-enameled metal handle and a four-inch blade. It was what some of the street punks called a gravity knife; if you folded the blade into the handle and flicked the handle hard enough, the blade would come flying out and lock in place. Sort of a poor man's switchblade, now that switchblades were illegal in the city. No fancy springs, just gravity and a flick and a click, and the blade was there instantly and ready to do some business. A gravity knife, but he had also heard it called a flick knife or a flicker. Dumb names.

Hank didn't have to look real close to see the blood. There was a smear of dried blood on the blade and on the handle both.

"This it?" Hank asked.

"Yeah, that's it," Marvin said. "At least, Mister Wizard down in forensics is pretty sure. He checked the blood against the sister's. Same type."

"Where did they find it?"

Marvin shrugged. "This is the weird part. You know that alley behind the convent and the school, the one between Washtenaw and Talman? Well, that's were they found it — in the bottom of a trash can about halfway down the alley toward LeMoyne."

Hank put the plastic bag back down on Marvin's desk. "Why the hell did it take them so long to find it? Didn't they check the trash cans up and down that alley last week, a few hours after the killing?"

Marvin shrugged again. "Yeah, they said they checked all the trash cans, and at first I was thinking like you're thinking. Some goofball rookie cop fucked up. Forgot to check some of the cans, forgot to lift the lids. But when I talked to the patrolmen, they swore they checked every single can there. Even left a white-chalk mark on each one they checked."

"So maybe they missed this the first time through, or maybe the knife is a recent addition."

"Yeah, that's the way it looks to me too. I figure it's a recent addition. The cans would've been picked up and emptied out last week when the garbage men came through. If that knife would've been there, those guys would've seen it for sure — they don't miss much, always looking for some kind of treasure in the trash. And if they didn't see the knife, it would've just gotten dumped into the garbage truck — it's too heavy to have stayed in the can when it got tipped in. So it pretty much has to have been thrown out after the garbage men did their thing."

Hank picked up the plastic bag again. He could see the knife clearly. He pressed his thumb against the sharp side of the knife's blade. There was no rust on it, but it felt dull, looked like it had been that way for a long time. Maybe had been made that way, and whoever bought it never sharpened it up properly to give it a good edge. But that didn't matter. A dull knife could kill as sure as a sharp one. It mostly depended on the strength of the man who was holding the knife. Or the woman. The important thing was the force driving the blade, and the angle. For straight stabbing, the edge wasn't too important. Fighting someone else who also had a knife was a different story.

"So somebody threw that blade into the trash can after the garbage was collected?" Hank said, turning to his partner.

"Yeah," Marvin said. "That's the way it looks. The fucker came back to the scene of the crime. Just like in the movies."

"Or maybe the killer never left the scene of the crime, or at least never went far away from it."

"Yeah, like you said on Friday to Father Anthony, maybe the killer is someone in this community, somebody in the neighborhood."

"That narrows it down."

"Yeah, all we have to do is check alibis for everyone in the neighborhood," Marvin said.

Hank looked at him, wondered if he was joking.

Marvin lit a cigarette, blew the match out, and flicked it into the trash can next to his desk. "Got any hunches?"

"Nothing that can stand on its own two feet."

"You going to ask me about the fingerprints?"

"Are you kidding? Okay, I'll ask: What about the fingerprints, Marvin?"

"There were a couple of good ones on the handle. Clear as the tits on an 8 by 10 glossy of Marilyn Monroe. The bad news is that the prints don't match any of the ones on file in the former-offender files. But they're still looking. The forensics guys are talking about checking the FBI files today."

"That'll take some time."

"Yeah," Marvin said. "So, let me ask you again — got any hunches?"

Hank had been a cop for a long time. He knew hunches were useless. Everybody had them, and they didn't mean a thing. Once in a while you got lucky with one, but usually they were wrong. What did his hunches tell him this time? That wasn't hard. The best bet was still that Father Ted was the killer. He had motive, plenty of motive. He would have kept his ass safe by keeping Sister Mary Philomena from spilling what she knew. But at the same time, it didn't seem all that likely that he knew Sister Mary Philomena was the one who had complained about him. And what about opportunity? Probably no opportunity to speak of. Father Ted was definitely at the hospital visiting sick and elderly parishioners that night, with plenty of witnesses. Slipping out, committing a bloody murder, cleaning himself up, and slipping back in before waltzing out again with his fellow priest and enjoying a late snack — all without anyone noticing anything — would be a pretty incredible bit of acrobatics. So Father Ted wasn't much of a hunch, but beyond that one, Hank didn't have any hunches at all.

"I'm still not in love with Father Ted, but if he's the perp I've got no idea how he could've pulled it off. So my best hunch is shit."

"What if it was just random?" Marvin said.

This time Hank just shrugged and didn't answer.

"No, listen. This is one fucking fucked-up neighborhood. I mean, imagine the area between Kedzie Avenue on the west side of Humboldt Park and Damen east of here, and between Lake to the south and Armitage to the north. Just a couple of square miles, and we've got three or four homicides a week, all year 'round. A lot of them are just kind of random. Guys killing people during a robbery, or some junkie or acid-head killing a dealer, or some pissed-off wife killing her husband, or some pissed-off husband killing his wife 'cause she wasn't happy with his being an asshole. Murder is just something that happens between people down here, like falling in love or one guy asking another guy for help making change. People kill each other sometimes — it's normal."

"Yeah," said Hank. "I guess if killing was so rare, God wouldn't have made a commandment against it."

"Absolutely. Killing may not be as frequent as fucking your neighbor's wife or missing Sunday school or synagogue on the Sabbath, but it's up there. People are killers, and people in this neighborhood seem to like it that way. I mean, it's not called Murdertown in the papers and the news shows for nothing."

"So what are you saying? Total stranger, no motive, nothing?"

"Sure, why not?"

"You're telling me that some guy stabs a nun in the basement of a convent 35 times, all for no reason?"

"It doesn't have to be a guy, remember. Some woman might have done it — we've seen a few like that. But sure, yeah, people kill, for no reason or for dumb reasons."

"So what's our job if this killing was like that — just random?"

"Our job? Same as always. Find the fucker and close him — or her — down."

Hank put the evidence bag back down on the desk. It would be nice if the prints on the knife led them to the killer; maybe they would, and maybe they wouldn't. The killer was either somebody they had prints for — like a guy who'd been in trouble with the law before, or a veteran, or a naturalized citizen — or he was like most other people in the USA, a person without prints on file. A crapshoot, that's all it was.

Hank looked up at Marvin. "So let's follow the shitty hunch we've got, and see if we can't pin this murder on Father Ted."

Marvin smiled. "Sure, that sounds like fun."

CHAPTER 26

HANK AND MARVIN stood at the reception desk at Norwegian American Hospital. There was a Christmas tree by the big picture window, with a crèche in front of it. Hank noticed someone had swiped the baby Jesus. What kind of world was it where someone would steal something like that? He didn't know the answer, but he was certain that if folks were stealing statues of Jesus already, it was probably time to take down the Christmas ornaments.

Marvin was working his charm on the receptionist, a middle-aged blonde in a yellow-and-red-striped dress. Her name tag said she was Claire.

"So, Claire, let me get this straight. You were on duty last Monday night when the two priests from Saint Fidelis were here, Father Ted Bachleda and Father Anthony Zak?"

"Yes, sir, I had a twelve-hour shift that night. I started at 4:00 PM and was scheduled to be here at the reception desk until 4:00 the next morning."

"That's a long shift. You must be ready to go home and sleep for a day after something like that."

Claire smiled. "Yeah, it's a long shift, but you get used to it. And it means I only work four days a week, not five. That's a good thing — gives me more time at home with my family."

"I know what you mean. I think I would work a single 40-hour shift if I could, just so I could spend more time with the people I love."

Claire smiled at him again.

"My partner here is getting impatient, so let me ask you again, just to be sure: You saw the two priests from Saint Fidelis Parish come in that Monday afternoon, Father Ted and Father Anthony?"

"Yes, sir, I saw the two priests. There were a number of priests here that Monday, from most of the parishes in the area. It was busy because of the snow, I guess. But I noticed Father Ted and Father Anthony, since it's pretty unusual for two priests from the same parish to show up together like that."

"You recognized them both?"

"Oh yes, sir, I've been here for seven years now, and I know all the local priests well. They come to Norwegian American religiously, after all."

She said that deadpan, then winked.

Marvin stared at her for a moment, winced, and said, "Oh. I get it."

She smiled and continued. "Every nearby parish has a priest visiting parishioners here at least once a week, and sometimes more often if there's a special situation. And we're not that far from Saint Fidelis Parish, so we see one of their priests here almost every day."

"What do you mean by 'a special situation'?"

The receptionist looked surprised and whispered, "You know, a parishioner dying, the priest needing to give them extreme unction — you know, last rites. Or if the parishioner remembers something he wants to confess, or just something he wants to tell the priest about while he still can."

Hank nodded to himself while Marvin asked her, "Do you like Father Ted?"

The receptionist leaned back on her stool. She seemed surprised by the question. "What do you mean 'like'?"

Marvin smiled and shrugged. "I don't mean anything much. You know...just whether or not he's easy to talk to, that kind of thing."

"Oh, okay, I see. Sure, the father is easy to talk to. He always makes a point of stopping by and chatting for a moment."

"How about Father Anthony?"

"Oh, he's more reserved. You know — old country. And sometimes Father Anthony is hard to understand, too, especially if it's noisy here. The Polish accent, you know? Of course, I like both of them, but Father Ted, well, he's a real hoot. He's always making some kind of joke or asking me how my family is. He's a nice man. I like to see him come to the hospital. I'm sure he does the patients from his parish a lot of good, brings them a smile or two." Claire smiled again then and fell silent.

Hank was getting antsy. After partnering with him for almost two decades, he knew Marvin's style. His partner liked to take his time in an interview, especially with the ladies they questioned. At this rate they might be here for another hour or two, so Hank stepped in and asked, "The night we're talking about, last Monday night. Did Father Ted seem...himself?"

"Oh sure. He asked me about Christmas and whether or not I got the presents I'd been wishing for. I told him I hadn't, mostly, but that was okay. For me the presents aren't a big part of Christmas. I guess that makes me old fashioned. And he said he was just the same. And then he said that really, the only present he ever worried about was the one for his mom. He always liked to get her something special, something she really wanted but was afraid to ask for. So I asked him what he got her this time, and he smiled, leaned up close to me, put his finger to his lips, and said, 'Shhh, it's a secret.' I laughed and he did too. Like I said, Father Ted is a real hoot."

"You remember what time he left?"

"What time Father Ted left? I think it was about 9 PM. That's when he usually leaves, just at the end of visiting hours."

"Did you see him leave?"

The receptionist looked down at her hands resting on the counter. It seemed to Hank like she was realizing for the first time that what she told the detectives might have some kind of significance beyond the usual patter, the usual back and forth. Claire glanced up after a moment.

"No...honestly, I can't say I saw him leave that night. Usually, there's a lot of traffic between 5 PM and 8 PM, but after 8 it really slows down. Visitors stop coming around then, since they know we're going to kick them out at 9:00 sharp anyway. So that's when I usually take my first break, around 8:15 or 8:30, but I think this Monday it was still kind of busy so I took my first break a little later, around 9:00. Even on a busy day, there's almost no incoming traffic at that point, just the last few visitors leaving. And it was still snowing like a son of a gun, you know, so that seemed like a good time to take a break. Have a cigarette, grab some coffee. I was probably doing all that when Father Ted and Father Anthony left. So no, I didn't see either of them leave."

"Since you didn't see him leave, he could have left earlier or later than 9:00?" Marvin asked.

Claire hesitated again, and then after a moment she said, "Yes, yes, I guess so. I really can't say. All I know is that I did see him and Father Anthony come into the hospital, but I didn't see either priest leave. But I'm pretty sure I would have seen them if they left before

I took my break, and I definitely would have noticed if they left after I got back at around 9:30 — the lobby was completely empty by then, and their being here so late would have been unusual."

Marvin leaned forward. He asked it again: "So you didn't see either one of the Saint Fidelis priests leave?"

Hank looked at Marvin, gave him a *back off* look. Claire was starting to tense up, starting to worry that she had screwed up somehow.

"Thank you so much, Claire," Hank said. "You've been very helpful. We're just going back over everything that happened last Monday, making sure all the time-lines add up."

The receptionist looked at Hank, and then she looked at Marvin, and then she looked at Hank again. "Does this have something to do with what happened to that poor sister at Saint Fidelis? Sister Mary Philomena? I knew her a little. She often came here to play with the sick kids in the children's ward. She was a wonderful lady."

Hank didn't say anything. He knew that Claire knew the answer was yes.

CHAPTER 27

HANK SAT AT his kitchen table that evening with a cup of black coffee in his hands and looked out the window. Even in the darkness outside, he could still see the snow drifting around the house. There was something magical about it. He remembered when he was a kid, maybe seven or eight, and he would stare out the window at night in the winter and wonder about the light the snow swirled in.

Where did the light come from? There was no sun and still there was light, and each snowflake flickered like there was a tiny candle inside, burning cold and bright.

He remembered when he finally asked his father about the light, about whether this was part of the miracle of Christmas that the priest talked about in church and the nuns talked about in school. His father was standing by the front window in the three-room apartment they were renting at the time, and he turned to Hank with a serious look on his face. His dad wasn't a guy who talked a lot, or talked funny ever. He was a serious guy in a serious time, what people would come to call the Great Depression. After a moment, his dad said, "Sure, kid, it's a miracle." And his father didn't say anything else. He just kept staring out the window with Hank, the two of them looking at the light flickering in the falling snowflakes in the darkness together.

Here now in his kitchen, staring out the window thinking about miracles, Hank knew that there *were* miracles, stuff that defied all logic and explanation. He also knew that the lights in snowflakes weren't miracles — they were just the product of light and reflection, the intersection of the absence of light and the presence of darkness, the presence of light and the absence of darkness, that kind of stuff. The mumbo-jumbo of science that explained whatever could be explained. But there were still miracles. Twenty years of being a cop and two years of being in the army before that, being married, raising a daughter, all those things had taught him that there were miracles. The dead that came alive. The living that were dead. The days that were darker than night, and the nights that were brighter than any day he had ever seen.

If he could pray, he would pray for a miracle. He would pray that his daughter Margaret would walk right through the door into this kitchen and say — just like when she was a kid — *What's cooking, daddy-o?*

But he couldn't pray for that miracle. He knew that wasn't how miracles worked. Miracles happened when they happened, and no amount of prodding or pleading or weeping or cursing God or begging Mother Mary or the saints brought them on any faster than anything else.

Hank heard the front door open then, and for a moment he caught himself listening as closely as he could. He listened the way a dying man listened to the swish and click of each of his own last breaths. He knew it couldn't be Margaret, but still he listened for the miracle.

"Honey, it's me. You home?" his wife Hazel called from the hallway.

"I'm in the kitchen. Having some coffee."

A moment later, Hazel was there in the kitchen with him. Hank looked at her and she looked at him. They both knew there had been no miracle, no light flickering in the darkness. Their daughter was still missing.

"I made a pot," Hank said as he motioned toward the Pyrex coffee pot on the stove. "It's half decaf and half the real stuff. Guaranteed to keep you half awake and half asleep, I guess."

Hazel smiled, got herself a cup of coffee, and sat down across from Hank.

"How's work?" he asked.

She smiled a little. "Work? It's there, like always. Everybody is still talking about what their Christmas and New Year's were like. What they cooked, who they saw, the gifts their kids got, the parties they went to. They'll get bored with that stuff soon, and move on to something else just as boring."

She didn't say anything else for a while.

Hank watched her look at her hands, pick up her coffee, drink some. She seemed to be listening to something, *for* something, just like he was.

Then she spoke again. "How's the investigation going?"

"Which one?"

"Any of them, I guess. Sister Mary Philomena's death? Margaret's disappearance? That drug dealer with the dog nailed to his wall?"

Hank didn't say anything. Now it was his turn to look down at the cup of coffee in his hands. He felt like a failure and a fool, like a man drowning in his own weakness and inadequacy.

Hazel had no trouble reading his thoughts. "Hank, don't... please don't," she said.

He couldn't look up at her. Couldn't say anything. Couldn't lift his hands off the table, couldn't smile or frown or weep. He needed a miracle — maybe a few of them at once.

"Hank, tell me about the Sister Mary Philomena case."

He lifted the cup and drank some of the coffee. It was lukewarm. "I told you we found what looks like the murder weapon, a gravity knife. It was in a trash can in the alley, about halfway between the convent and the next street north. They're still trying to match up the prints on the blade with the prints in our files and the FBI files. It's not easy. It'll be great if they have something by the end of the week. But we're not too optimistic."

"Why not?"

Hank knew what she was doing: trying to get him out of his funk. Trying to work him back to the surface. He was grateful for the help.

"You know... it's the difference between the way prints work in the real world and the way they work on TV. It would be one thing if everybody in this country had his prints on file. We'd send the prints in, and *Shazam!* we'd have the name of the killer and his picture and his address. But the problem is that they don't have all those prints on file. They've got prints on maybe 20% of the people in this country, mostly criminals and military, plus immigrants. If you aren't in one of those groups, you're not likely to be identifiable from your prints — so the only good news is that the neighborhood's full of criminals and immigrants. But we're hopeful anyway. You want to know what the best news is we've heard so far?"

Hazel nodded her head and said, "Yes. Tell me."

"The best news is that we're still looking at one of the priests for our killer."

"You mean the young priest, the one who handles the Teen Club at Saint Fidelis?"

"Yeah, he's the one — Father Ted Bachleda. He has an alibi for the night of the murder and we thought at first that it was rock-solid, but now it turns out it's not as solid as we thought. There's good evidence for the start of his alibi — showing up at the hospital where he was visiting the sick — but the evidence that he was there until nine o'clock is looking a little shaky. He definitely showed up at the hospital before the crime was committed, but he may have left in time for him to get back to the parish to do it."

"But what about the other priest, Father Anthony? Didn't he say he was with Father Ted the whole time?"

"Yeah, he did, but maybe he's lying, or maybe Bachleda slipped out while Father Anthony was with a parishioner and then got back in time for them to leave together. They mostly didn't visit the same patients while they were there; the whole reason Father Thomas sent them both was that there were too many parishioners there for one priest to handle."

Hazel shook her head and took another sip of her coffee. She looked tired. Hank could see it in her eyes, the color of her face — a yellow that was giving way to something darker. He had seen it before, the look she had, on the faces of the men he'd been with in the army. They called it shell shock back then, or combat fatigue, or battle weariness. A lot of different things. The look of someone who had lost hope and was waiting for the next piece of bad luck, the bullet or shell that would end it all.

"Anything new about that drug dealer, Willy Something?" Hazel asked.

"I talked to the detectives up at the Rogers Park Station. One of them said that this guy was small potatoes, mostly just selling grass to college students and people like that. Nothing harder, nothing wholesale. He was apparently getting his supply from another small-time dealer. Other than the marijuana, they haven't found anything on him."

"Whoever left his dog like that, crucified on the wall, must have really wanted to hurt him."

"Yeah . . . and it wasn't easy to do. Whoever did that must have had somebody helping him, holding the dog up while he nailed the poor thing to the wall. Maybe even two helpers — golden retrievers are pretty big dogs."

Hazel picked up her coffee cup again, held it to her lips. She didn't say anything and neither did Hank.

He knew what she was thinking. The unthinkable: that maybe their daughter Margaret, the little girl who loved books and dolls and puzzles, had lifted and pressed the body of a dog to a wall as someone took a hammer to its paws.

CHAPTER 28

THE CALL CAME in at about five that afternoon.

Hank and Marvin were driving west down Division Street headed toward one of the old Polish neighborhood bars on Washtenaw, the White Eagle Tap. There had been a report of a theft. When the owner opened the storage room down in the basement, he found that it was empty — the twenty-three cases of bourbon and scotch and vodka that were supposed to be there were gone. The patrolman had called for some investigators, so Hank and Marvin were tagged and were just about to turn onto Washtenaw.

That's when the police dispatcher's ragged, staticky voice came through on the car's radio and told them to forget the missing booze and get up to 1523 Washtenaw instead. A dead body. A boy, maybe ten, maybe eleven.

Hank recognized the building as soon as he pulled up in front of it.

And he recognized the kid, too, as soon as he saw him hanging from the bar in the coat closet. It was Tommy Sawa, the nice kid they'd talked to a few days ago, a couple days after Sister Mary Philomena was killed. The altar boy with the screwed-up father, the guy Hank thought of as "the wrestler". The kid they took to his friend's house to wait for his mom — the mom who would keep him safe.

She didn't.

Most of the facts were pretty obvious, but Hank and Marvin listened to the patrolman talk them through what had happened anyway. He was a young cop, maybe twenty-two, maybe even a bit younger. The name on his nameplate was Thomas Morrison. He pulled a notepad out of his back pocket and read from it, straight and slow just the way the instructors at the Police Academy had taught him.

"Well, Detectives," Morrison said, "apparently the boy was a student at Saint Fidelis School just down the street. School let out as usual today at three o'clock. It looks like he had just gotten home from school; he was still wearing his grade-school uniform: a light-tan, long-sleeved shirt, a dark-blue tie, and dark-blue pants. It looks like he pulled a wooden step-stool that's kept in this closet to a position right under the bar, then he stood on the stool and tied a rope around the bar. It's meant to hold winter coats, so it's pretty sturdy. He'd probably already tied a noose on the other end of the rope. Then he placed the noose around his neck and jumped off the stool. It looks like a suicide."

"What the fuck," Marvin said. "What the fuck."

"You got the kid's name?" Hank asked the patrolman.

"Yes, sir, it's Tommy Sawa. We got it from his mom."

"Good God, is she here?" Marvin said.

"Yes, sir, she's the one who found him. She's downstairs now, in a neighbor's apartment."

Just then Hank heard it. It came from the apartment below them: one long piercing cry of pain, a cry that went back, way back, back to the first mother who found the dead body of her first murdered son, Eve and her little boy Abel, killed by the other boy she gave birth to, nursed, and loved. Then Hank heard it again.

The wailing lasted for at least two minutes — a long, long cry of grief and pain.

When it finally sank into sobbing, Marvin turned to Patrolman Morrison and asked, "How did she find Tommy?"

"She came home from work around 4:30 PM and went looking for the boy. Usually, she knocks and he opens the door for her. We got this from the lady downstairs. But this time he didn't open the door, so she entered the apartment and called for him. When he didn't answer, she went from room to room looking for him, noticed the closet stool lying on its side on the floor, and decided to look inside the closet. When she opened the closet door, that's when she saw her son and ran downstairs for help. It was the lady downstairs, Mrs. Pytlok, who called the police to report it."

Hank didn't want to look at Tommy Sawa, didn't want to think about this. He liked the kid. Liked his pluck. Saddled with a crazy dad built like a truck, he dealt with it the way the best kids deal with bad situations: putting up with the bullshit and meanness and troubles without letting them get him too far down. He'd seemed like a good boy who deserved a good life, and now this.

Hank walked up to look at the body. He had seen suicides before, seen the faces of men and women who had hanged themselves. It wasn't something he liked to look at.

He had seen men and women who had been shot to death, beaten to death, stabbed to death, even starved to death. And their faces, mostly, suggested some kind of repose. It was like their death, no matter how brutal and terrible, did what it was supposed to do — bring some kind of relief, some kind of peace.

It wasn't that way with folks who'd hanged themselves. He guessed that's why in the old days they put sacks over the heads of the people who were being executed by hanging — to spare the living the look of the sorrow and brutality written on the faces of the hanged.

Hank looked at Tommy Sawa's face. It was the kind of face you only saw in nightmares: the skin growing purple, the eyes bulging wide, the pupils wide and stark in horror, the tongue swollen and trying to escape the mouth, trying to find some last taste of life. He remembered one of the concentration camps he and his platoon came upon at the end of the Second World War. There was a gallows there, and hanging from a center pole there were six emaciated bodies in striped rags, the shit and piss coloring those rags black, the faces of the dead speaking of the horrors they had seen in the camp. There was no peace for them.

Tommy Sawa's face was like that — it also spoke of horrors. If he'd killed himself because he was looking for some kind of peace, his face told Hank he hadn't found it. What the little altar boy had found was some other kind of hell.

"Jesus," Hank said, and he stepped even closer to the body, to the face that once before had said, *help me, help me*. He wanted to touch that face with his hand, say something to the boy that would ease his leaving, his dying, but Hank knew that was all useless. The dead only wanted one thing — to be left alone with their silence and the darkness. And the forensics guys would give him hell if he touched the victim.

Behind him, Hank heard the door open, and then there were voices and the sound of bags being put down. He turned around and saw Billy Tate and his three-man forensics team. Billy was saying something to the short guy on his crew and smiling. The short guy shrugged, and then he smiled back.

Hank wanted to tell Billy and the short guy to shut the fuck up and to stop smiling, but he didn't. He waited till Billy stepped closer and said, "Hey, Billy, we knew this kid. Marvin and I interviewed him last week, about the Sister Mary Philomena murder. When you're doing your work, make sure you look over the kid's body carefully. His dad seemed to be a bastard who beat the kid pretty severely, for no reason other than meanness. Let us know if that shows up in your workup."

"Sure, Hank," Billy said, "we'll keep our eyes open. Terrible, something like this. A kid killing himself."

"Yeah," Hank said, and then Hank knew it was time to leave. He looked at Marvin. His partner seemed lost in his own memories. Hank and Marvin had to go where there was no smiling. They had to go talk to Tommy Sawa's mom downstairs.

CHAPTER 29

TOMMY'S MOM SAT in the kitchen weeping, her hands twisting together, a damp yellow handkerchief in her lap. Her husband, the big tough guy who had been so hard on his son, sat on a wooden chair next to her. He had an arm around her shoulder, and he was patting her hands. He wasn't crying; instead he seemed confused, shocked. Something had happened that he didn't understand and would never understand. His son — the boy he bullied and razzed and beat the shit out of — was dead. The kid who always came back from the hard times his dad gave him was dead, a suicide.

Hank hated this part of his job.

He walked up to Tommy's parents and stood there for a moment. The boy's dad finally looked up at him and Marvin.

Hank took off his hat and said to Tommy's mother, "I'm sorry, Mrs. Sawa, but I've got to ask you and your husband some questions."

"This can't wait?" Tommy's father asked in a gravelly whisper.

"I wish it could. I promise you, it won't take long, and then we'll leave you alone."

Mrs. Sawa didn't say anything. She just kept looking down at her hands and weeping.

After a moment, Tommy's father nodded his head, and Hank sat down on one of the kitchen chairs. Marvin stood next to the refrigerator, a few feet behind Hank.

"Can you tell us what kind of mood your son was in recently?"

"Mood?" Tommy's father said, glaring at Hank and then at Marvin. "What the fuck are you talking about — mood! He was always the same. From the time he was a baby. A good boy, quiet. He liked to sit and read, liked to play with his puzzles, liked to help the priests with their Masses and holy days. Stuff didn't bother him. It rolled off his back. I don't understand this, what happened. It don't make no sense. Why'd he do it?"

Hank nodded. "That's what we're trying to find out here, Mr. Sawa. What happened and why it happened."

Sawa grunted, shook his head, and turned his face away from Hank.

Hank looked at the boy's mother then and said, "Mrs. Sawa, I know this is hard, but if you could just give us a moment. Tell us about your son. Did you notice anything unusual about him, his actions or his attitude, these last couple of days?"

Mrs. Sawa looked up at Hank and tried to rub the tears from her eyes. Her lips were pressed shut, but they were moving, as if her soul was preparing some kind of message from its deepest parts. Hank waited.

Finally, she spoke. "Like his father said, officer, Tommy was quiet, a good boy. Even when his father was rough with him, hard on him, Tommy still was a good boy. He always forgave his dad for everything. I don't know why our son did this. It wasn't like him. He never complained, never seemed angry or hurt. He was always quiet, good, kind, cheerful. Even when he was a baby. Always smiling, always making happy noises. I just don't understand it."

As she spoke, Mrs. Sawa's Polish accent grew stronger.

"Can you tell us what he was like the last time you saw him?"

Hank asked.

"This morning? He was the way he always was. We sat there having breakfast. He liked to read at breakfast, and I always let him, even though it's not really polite. He was reading a comic book. Something with Spiderman — he liked Spiderman. He ate his Cheerios and he read, and then he started laughing — I guess there was something funny in the book. I looked up and asked him why he was laughing, and he told me...but I wasn't really listening, so I don't remember what he said." She choked up and made a small gasping sob.

Her husband was suddenly angry again. He looked at Hank and shouted, "For Christ's sake, can't you leave us alone? Don't you see what you're doing?"

"Bruno, please," Tommy's mom said, "I want to help the police. Please let me talk."

Hank didn't take his eyes off her. "Ma'am, please take your time."

"There's not much more. He finished his cereal, and then he made his lunch — a cheese sandwich. He packed it in a paper bag with an apple, took his books, said goodbye, and he was gone. That's the last time I saw him."

She stopped then and looked down at her hands again like she was finished, but Hank felt there was something else she wanted to say.

And there was. She looked back up at Hank and said, "He didn't let me give him a kiss. He felt like he was supposed to be a big boy, and I guess he thought big boys don't let their mothers kiss them goodbye. He was only eleven, but he left without a kiss. I couldn't kiss him goodbye. I didn't kiss him goodbye."

Hank waited for a moment before he asked his next question. "Mrs. Sawa, did Tommy say anything recently about how he was doing at school? Or maybe about his duties as an altar boy?"

"Of course, he talked about his friends and the priests and the nuns, but there was nothing unusual. It wasn't like he was having any trouble there."

"Nothing about being at the rectory, or how the priests were treating him?"

"No, nothing special. Tommy loved serving at Mass, loved helping the priests. He didn't say anything more than that about them."

Hank nodded. If there was something going on between Tommy Sawa and the priests, his mother didn't seem to know about it. He tried again, just to be sure. "How about Father Ted? How did your son get along with him?

Tommy's mother didn't look up. "Tommy liked Father Ted a lot. He thought he was funny. He liked the way he was always telling jokes, especially about Elvis Presley and rock and roll and things like that."

"Did Tommy ever seem nervous or confused, or maybe more quiet than usual, when he came back from seeing Father Ted?"

Mrs. Sawa raised her eyes, looked at Hank, and shook her head. "No, nothing like that. He was always smiling when he came home from serving Mass with Father Ted. All Tommy wanted to do was tell us the jokes Father Ted told him, so we could hear them before he forgot them. When Tommy told the jokes we'd all start laughing. Even his dad."

The wrestler nodded his head slowly and said, "Tommy loved those jokes."

Hank waited a moment and asked Mrs. Sawa his last question, "How have Tommy and his dad been getting along? The last time we saw them together there seemed to be a lot of tension between them. Mr. Sawa seemed real angry at Tommy."

She didn't speak at first. She looked at her husband, and he dropped his eyes. Then she said, "Detective, I know what you're saying, but it wasn't like that recently. These last few days have been different. Tommy and his dad were getting along. They were working together on some kind of project, some gift for me — I think it was for my birthday."

Hank looked at Tommy's father. The big man's head was cradled in his hands, and Hank could hear him softly weeping.

Mrs. Sawa put her hand on her husband's head and brushed it softly. Then she looked at Hank and asked him again what she had asked him earlier: "I just don't understand, detective. Please tell me why our son did this, why Tommy hurt himself so much. Can you tell us that, please, officer? You're a man who has seen such things before. Maybe you know? Maybe you can tell us?"

Hank sat across the table and didn't say anything, didn't nod, didn't shrug, didn't frown, didn't sigh. There was nothing helpful he could do or say, nothing he could tell her. She was right — he had seen such things before, but none of what he'd seen had prepared him for what had happened upstairs in her apartment. No other death prepared him for the one he'd seen upstairs, and this death wouldn't prepare him for the next one.

But Hank knew what to say to her, even though he knew it wouldn't really help. He was about to tell her what he always told the people left behind when they asked him what Mrs. Sawa had asked him, the question they all asked, when he heard a sound behind him, someone knocking on the door in the front room. Mrs. Pytlok, the Sawas' downstairs neighbor, answered it.

"Come in, Father," Mrs. Pytlok said.

Hank turned around.

Father Ted Bachleda came into the apartment, hugged Mrs. Pytlok, and said, "Such a terrible, terrible day."

Hank looked up at Marvin. His partner, who had been quietly leaning against the refrigerator this whole time, suddenly wasn't — jaw clenched, he started toward the front room.

Hank knew what was coming. He grabbed at Marvin's arm. "Don't."

Marvin shook off Hank's hand and said, "I got this one."

He rushed to the front room.

Hank jumped up. "Excuse me," he said, and followed his partner. As he crossed over into the front room, Hank saw Marvin step up to Father Ted. The detective stood there for a moment facing the tall priest, not saying anything.

"What?" the priest finally said, looking impatiently at the detective blocking his way.

Marvin still didn't say anything. Instead he jerked back his right hand and punched Father Ted in the face. The priest fell back hard a step, swayed, but caught himself from falling.

Then Marvin did it again. He punched the young priest in the face with all the strength he had, right between the eyes.

This time, the priest dropped to the floor before Marvin could slug him again.

Hank said, "Jesus," and ran up to Marvin, pushed him out the door, and turned to the priest. "Sorry, Father. My partner's got a temper."

CHAPTER 30

HANK STOOD IN the Wood Street Police Station's third floor men's room and straightened his gray-checkered tie. It was one Margaret had given him for Father's Day last year. He wondered if she would be around this year for Father's Day. He shook his head.

Lieutenant O'Herlihy's decision didn't surprise him. It was fast but understandable. You don't punch a priest in the face twice, knock him out, and just walk away from it. Two days after laying out Father Ted, Marvin had been suspended for two weeks without pay. A couple weeks wasn't so bad, Hank figured. It could easily have cost his partner his job, except that the father didn't want to press charges. Hank guessed Father Ted was trying to show himself to be a decent guy — not a bad strategy for a suspect.

But still, Hank knew the suspension would be hard on his partner — not the money, but the inactivity. Marvin had never been the kind of guy who liked puttering around the house, planting geraniums, working on his stamp collection, standing at the kitchen window and staring out at the falling snow. That kind of stuff was nice, but not for Marvin.

The toilet flushed just then, a rough raucous sound. The stall door opened, and Hank's partner came out of the stall.

"Well, that wasn't too bad," Marvin said as he lathered up his hands. "Two weeks without pay is kind of a drag, but you figure that's about seven days' suspension for each punch I got in, including weekends. That's not so much on a per-punch basis. I was about to kick that motherfucker in the balls when you pushed me out of there. That kick would have cost me my job, I bet, even if he's not supposed to be using them for anything."

"Yeah," Hank said. "And then where the hell would you be? Most employers don't have much use for a middle-aged cop with a drinking problem *and* an aggression problem."

Marvin turned off the faucet and laughed. A long, serious laugh. Then he said, "If they start firing middle-aged cops who like to get drunk and throw a punch every so often, there'll be nobody left to pass out tickets and eat donuts."

"Yeah, I guess," Hank said.

"Hank, I never believed what the other guys said about you — that you were a real prick with no sense of humor. But after all this time, I realize the guys were almost right. You really are a prick, but you do have a sense of humor. Problem is, it's one that I wouldn't dump in the toilet of anyone I liked." Marvin laughed again.

Hank didn't smile. "Where you going now?" he asked.

"Where are *you* going now?" Marvin answered.

"I'm heading back to my desk."

"Mind if I tag along?"

"You kidding? Don't you have anything better to do?"

"Nope. I'm going to practice my detecting skills by trailing you for the next two weeks. Maybe I can learn how to be a real detective."

There was a file on Hank's desk when they got back to his office at the Shakespeare Substation. He picked up the manila folder and sat down. It was thin, not much to look at. "Tommy Sawa's file," he said.

"Jesus, already?" Marvin said as he sat down across from his partner.

"I guess."

"Open it up."

"You want to read it?"

"Are you kidding? I'm suspended — I'm not allowed to read exciting cop paperwork for the next two weeks. You read it and tell me the good parts."

Hank started reading. It didn't take long; there wasn't much there. The kid had no record, no history with the police. It didn't take Hank more than a minute to find what he was looking for; and when he did, he dropped the folder back down on the desk.

"The prints?" Marvin asked.

"Yeah, they got them here. They compared his to the ones on the knife. Same prints. It looks like now Tommy Sawa is our prime suspect. Or rather, was our prime suspect."

"What the fuck? Are you kidding? That kid didn't kill Sister Mary Philomena. You and me both heard him talk about her. No way he did it!"

"That's not what this file says. It says here that he wasn't home for most of the evening when Sister Mary Philomena was killed. His parents said they thought he was either at the library or at his friend Eugene Wosh's house, but the patrolmen checked, and that's not where he was. The librarians at the Humboldt Park Branch of the Public Library knew Tommy well, and they said that they didn't see him that night. Ditto with his friend Eugene, and his other friend Donald Walton, the one he used to stay with when his father was in a hitting mood."

"Yeah, but there's no suicide note, no confession."

"Come on, Marvin, you know as well as I do that most suicides don't leave a note."

Marvin stood up and picked up the folder. He read a couple pages. Then he looked back at Hank.

"I don't know," Marvin said. "This kid was eleven years old, and there wasn't much to him. A good lawyer would say that he didn't have the size or the strength to take on anybody, even a nun, and stab her to death."

"A better lawyer would say that if the attacker took the nun by surprise and his adrenaline was jacked up to the sky because of some kind of crazy rage or fear or hate or love, even a scrawny kid like Tommy could pull it off. You've seen this kind of stuff. You know what people can do."

Marvin dropped the file on Hank's desk. "Yeah…you know, I once got called to a bar on Milwaukee Avenue where a mom took out two drunks with her handbag when they tried to touch her little girl. She beat them to the ground and kicked their asses for twenty feet before they managed to get away from her. What was even crazier was that she was pregnant, maybe eight months, big as a house."

"I think they're going to declare this case closed, Marvin, real fast," Hank said. "The kid's fingerprints are on the knife. He knew the victim, had the opportunity, didn't have an alibi. And probably they could make an argument for motive. Like Sister Mary Philomena told me, Tommy saw her when she spotted him and the priest together in that room behind the altar. The prosecutor would have argued that the kid was trying to keep word from getting out that he was doing this bad thing with the priest. And maybe he figured he was doing the priest a favor, saving the father's soul or reputation or something. Saving his ass, in any case."

"Hank, come on, you listened to that kid. You saw what he was like. There's no way he could have done it, killed Sister Mary Philomena."

"Yeah, I feel the way you do, Marv, but I don't see what we can do here."

Marvin pushed the office door closed and leaned close to Hank. "We can do what we did before. We can do the law's work for it."

Hank said, "Yeah...."

And then he thought for a minute about doing the law's work for it. There were times when Hank and Marvin had done that, been judge and jury. They had meted out punishment with fists and feet and sometimes Marvin's sap. And once or twice they had even been executioners. That part of the business had troubled Hank for years — fucked up his dreams, fucked up everything he thought and felt. He shook his head. "But it ain't that easy this time. Anyone we ever killed, we knew everything we needed to know about them. We knew they were killers — they admitted it to us, right to our faces, and laughed at us 'cause they knew we couldn't touch them, because they were too important, too connected, too much of a big shot."

"Come on, man," Marvin said, sitting down again. "We got proof here, too. Sister Mary Philomena sees the priest with Tommy. Tommy sees the nun. The next thing we know the sister is dead."

"What links the priest and the sister?"

"The kid tells the priest. The priest is worried about the nun turning him in. The priest kills her."

"Maybe," Hank said. "But *maybe* isn't good enough. *Maybe* doesn't give us the right to kill someone."

"And then he frames Tommy the altar boy for the killing. Holds onto the knife till he can plant the kid's prints on it, then ditches the knife in a trash can near the boy's house."

"Then he kills the kid and makes it look like the kid committed suicide?" Hank asked.

"Yeah, for Christ's sake. That sounds right."

"Maybe that's the way it happened. It's a possible scenario, but I think we're going to have to have some pretty strong evidence to back it up. And we don't have that — not any more today than we had the day Sister Mary Philomena's body was found."

Marvin leaned back in the chair and didn't say anything.

Hank knew what his partner was thinking. Marvin was trying to get his mind around the killing, trying to remember some little piece of it that would be the key that started the scenario up, got it moving and skipping along.

Hank wanted to find that key too, but he didn't think there was much chance of it. All of the brass of the Chicago Police Department were going to be delighted with the way this case was heading now, the way it was closing up neat and tight, with a killer everyone could believe in and no need for a trial where the prosecutors might have to do some actual work to get a conviction. And tomorrow when the *Chicago Tribune* and the *Sun Times* ran their articles about the altar boy Tommy Sawa and the nun he killed by stabbing her 35 times in the gut, a lot of the police bigwigs would be bowing their heads and modestly accepting the good wishes of the city upon their brows.

Accolades too, all around, for all those guys who didn't know anything about Sister Mary Philomena and Tommy Sawa, the kid who wouldn't have killed her in a million years.

The case would be closed, no question.

Marvin leaned forward. "Hank, I can see you're thinking. That's good. I like thinking, especially when I'm not the one who has to do it, but knowing that there's thinking going on is only half the fun. I'd like to know *what* you're thinking, you know? Can you share that little pittance with a brother?"

Hank nodded. "I think we're not done thinking. And I think that while we keep thinking, we're going to look for Margaret."

CHAPTER 31

HANK AND MARVIN stood in the living room of Willy Reich-ard's apartment. The dealer with the phony beard wasn't home. They didn't expect him to be. He had disappeared before his dog was found dead, and he didn't seem to be in any hurry to come back.

They got the key to the apartment from the super. Hank told him they were detectives and wanted to look around; the super stuck his cigar in his mouth and said, "Knock yourselves out, guys."

So that's what they were doing.

Hank stood in the living room and sniffed. The smell of the dead golden retriever was still in the air, the sweet and burning smell of shit and death. It would probably be in the air for a long time. Death and shit were smells you couldn't get rid of with Lysol or Ajax cleanser. Hank imagined it wouldn't be easy renting out this apartment for a good long while. Nobody wanted to live someplace where the smell of shit and death wouldn't go away.

The detective walked into the kitchen and pulled open a drawer. Nothing but cheap, shitty cutlery, mismatched plastic-handled knives and forks and spoons. He moved through the kitchen, pulling open more drawers and opening cabinets. They were all stuffed with stuff, but it was stuff that he didn't want to bother looking through. Dishes, cans of Campbell's Tomato Soup, towels and dishwashing detergents.

It was funny to see all that normal stuff. Hank was surprised, although he knew he should know better. He kept shaking his head and thinking that junkies lived pretty well — they had their domestic sides, just like the housewives you saw on TV, the ones in *Bewitched* or *Donna Reed*, even if the kitchens on TV were cleaner and the dogs on TV weren't nailed to anything. The world was a crazy place.

In the living room, Marvin was singing some Christmas song, something about Santa Baby hurrying down the chimney tonight. There was something sexy about it, even hearing Marvin's gravel voice stumble through it. Hank didn't know the song and wondered who'd recorded it. He'd have to find out. If Margaret was around, she'd be the one to ask.

He reached for the refrigerator door while he watched Marvin slowly turn over one pillow and then another on the couch. Hank was surprised his partner was being so careful; it was easy to forget that Marvin was a very good detective when he didn't think anyone would catch him at it.

Hank opened the refrigerator. The milk was old, smelled of dairy rot, had an odd green tint to it. He felt like gagging. He poured the milk down the sink and washed it down with water from the faucet. He figured that spoiled milk didn't count as evidence of anything interesting. Then he opened the freezer. Behind a half-gallon container of Borden's vanilla ice cream, he found a plastic bag full of grass, maybe five ounces. Behind that was another half-gallon container of vanilla ice cream. There were two more on the other side of the freezer — four altogether. Willy the Dealer must really like vanilla ice cream.

In the living room Marvin was on his hands and knees now, looking under the straw-colored couch. He was reaching for something.

Hank placed the four half-gallon ice-cream boxes on the Formica table in the kitchen and opened the first one. Vanilla ice cream, as advertised, with a few scoops gone. The second one was the same, but full. The third one was the surprise. It felt lighter than the first two, and he figured maybe this was the one Willy had been mostly working on before he disappeared, but then when Hank accidentally gave it a little shake, it didn't sound like ice cream in there. He shook it again and listened, like a kid shaking a box of Cracker Jack trying to figure out what the prize was. The last box was also full of some kind of goodies other than what Elsie the Cow had put in there.

"Hey, Marvin, get over here."

Marvin looked up from beside the couch and grunted. "Can't you see I'm busy? I'm an *alter cocker* — you think it was easy for me to get into this position?"

"You got to see this."

Marvin stood up slowly and walked over to the kitchen table.

"So Willy the Dealer liked his ice cream. So what? Borden's is pretty good stuff."

Hank took one of the containers in both hands and gave it a shake. "This one doesn't feel like ice cream. Or sound like it." He opened the box and spilled its contents on the table: a couple hundred little squares of red blotter paper, each one in a little plastic bag.

"Holy shit, LSD!" Marvin said. He picked up one of the bags and read the label on it. "Red Dog? What kind of shit name is that? I don't think I'd ever want to try something with a dumb-ass name like that."

"What I don't get is what it's doing here. How come the patrolmen didn't check out the icebox?"

Marvin shrugged and smiled. "Too fucking busy jerking each other off in front of the dead mutt, maybe?"

Hank picked up one of the packets of acid and held it between his thumb and index finger. Suddenly, he snapped the bit of blotter loose from its plastic bag.

"Remind me again what this stuff's like, Marvin?"

"You like to see black snakes crawling out of a burning refrigerator? How about some beautiful naked chicks suddenly turning into leopards with long, curling teeth and trying to take a nice big bite out of your prick?"

"Doesn't sound like a lot of fun."

"Yeah. I've dropped acid about four or five times. Mostly it's like that — one bad fucking trip after another."

Hank shook his head.

"…But you know, probably that's just me," Marvin continued. "It ain't always that way. If it was, you could bet your ass you couldn't sell this stuff for a red cent, let alone the five bucks per hit that this shit probably costs on the street. You know a Jew patrolman named Max Shapiro, works Rogers Park?"

"Yeah," Hank said, sitting down at the table. Marvin pulled out the other metal chair and sat down across from him.

"Well, Max, he tells me he takes it about once or twice a month, and every time it's rainbows and golden sunshine dripping down from heaven, and Buddha sitting on his fat ass and smiling at him like he was the Prince of Peace, God's Great Gift to Mankind riding on a white unicorn. Max is a walking ad for acid. You hear him tell it, there's nothing better for your mental and physical condition than a regular hit of LSD. So I keep trying it, but if I got a unicorn it'd probably stick its horn up my ass."

Hank sniffed the plastic bag. It didn't smell like anything. He brought the thin red blotter of acid up to his nose, sniffed again. Still nothing.

"You're not going to smell anything, Hank, but I wouldn't let that shit get anywhere near my big Jew nose, my man, and you shouldn't either. You don't know what kind of crap might be in that thing — I wouldn't trust this Willy to be selling good-quality stuff."

Hank stuck the blotter paper back in the bag. "What's this haul worth?"

"I'm thinking there are maybe about two hundred little bags in each carton. Each bag is worth maybe five bucks. That's a thousand bucks a box. Two boxes are two thousand bucks on the street, more or less. One more carton and you can buy yourself a pretty little Mustang convertible, with plenty left over for gas and girlfriends."

"That's not bad for a couple half-gallons of ice cream. Which reminds me — we should put the real ice cream back. No sense letting good evidence melt, and Willy might be figuring on a snack when he gets home."

"Yeah. My guess is that he was planning on eating more ice cream *and* selling more acid. Let's see if we can find some more interesting stuff stashed around the place."

———

They didn't.

After another hour of searching, they were back in the kitchen standing over the Formica table.

Hank looked at the two vanilla ice cream cartons sitting there. "What makes no sense to me is why this stuff is still here. Our junkie friend Willy wouldn't have walked away from it, not two thousand bucks' worth. He probably paid a half a grand for this, so why would he leave it behind? And if he didn't leave it behind intentionally, how come whoever chased his ass out of here didn't grab the stuff?"

"Yeah," Marvin said. "Nobody leaves this kind of shit sitting around. A typical junkie might do something that stupid, but Willy-boy doesn't seem to have been using the hard stuff—there's no needles around, and most junkies would just dump the ice cream in the toilet instead of eating it."

"Anyway, we've got to turn it in," Hank said. "This is some haul. It means this guy wasn't just some street dealer selling college kids a nickel bag here, a dime bag there. There's real money and real drugs here, maybe real enough to get the Chicago Police Department interested in Willy the Dealer."

"Yeah," said Marvin, "and if they shine some light on him, maybe a little bit of that light will splash over onto Margaret and help us find her."

Hank nodded his head. That was what he was thinking, too.

"…It's a shame though," Marvin said. "For a moment, I was thinking that maybe I could hold back just a little of this possibly very good quality acid. Maybe one box of it? Or even half a box? I mean, even the Chicago Police Department doesn't usually need *that* much encouragement."

CHAPTER 32

STANDING OUTSIDE THE brick bungalow off Addison, Marvin looked at the way the cool January sun glistened off the snow in the front yard. "I like the sun on the snow, Hank. How about you?"

"Me too," Hank said. "Although I wish it were a little warmer so the sun would melt it already."

"Hmm. I don't mind the snow, really . . . . What do you think Mr. Reichard will be like? A proper kraut? A sieg-heiler? I like the ones with the accents. The ones who stand stiff and proud like they won the war."

"The war ended twenty years ago, Marvin, and you never saw a German the whole time you were in it. You going to ramble on about that shit, or are we going in?"

"You realize less than a thousand Nazis were tried for war crimes? That there are Germans who fried Jews like they were burgers on a barbecue walking around free as you or me — and drawing a pension from the German government?"

"Why don't you bring it up with Willy Reichard's dad when we finally start interviewing him?"

"Maybe I will. Maybe I will."

Hank rang the doorbell of the bungalow and waited. There was no answer. Half a minute later, he rang it again. This time he heard someone on the other side of the door fumbling with a lock.

Finally the door opened. A gray-haired gent in his late forties, dressed in a checkered sport coat and black tie, stood in the doorway. At first he didn't say anything, just stared at the detectives. Then he said, "Yes?"

Hank recognized the accent easily — South German, or maybe Austrian.

"Can I help you gentlemen?"

"Yes, Mr. Reichard, we're detectives with the Chicago Police Department, and we've got some questions regarding your son, Willy Reichard."

"Professor Reichard," the man standing at the door said.

"Sorry?" Hank said.

"*Professor* Reichard," the man at the door repeated.

Hank got it. "*Professor* Reichard. Sorry."

Professor Reichard nodded his approval. "I already told the police officers who were here last week everything I know about where my son is. I don't see what else I can tell you now."

Hank sensed that this wasn't going to go well. "We've discovered something about your son that we think you'll want to know. It's something you won't want us to talk about here on your front porch."

The professor didn't move from his position blocking the door.

"I'll be the judge of that. What have you learned?"

"Okay," Hank said. "We found several hundred doses of LSD in his apartment, in bags ready to be sold. We want to talk to you about it."

Professor Reichard stood in the doorway for a moment longer, silent, his face expressionless. Then he pulled the door open further and gestured them in. He led them into a living room and pointed to the couch.

"So tell me about these drugs you found, the LSD. Are you sure that it is my son's?"

"We found the drugs in the refrigerator in his apartment — " Hank began.

Marvin jumped in, "Yeah, the bags didn't have little 'Willy Reichard' labels stuck on them, but they were hidden in ice-cream containers in his freezer in his apartment, with his fingerprints on the boxes. They were the only readable prints we found there. That suggests to us that your son is involved in selling some very serious, dangerous drugs. He's a fucking dealer, a big one, and we're going to prosecute his ass."

Hank glanced at his partner for a moment; he suspected they were heading toward trouble, especially if the professor called Marvin's bluff about the fingerprints.

Professor Reichard said nothing at first. He just stared at Marvin while Marvin stared back at him.

Hank figured maybe the professor was pissed off at his partner, or maybe not. Maybe the professor was just thinking through his options — what he should tell, what he should hold back, whether or not he should contact a lawyer.

Finally, the professor spoke. "Detectives, my son was a good boy. Through grade school and high school, he was an excellent student. He attended and graduated from Lane Technical High School — I'm sure you know what that means. He was going to attend Northwestern University in the autumn after he graduated…and then he didn't. Instead, he fell in with bad companions that summer and started smoking marijuana. You know where it has led him. He moved away from home, seldom spoke with us after that, and now this trouble. First with the dead dog in his apartment, and now this LSD. I don't know if you know this, but that golden retriever was his pet from just before he started high school — we bought it as a present to celebrate his getting into Lane Tech. He loved that dog. Cappy...he called it Cappy."

Hank looked at the professor, looked around at the room they were sitting in, wondered what kind of baggage this German carried with him. Was he a sieg-heiler like Marvin suggested when they were outside the bungalow? Did he have his own ghosts trailing behind him rattling their chains and moaning? Was all that stuff about Cappy the golden retriever just some bullshit that was supposed to melt the hearts of a couple of stupid Chicago cops?

Hank leaned toward the professor. "You know, it appears that my daughter probably knows your son."

"Yes...?"

"I don't know how well she knows him. I didn't even know she knew him until the day the dead dog — Cappy — was found. I was the one who found it there in your son's apartment; I was there because I was looking for my daughter, Margaret, who had disappeared a few days earlier. I got your son's address from my daughter's friend, who said Margaret and Willy were spending time together. I was hoping your son could answer some questions for me about where my daughter might be, or who her other friends might be. Everything else we learned about Willy was kind of an accident — we weren't going after him at all, just trying to find my little girl."

The German nodded and sighed. "Yes, our children our mysteries to us. They are with us for years, and we think we know them so well, so completely, and suddenly they aren't with us any longer, suddenly they are gone, and we are left with questions for which there are no answers. You ask where is your daughter. I ask where is my son. This question joins us. Are our children together, do you think?"

Hank looked at Marvin. He was sitting with his notepad in one hand, his pen in the other, his *do you believe this bullshit?* look on his face.

Hank turned back to Professor Reichard. "You told the police officers who came here that you didn't know where your son was, and that you didn't know how to reach him."

Professor Reichard nodded and said, "Yes."

"Can you help me find your son? Can you help me find my daughter? What *do* you know that might help?"

The Professor didn't hesitate. "The companions he was closest to were two boys from this neighborhood, boys from good solid German-American families. They were friends from grammar school and before, inseparable for a long time, and I think all three of them fell under some bad influence about the same time, toward the end of high school. I found out later that these two were the boys he started drinking with, and later smoking marijuana with. One of them still lives at home; his name is Richard Houser. The other one is Helmuth Muller. Like Willy, Helmuth has left home. Perhaps, like Willy, he too is selling drugs. I don't know."

"Professor, do you have the addresses of these friends? This is just the kind of information we need to help track down your son and my daughter."

The professor stood up. "I don't have the address of Helmuth Muller, the boy who has left home, but I do have one for Richard Houser, since I've known his family for many years. I have it in the kitchen. I'll get it for you."

"Thank you," Hank said as he watched the Professor move toward the kitchen.

Marvin smiled. "You can thank me for this," he whispered.

"What are you talking about?"

"He knew I'd have his Kraut ass in a sling if he didn't come clean with what he knew."

Hank nodded his head. In a sense, this was just more of Marvin's bullshit. But Hank also knew that "Good Cop / Bad Cop" was the oldest game in the book, one that every detective could play in his sleep, and he'd just played Good Cop to the hilt even if everything he'd said was God's honest truth. It was just that after all these years, he still hadn't figured out whether Marvin had any fucking idea that it was a game. At least they were getting something from the professor that might help. "Let's see what he's got for us."

Professor Reichard came back with a slip of lined yellow paper and handed it to Hank. "This is Richard Houser's address. He lives with his parents only a couple blocks away. A good boy. He did what I hoped my son would do — straightened himself out. Richard took a year off, then went to college. Now he's studying to be a doctor at the University of Illinois. I think he may be able to tell you where their friend Helmuth Muller is, and maybe he will also know the names of some other friends he shared with my son. I've also given you Helmuth's parents' address, although I do not think they have any idea where their son is now."

Hank took the paper, looked at the addresses, and handed it to Marvin so he could copy them into his notebook.

"I hope you find my son and your daughter, and I hope they are safe and can come home and live the way they used to live, before all this madness started."

Hank stood up and shook Professor Reichard's hand. "We'll do our best, Professor. Thanks for all your help."

The Professor stood up straight and tall and gave a slight bow.

CHAPTER 33

THE PROFESSOR WAS right. Rick Houser was a good boy, and he gave up what the Professor said he would. He was more than ready to give them all the information he had on Willy Reichard and Helmuth Muller: he told them how Willy had started out selling grass to a couple of his friends, and soon was selling it in pretty serious quantities and starting to branch out into acid — and lately, even a little heroin. He was buying it from the Outfit guys, the Chicago mob operators who ran the bars around Old Town, the hippie section of Chicago. And he was selling it to whoever wanted it, through the usual network of friends, friends of friends, and friends of friends of friends.

Listening to Rick Houser, Hank felt that the doctor-to-be was telling it all like he was confessing to a priest, trying to get a *te absolvo* for his own wild times and whatever guilt might have scattered onto him from the sins of his friends.

Some friends they were....

The last thing Rick Houser gave Hank and Marvin was the address of Helmuth Muller, Willy's high school buddy and fellow junkie. He made them swear not to tell Muller where they'd gotten his address.

———————

The address Rick Houser gave them was a two-story walk-up on Wells Street, just south of Old Town with its tourists and weekend hippies, and just north and east of the black junkie area that was part of the Cabrini Green Projects. The first floor was occupied by a hippie book store and t-shirt emporium.

Marvin was staring at the titles in the window. "Say, Hank, I got to come back here when I have some time and some cash. I mean, dig it — here's all the books I need to educate and expand my mind, get me thinking and breathing like I'm thinking and breathing for the very first time, help me 'turn on, tune in, drop out,' my brother."

Hank looked at the window, the display of books and psychedelic t-shirts. "What the hell are you talking about?"

"I'm talking about my guru, Timothy Leary. Guy was a Harvard professor who turned himself into the great prophet of LSD — practically started a new religion around it. Like on that t-shirt there. I'm telling you, dig it."

Hank looked where Marvin was pointing. It was a bright red and yellow t-shirt with a cartoon of a short bald fellow with a long, flowing white beard and a goofy grin. A big word bubble was exploding out of his mouth: "Find the divinity within: Turn on, Tune in, Drop out!"

"What the hell?" Hank repeated.

"Listen, this 'turn on, tune in, drop out' guy, Timothy Leary, is like the new Jesus. Or at least the new John the Baptist. He's this Harvard psychology prof who did research into LSD, and now he's going around telling kids it's time for a new religion, the Religion of Acid. You don't need no stinking bible, no stinking church, no stinking preacher, no stinking savior. All you need is a hit of acid — it'll open your mind, excite it, expand it, make you feel like a whole new man."

Hank looked at the psychedelic t-shirt again and the books in front of it in the window. He had heard of a couple of them — the older books like Herman Hesse's *Siddhartha* and *On the Road* by Jack Kerouac — but most of the others were a complete mystery: Aldous Huxley's *The Doors of Perception*, *Stranger in a Strange Land* (he hadn't read any of Robert Heinlein's stuff in years), *Howl and Other Poems* by Allen Ginsberg — does anybody actually buy poetry books? he wondered — and another book called *Been Down So Long It Looks Like Up to Me*. Hank hadn't heard of those, or a half-dozen other titles scattered in front of the t-shirts.

"So I'm supposed to take a hit of this acid and read these books and that will give me a religious experience?"

"That's what Tim Leary and the kids are saying."

"But you said that you had a miserable time when you took LSD."

"Yeah, for me it was a real hell, one bad trip after another," Marvin said, shrugging. "But you know, that was probably just because I'm old and all fucked up from years of boozing and bad living and not having read enough of these books. It couldn't hurt both of us to maybe read that one there, *Siddhartha*, with the picture of Buddha on the cover. It's supposed to be good, and it's pretty short."

Hank shook his head. "Maybe later. Let's go see if Willy's boyhood buddy Helmuth is home."

Marvin smacked his lips. "You know, I love these Kraut names. Willy Reichard, Richard Houser, Helmuth Muller....every one so crisp, precise, and well defined! Makes me want to take some orders and march on Warsaw or Paris or Moscow."

"So let's march upstairs and see what Herr Helmuth Muller has to share with us."

"Yeah, man. Let's turn on, tune in, and drop in on him!"

⌇⌇⌇

The second floor above the bookstore was cobbled up into five two-room studios — two on either side of a long, narrow corridor that ran the length of the building, and one at the very front.

They checked the 3 x 5 cards taped to each door for names; the apartment all the way in the front was Helmuth Muller's. Hank and Marvin listened to see if anyone was inside any of the apartments. The only one with any sound coming from it was the front one, Muller's. It was the sound of plates; maybe he was putting dinner on the table, or else cleaning up. A thin strip of light peeked out from under his door; the rest of the apartments were all dark. Some neighbors were early sleepers, and the rest hadn't gotten home yet, Hank figured.

Hank and Marvin stepped back to the dark at the top of the stairs at the other end of the corridor.

"What do you think?" Marvin asked in a whisper. "We go in like Gang Busters, or quiet like Charlie Chan?"

Hank pursed his lips and thought for a moment. "Nice of you to ask for once. Maybe all those books are helping, even if you haven't read any of them yet. I think it's every man for himself."

Marvin smiled and put on a fake Chinese accent. "Ahhh, you make most excellent choiceless choice, Number One Partner."

They walked softly back down the corridor. Marvin stopped about a foot from the door and turned to Hank, waiting.

"You ready?" Hank asked.

"Oh yeah! Ready, Freddy!"

Hank nodded, and Marvin threw himself against the dark door, shoulder first. It shattered the frame and cracked the lock free. The noise was enough to rouse the sleepers and bring them running;

Hank turned back as he heard rapid footsteps and one of the doors behind him opening up. He flashed his badge at the long-haired hippie coming through the door and said "Police business." The guy nodded and scooted right back to bed.

Hank turned back to Marvin and the remains of the door. Standing in the doorway with his revolver drawn and pointing at the ceiling, he yelled, "Helmuth Muller? Are you alone in there?"

A guy who looked like maybe he had once been an athlete, but now had the unhealthy, pale, skinny look of a junkie, stood at the sink with a soapy wine glass in one hand and a scrub brush in the other. He looked at Hank and Marvin and shouted, "What the fuck is this? You screwed up my door, broke the damn thing. You're going to pay for that. Jesus Christ!"

Marvin ran up to Muller, shoved him face-first against the refrigerator, and slammed his elbow hard against the junkie's skull. The wine glass dropped out of Helmuth's hand, shattering on the floor and rocketing glass slivers everywhere. Marvin pressed the barrel of his .45 against the back of Muller's head.

The junkie shouted again, "Jesus Christ, you're going to pay for this! Jesus Christ!"

"Fuck you, Kraut motherfucker," Marvin shouted back. He jammed his left fist into the junkie's kidney, jammed it hard.

Helmuth Muller let out a groan and dropped to his knees, his face still pressed into the white-enameled steel of the refrigerator. He wrapped his arms around his stomach like he was trying to protect himself and keep from puking.

"Please," he choked out. "Please."

"Another? You begging for another one, motherfucker?" Marvin said, and kicked the junkie in the ass. Muller slid to the checkered black and white linoleum on the kitchen floor and didn't move.

Everything went quiet, except the junkie moaning on the floor like a baby.

Hank closed the busted door behind him as best as he could, pushed it tight and forced one of the kitchen chairs against it to make sure it wouldn't fall open. He didn't want anybody coming in or peeking in to see what was going on. He looked at Marvin then, nodded, and sat down on one of the other kitchen chairs.

"Helmuth," Hank said, "my friend and I are here to ask you some questions."

"Yeah," Marvin added, "official police questions."

The junkie didn't speak, didn't move. He was still suffering from the elbow and the punch and the kick, still lying on the floor, tucked into himself like an aching jelly roll filled with pain. After a minute or so, his shallow breathing started getting heavier, deeper. But he still didn't move.

Hank wondered if the guy was falling asleep.

Marvin must have been wondering the same thing. He softly touched the toe of his shoe to Helmuth's side, near where he had just delivered a kidney punch. Muller groaned.

"Helmuth, listen to me," Hank said. "We ain't got all day. We've got other calls to make, and we've got to finish with you before we can move on to the rest. So let me ask you: Do you need any more encouragement to cooperate?"

A whisper came out of the pain-filled jelly roll. "No."

"Good. It won't take too long. After you answer a couple questions, you can go back to your pain and your dishwashing."

"Okay, sure," Helmuth whispered. "Water?"

"Sure," Hank said, nodding to Marvin.

Marvin went to the sink and filled a glass, carried it to the junkie on the floor, held it to his lips when he raised his head. Muller drank a little, and then he whispered that he'd had enough.

"Okay," Hank said, "here's what we want to know. First, I want you to tell us about your friend Willy Reichard."

Helmuth Muller was still hurting, hurting a lot. He coughed and the coughing came up from deep in his chest. Hank knew it was from Marvin's punch to the guy's kidney. Marvin had big fists for a little guy, and he punched way above his weight. Hank had seen his partner break a guy's jaw with one solid punch, kill a man with two. They came like hammer blows when they came.

The junkie coughed again, and then he leaned over and vomited. The remains of his dinner came out of his mouth like a backed-up toilet.

"Jesus," Marvin said as he reached for a towel and threw it down to Muller. "You're making a mess in your kitchen, man."

Hank waited for the kid to stop puking and heaving, then he grabbed a fresh towel and held it to the kid's face. The kid coughed a few times; then he looked at Marvin.

"I'll kill you," Helmuth said. "I swear."

"Yeah, but first you're going to tell us about Willy."

Helmuth shook his head and tried to rise, and then he sat back down, his back to the refrigerator.

Marvin slipped his .45 into his shoulder holster and took a step forward.

Hank knew his partner. "Let me take it from here."

"Shitting faggot," Marvin said. "Always the Good Cop. Someday you're going to be made into a fucking saint because of your charity to thugs, squirrels and sparrows, and goddamn junkies."

Hank ignored his partner and moved his kitchen chair closer to Helmuth. "You can make this easy, kid. Just talk. Tell us anything. Ten minutes of good talking and we're out of here, and you can start patching yourself up and get on with your life. Just give us something about Willy."

Helmuth didn't smile, didn't whimper, didn't seem thankful for being able to talk to the Good Cop rather than the Bad one. He coughed again and cleaned some of the puke off his face with the towel. "Willy's an asshole," he croaked out. "He thinks he's hot shit, but he's just an asshole."

Hank leaned forward. "We've already heard that much about Willy. Put that aside for now. You know anything about this girl he might have been seeing, a girl named Margaret?"

Muller pressed his back against the refrigerator again and closed his eyes.

Hank could see how much the guy was hurting. He lifted his foot and prodded Muller's knee gently with his toe. "Tell me about this Margaret."

"He's always got some teenybopper hanging around, some new chick from the sticks."

"Margaret," Hank said. "Tell me about Margaret."

Helmuth coughed again and shrugged.

"Come on, Helmuth. This girl was nineteen. Probably wearing an old Ike jacket, an army jacket. Short brown hair — a pageboy. She might have been with a heavy-set girl, her friend Maureen. With red hair. This Maureen, she's always trying to talk and act like a hard case, a tough broad, a real doper."

Helmuth looked at Hank for a long moment. He looked like he was thinking about what he should say next, and maybe what he shouldn't say.

"Yeah, I remember the friend. The fat one, the redhead. Got a mouth on her — every other word was 'fuck', but it never sounded natural. Yeah, I remember her."

"Did you ever see her at Willy's?"

"Yeah, he was fucking her, fucking her and the chick with the pageboy too, the two of them giving him blowjobs like he was Mick Jagger or something."

Hank punched Muller in the mouth, hard, and then he did it again. That was out of character for the Good Cop, but Marvin wasn't officially a cop right now, so the hell with it.

"What the fuck!" Helmuth said through the blood spreading across his face.

Hank looked at the blood on his fist. He picked up a dish towel from the table and tried to clean it some. "I don't want to know about whether he was fucking the girl with the pageboy. There was a dead dog in Willy's apartment when I got there. The thing had been crucified, nailed to the wall. What was that all about?"

Helmuth Muller leaned forward and picked up the glass of water that was sitting next to him. He drank it down slowly, and then he coughed some more. "The golden retriever?"

"Yeah, that's the one."

"It was Ernesto's dog. Willy was watching it. He was trying to keep it safe."

"Safe from who?"

"The Blackstone Rangers."

Marvin kicked Helmuth in the ass. "What kind of fairy tale you telling, Hell Mouth? We heard from Willy's father that it was Willy's own dog."

"No, honest to Jesus, that's what it was. Willy was watching the dog, protecting it from the Blackstone Rangers, the black gang from the South Side, you know?"

"And this golden retriever was Ernesto's dog? Who the fuck is Ernesto?" Marvin asked.

"He's this Latin Scorpion guy Willy was getting some of his stuff from, his grass and his acid. He told Ernesto he would watch the dog, keep it safe, in exchange for two hundred bucks' worth of nickel bags."

Hank leaned back on the kitchen chair. This did all sound like some kind of crazy story, a fairy tale. Or like Marvin would say, a *bubbe meiseh*. Professor Reichard had said the dog was Willy's, a beloved pet named Cappy. Hank shook his head. "So the dog is Ernesto's. He's with the spic street gang, the Latin Scorpions. Are you saying the Blackstone Rangers killed the dog because of some kind of dispute between them and the Scorpions?"

"Yeah, that's it," Helmuth said. "It sounds crazy, I know, but that's what I think happened. The Rangers took it out on that dog."

Hank shook his head. "And this dog wasn't Willy's golden retriever? Not Cappy?"

"No, no way. Cappy died a while ago. Willy told me they don't usually live super long. This one was Ernesto's. Same breed, different dog."

"And how do you know this?"

"Willy told me."

"Jesus," Marvin said, pushing back his fedora. "Golden retrievers everywhere.... So where's Willy? And the chicks he was with?"

Muller looked at Hank. It was clear he was afraid of saying anything about the girls, and also afraid of keeping quiet about them. He was frightened of Hank's fists too now, not just Marvin's.

Hank nodded.

"Yeah, it's okay," Marvin said. "He won't punch you again. We're friends now. Everything is hunky-dory."

"I don't know much," Helmuth said. "I figure maybe he ran off with the girls. The dog he was supposed to be watching got killed, so probably the Latin Scorpions are after him now, and he's hiding out from them somewhere. Or maybe the Scorpions got him, or maybe the Rangers. Willy was always fucking up — pretending to be a big shot, pretending he had all these connections, that he was some kind of Outfit guy, you know, like with the Mafia. But he was nothing like that. He fucking penciled in his beard. Like I said — an asshole."

"What's Ernesto's last name?" Hank asked.

"I don't know for sure. Honest! Something like Roverez or Romerez. Something that starts with an R."

"Ramirez, maybe?"

"I don't know. Some spic name that sounds like that."

Hank nodded. He looked at Marvin, then he looked back at Helmuth, the slimy mess all over the floor, the puke and broken glass, the blood and the dish towels, the wooden pieces scattered from the shattered door frame. None of that stuff made him feel very good. He knew what he had hoped to find: some straight path from here to Margaret, some clearly defined way of finding her and bringing her home and putting her back where she belonged so his life and Hazel's life and Margaret's life would again be the life it had been when she was a kid and he was just a cop chasing bad guys who lived far, far away from Hazel and Margaret and him.

But now Hank realized that all that was the fairy tale, not this crazy shit about the dog and the rival gangs. The life he imagined bringing Margaret back to existed only in his head and nowhere else anymore.

And looking around Helmuth Muller's kitchen, he didn't feel like he was Prince Charming, some hero out of Hans Christian Anderson or Walt Disney who could remake the world into a technicolor cartoon paradise that maybe it used to be but never would be again, not ever.

Hank looked at Marvin again. His partner was standing next to the sink, his .45 holstered but still very much present. Hank knew what he wanted to say to Marvin, but he didn't say it, so Marvin said it for him.

"You want me to kill this motherfucker?"

Hank stood there staring at the junkie punk on the floor, at the puke and broken glass and splintered wood around him.

Helmuth Muller looked up at Hank. "You're joking. You're cops. You won't kill me. You can't."

Hank still didn't say anything. He wanted to kill this guy, wanted to kill him bad, because Muller knew his daughter and the kind of kid she had grown into, and maybe if nobody knew all that, it wouldn't be real. He wanted to say to Marvin, *Yeah, I'm done with this prick, and the world's done with him too. Send the motherfucker to hell.* He wanted to say it, but he didn't. Instead he turned, kicked away the chair that was propping up what was left of the door, and walked through it.

Behind him, Marvin walked up to the junkie, pressed the heavy barrel of his .45 against Muller's forehead, and pulled the trigger.

The junkie screamed. The pistol clicked.

Marvin smiled at Helmuth Muller and said, "Fuck you later, Hell Mouth. And oh, yeah, one more thing: Call your mother!"

CHAPTER 34

HANK AND MARVIN sat in their unmarked cruiser on Potomac just off of Western and waited for the callback from Joe Dubchek, a veteran detective they knew who worked out of the Wood Street Station. Although Dubchek was fat and old and tired, he knew pretty much all there was to know about the Latin Scorpions and the other Hispanic gangs in the Humboldt Park area, and Hank had called him asking for Ernesto Ramirez's address. Dubchek said he didn't have it himself, but he could make a call or two and get it if Hank gave him thirty minutes. So Hank and Marvin waited.

Hank remembered when the town was run by the Irish gangs and the Italian gangs and the Jewish gangs, back when he was a kid. For the better part of the first half of the century, the O'Banions and the Morans, the Capones and the Torrios, the Hymie Weisses and Jacob "Greasy Thumb" Guziks owned the city. They shot it up and they blew it up, they killed one another and a lot of civilians that got in their way. They bossed it over the politicians and the cops and just about everybody else.

Those gangsters did their work just like in the movies he loved as a kid, films like *Little Caesar* and *Scarface* and *The Public Enemy*. And those television shows he used to follow in the late 50s — *M Squad* with Lee Marvin playing a cop right here in Chicago, and *The Untouchables* about Eliot Ness and his crew of Feds taking down the Chicago crime bosses of the 30s. *Dragnet* and *Naked City* were okay too, but he could never get very excited about them. But what didn't get into those movies and TV shows was the real human debris, the streets left sticky with blood and body parts, the eyes and hands and fingers left at what those shows always loved to call "the scene of the crime".

Hank sometimes wondered if the new gangs even came close to the kind of messiness those old gangs worked up. The old gangs warred with one another and sometimes with the cops, and a lot of times it felt like a real war, sometimes with some pretty heavy weapons.

The new gangs? Maybe some guerrilla warfare like the US was now stuck doing in Vietnam, but they didn't seem to be fighting as much with other gangs — a skirmish here, a shooting there, but no pitched battles. More often than not the only ones hurt were civilians who got in the way of whatever the gangs wanted to do, and paid the price. On the South Side it was black gangs like the Blackstone Rangers, and on the North Side it was bunches of little Puerto Rican and Mexican gangs like the Latin Scorpions that thugged it over the small corner-store owners and the guys who owned the bars — extortion mainly, but now with the growing demand for marijuana and LSD and other stuff, the gangs seemed to be turning to drugs just like Capone and his boys turned to alcohol. Maybe there would be more of the inter-gang fighting as the drug business got bigger, richer, and more competitive.

"Say, Marvin," Hank said, lighting a cigarette, "remember when the Latin Scorpions first started up?"

"Yeah, sort of."

"You remember the first time you heard of them?"

"Yeah."

"The spelling?"

"What're you talking about?"

"We were driving through an alley, maybe between Hirsch and Evergreen, heading toward Humboldt Park, and we got to the end of the alley, and you looked up and saw some graffiti on a garage door."

"How do you remember this shit?"

"And you remember what the graffiti said?"

Marvin shook his head. "Where's all this going?"

"It said, 'Latin Scorpions Rule.'"

"Yeah…so what?"

"Remember the spelling?"

"*What spelling?*"

"The word 'Scorpions' — they misspelled 'Scorpions'. They spelled it with a T: S, C, O, R, P, *T*, I, O, N, S, scorp-shuns."

"Jesus, how do you remember this shit?"

"Lucky, I guess."

The Motorola police radio squawked on, and Marvin picked up the mike.

It was Joe Dubchek with an address for them.

"Hey, Hank, hey Marv, it's me. Ramirez is at 2433 Potomac, second floor in the rear. It's his apartment. He lives there with his little girlfriend, wife, whatever she is. Go easy on him. He's a good snitch, and we don't want to lose him. Got that, Marvin?"

Hank looked at his partner, who clicked the talk button on the mike. "Roger that, Joe, we'll go easy on him. I won't let Hank hurt your informant."

Hank looked at Marvin. "You think Ernesto was one of the Puerto Ricans who rioted last summer?"

"What difference does it make?"

"What difference does it make? You were there too. You saw what the bastards did. Houses burned, innocent people beaten by the gangs, even some shootings. I was surprised nobody got killed."

Marvin gave Hank one of his big smiles. "Don't be a spoil-sport. Everybody deserves to party once in a while."

The early evening sky was clear and cloudless and dark cobalt blue. Hank stood at the back door of Ramirez's apartment and waited for Marvin to make it up the wooden staircase from the back porch. The going was slow; whoever was responsible for keeping the snow and the ice off these back steps must have decided to take the winter off and spend it in Florida. There was about half a foot of snow still on the stairs, with ice hiding under it. The moon was just coming up, and it made even the dirty snow seem clean.

When he finally reached Hank on the second floor landing, Marvin whispered, "You know, I think I'm getting too old for this shit."

"Yeah, I know what you mean," Hank said, and stepped over to the window just to the left of the back door to take a peek. The kitchen light was on, and he could see through the plastic yellow curtains into the kitchen, but the kitchen — except for a table and some chairs — was empty.

He knocked on the door then, and after a minute it opened a crack, and a pretty young woman stood on the other side. She looked out past the chain lock at Hank, and Hank looked at her. She was Hispanic, maybe eighteen or nineteen — Margaret's age. She didn't say anything...nothing at all. After a moment, Hank pulled out his badge and held it up to her face.

She looked at it for a long time and said, "*Sí,*" and then she didn't say anything else.

Hank turned to Marvin. "How's your Spanish, Marv?"

"Better than yours, *jefe.* Let me give it a try."

Marvin took Hank's place at the chained door and pointed at Hank's badge.

The girl gave it the slow look again.

"*Policía,*" Marvin said, pointing at Hank and then at himself.

The girl nodded her head and again said, "*Sí.*"

"Now we're getting someplace," Marvin said as he grinned and pointed at her. "*Tú sabes* Ernesto Ramirez?"

She pressed her lips together and looked puzzled. Then she said it again, slowly: "*Sí.*"

Hank looked at Marvin and said, "Tell her it's cold and getting dark out here, and we want to come inside and talk to her boyfriend. And we want to do it fast."

Marvin looked at Hank for a long moment and said, "Sure." Then he turned back to the girl. "*Chica, por favor, que es frío, y … oscuro aquí, y queremos … entrar, y hablar con su,* uh, *novio. Y queremos hacerlo rápido.*"

She shook her head and said something back in Spanish.

Hank looked at Marvin.

"She said she can't let anybody in. That her husband is sleeping, and he told her before he went to bed not to let anybody in."

"Jesus Christ," Hank said. "I don't know how they do things in Puerto Rico, but you'd think that having a cop with a badge standing at your door asking to come in would be all the key we'd need to get the damn door open. Try some more of your Spanish, and maybe throw in a little of your famous charm."

Marvin stepped up to the door and was about to say something when Hank saw a movement behind the girl. It was a guy in a red flannel shirt and bluejeans coming quickly toward the door.

"What the fuck is this?" he said with a slight Latin accent. "I'm sleeping. What's all this noise?"

"We're cops. You Ernesto Ramirez?" Hank asked.

"Yeah, I'm Ernesto," he said to Hank, and then he added to the girl, "*Abra la puerta, chica.*"

She shrugged, undid the chain, and pulled the door open.

Hank and Marvin walked into the kitchen. It was small, just big enough for a table and some chairs. The room was cold, even though the door of the stove was open and Hank could see the gas-fed flames dancing around in it.

Ernesto motioned with his hand and started walking toward the front room.

"I guess we tag along," Marvin said.

"Yeah, I guess," Hank replied.

Following Ernesto down the short hallway to the front of the apartment, Hank thought about how he had seen a million apartments like this, all over the city — 'flats', they called them here for some reason. This flat was small: four little rooms, a toilet, and a couple of closets, just enough room for two people — but usually in a flat like this you'd have a whole big family, mom and dad, a half dozen kids and sometimes more, crowded and noisy, cold in the winter, hot in the summer. But this is where the Poles and the Germans, the Puerto Ricans and the Mexicans, the Italians and the Chinese, the Blacks and the American Indians, the Kentuckians and the Tennesseans came when they first came to Chicago. And all Hank could think of was that these little miserable rooms with their roaches and their rats and their lack of this and that were probably 100% better than anything those folks left behind in their old homes in their old towns in their old countries.

The front room was warm, at least. A small kerosene stove stood in the corner, and Ernesto sat down on an easy chair next to it. He didn't look to see if the detectives would stand or sit, or where they'd sit if they did sit. He didn't seem to give much of a fuck.

Marvin sat down on a rocking chair near the TV set, a big old Crosley with a crack running diagonally across the glass screen. Hank waited for a minute to see if Marvin would try using some more of his high-school Spanish. He didn't. He pulled out his notepad and a pen instead.

Hank didn't sit down, didn't pull out a notepad. He stood. He knew his job, and he started right in. "Ernesto Ramirez, Joe Dubchek says you're a good guy, someone we can trust. Is that right? Is that who you are?"

Ernesto pressed his lips together and smiled. "Yeah, yeah, Dubchek is my friend, a good cop. We got a thing going, him and me. You better not let the *chica* know — you know, my wife." Ernesto paused, then gave the two detectives a big grin and laughed.

Hank didn't like Ernesto's smile. The bastard was sitting around enjoying his home and his young wife's company, cracking his little jokes, and Margaret was out there somewhere in the cold and the shit. Hank wanted to fuck Ernesto up bad, but he needed to act like he didn't. "Dubchek thinks you can help us with a case we're working on."

"Maybe," Ernesto said, sitting comfortably in his chair.

"Maybe? That's not what Dubchek said. There were no maybes when I was talking to Dubchek about you."

"Okay, sure, no maybes," Ernesto said, putting up his hands, palms turned toward the detectives. "Come on, man. I'm just funning you guys, you know? I don't mean to piss you off. Sure, I'll help any way I can."

"Good," Hank said. "Let me ask you then...you know anything about the disappearance of a dealer up by the lake, over near Diversey, a guy named Willy Reichard, and a dead dog, a golden retriever that was found in his apartment?"

Ernesto leaned forward. "Yeah, sure, I know something about it. Somebody killed that dog, a beautiful dog, a sweet, good dog."

"Your dog?"

"Yeah, sure it was my dog, my golden retriever."

Marvin glanced up from his notepad. "Ernesto, what the fuck was Willy Reichard doing with your golden retriever?"

"He was watching it for me. Protecting it from the Blackstone Rangers. Those motherfuckers murdered it."

"How come?"

"They wanted to even a score. They figured they owed somebody something, and they took it out on a dog that wouldn't even chase a cat."

Hank was starting to feel that this was going to take longer than he'd thought at first. He sat down on an easy chair across from Ernesto. This stuff about the dog wasn't making any sense, or at least it wasn't making enough sense. And how come Willy's dad thought the dog was Cappy, but it wasn't Cappy? Why would the Rangers come looking for a dog? Who the hell would care so much about a damn dog?

Hank decided it was time to take another tack. "Ernesto, let's leave the dog aside for a moment. The Chicago Police Department doesn't in fact give a good goddamn about your dog, although my partner and I understand that you do. Let's talk about Willy for a minute. He's the guy we're looking for."

"I don't know what the fuck happened to Willy. I took the dog to his place up near Diversey. He was supposed to take care of it, and he didn't. The next thing I hear, my dog is dead — fucking crucified like Jesus on a fucking wall!"

"Why'd you take it to Willy, though? Why not someplace else?"

Ernesto took a pack of Lucky Strikes out of his shirt pocket, popped one out of the pack, and lit it. He watched the smoke for a moment, then he said, "You boys want one of these smokes?"

Marvin said, "Fuck the cigarettes. Answer my partner's question."

Ernesto smiled and lifted his hands a little. "Sure, no problem, man. Willy owed me a favor, and he's used to taking care of a dog. And he was living up on the North Side. I figured the Blackstone Rangers would think twice before hustling their black monkey asses up there, so far from their turf."

"When you dropped the dog off, was Willy alone in his apartment?"

"No man. He's never alone. He had this teenybopper chick with him. Hippie girl — a skinny one with an army jacket, you know, like what they call an Ike jacket around here."

"You talk to this girl at all?" Hank asked.

"Sure, why not? I said 'hey' and 'what's happening'. You know, that shit. She didn't say much back. She seemed pissed off. Angry, I guess. Like something was bugging her. I don't think she wanted to be there with Willy and my dog and me."

"So you dropped the dog off and then you left Willy and the girl there. You got any idea where they went?"

"They weren't supposed to go anywhere, man. Willy said he was going to stay there and keep an eye on my dog. Protect the fuck out of him. I figured Willy would do that until I came back."

"Why did the Blackstone Rangers want your dog, Ernesto?"

"Oh, man," Ernesto said and shook his head. He had been forthcoming, a ready talker...and now he wasn't. Suddenly he clammed up. It was like he had nothing more to say. He took a drag on his cigarette, and then he played with his book of matches for a minute, flipping and snapping his finger at the matchbook.

Marvin leaned into the conversation. "Come on, Ernesto, be a big boy — tell us what happened."

"Stupid story, man. We had a meeting with them, down on the South Side. You know, around the Woodlawn area, 63rd or 64th, somewhere near the lake, and we went down there a couple of days early just to check the place out. We'd been talking to the Rangers about this and that, and we wanted to check it out, the scene there. You know. Well, we got to the place kind of late and there was nobody around, and one of our guys broke into the place and there was this dog there — I mean this fancy kind of dog, some kind of little poodle or something, I don't know, and it was yapping and yapping, and one of my guys got worried and hit it with a baseball bat, fucked it up real bad, and we thought it would be funny to stick it in the refrigerator and that's what we did, stuck it in the icebox next to the beer bottles and the apple pie."

Marvin smiled. "Yeah, that'll do it. You kill a dog belonging to the Blackstone Rangers and stick it in an icebox? It don't take a genius to know that's a situation that's going south real fast."

Ernesto laughed a small, rolling laugh. "Going south, that's funny, man. That's real funny."

Hank could see that Ernesto knew that this dog business was stupid, and it was the kind of stupid stuff that got stupider and stupider, more and more dangerous, as time went on. What started with a yappy little dog could easily end with dead people.

Hank got out of the easy chair and started buttoning his coat. "So what do you think happened to Willy and the teenybopper, Ernesto?"

Ernesto shook his head and scratched his chin. He'd been doing that a lot during this conversation. "I don't know, man. I figure it had to go one of two ways. Either Willy and the chick scrambled out of there before the Rangers showed up, or the Rangers grabbed them and took them down south, to their hangout."

Ernesto's wife came in with a tray and set it down on the coffee table in the middle of the room. It held a bottle of Jack Daniel's and four short glasses.

Hank watched the girl pour a couple fingers of whiskey into each glass. When she was done, Marvin got out of his seat, took two of the glasses and handed one to Hank. The girl gave a glass to Ernesto and took one for herself.

The four of them stood for a moment in the living room. Hank turned the glass and looked at the liquid, then he lifted the glass to his lips and paused. He didn't have to take a sip to know it would go down burning but good.

Marvin said, "What are we toasting, Ernesto, my man?"

Ernesto smiled. "Soft winter, early spring."

Hank nodded and threw the liquor back. A good burn, but cooling too fast, like always. He looked at the empty glass and tilted it back again, looking for just a little more.

Marvin turned to the girl and then glanced at his glass. "*Por favor?*"

She looked over at her husband, who nodded at her and answered, "Sí," then she poured Marvin another couple fingers.

Hank finished buttoning his coat and then rolled on with his questions again. "Ernesto, you got any idea where Willy and the teenybopper might have gone to if the Blackstone Rangers didn't take them?"

"Sure, I got some guesses. Maybe they went to a friend's house. Willy, he had some friends, guys he was doing business with on a regular basis. There was one short, skinny guy up on the North Side, way up on Wilson or some kind of shit like that. You know, Uptown, near the lake. Guy's a dealer, lives with his mother. Older guy, but lives with his mother. Maybe he's a fag. Weird. Anyway, Willy always said this guy had the best-quality stuff in town. Him and Willy, they was friends from way back."

"You know his name?"

"Yeah…some kind of weird pussy gringo name. Not one like Tom or John. Last name is like the name of an airplane or something. That's what I remember, at least."

Hank looked at Ernesto. He still wanted to punch him in the stomach, smash him again and again, and then kick him when he fell to the ground. But he also knew the feeling was irrational — the guy was Puerto Rican, a gang member, but he did seem to be trying to be as helpful as he could. He said, "You figure out that name, Ernesto. You figure it out, and you tell it to Dubchek. He'll get it to us."

Marvin nodded and put his glass on the tray. "You've been helpful, Ernesto. We'll tell Dubchek that, make sure you're in solid with that old Polack."

Ernesto gave Marvin and then Hank a big smile and raised his glass. "Thanks, but remember not to call him that. Old Joe may look fat and slow, but he'll kick both your asses while he reminds you that he's a Czech, not some dumb Polack."

Hank put his hat on. "So what if Willy ain't with this guy in Uptown? What then?"

Ernesto smiled even bigger, his mouth a cave full of busted teeth and gaping holes. "Then maybe he and the *chica* — they're with the Blackstone Rangers, those devils on the South Side. You know. And then nobody gets them loose, man. They are fucked."

Marvin said it too: "Fucked."

After Hank walked out the door, Ernesto said quietly to Marvin, "Take the bottle with you — I think your friend needs it."

Marvin took the bottle of Jack Daniel's off the coffee table, screwed the top on tight, and turned to follow Hank out of the apartment and down the icy back stairs.

CHAPTER 35

HANK SAT IN the dark-blue Ford, and through the front windshield watched the night snow falling. The flakes were dry and light, and there was just a little wind blowing, so they came down slowly and in a slight swirl, moving almost like waves, back and forth. He thought about the beach at Normandy, D-Day morning, how dark the dawn waves there were. That was a dawn that never seemed to break, and then it did and he wished it hadn't.

But this darkness wasn't anything like that darkness. Street lights down the block made it all look beautiful, like something out of a Christmas movie, that one with Bing Crosby and Rosemary Clooney, about the time just after that war. Hank listened to the wind. It wasn't playing "I'm Dreaming of a White Christmas".

Marvin unscrewed the bottle of Jack Daniel's he'd taken from Ernesto's apartment and passed it to Hank. Hank tilted the bottle back and let it come. He didn't want the burn to stop this time. He wanted it to go on and on.

"Hey, save some for the fishies, man," Marvin said.

Hank looked at his partner and handed the bottle back to him.

"You know what I hate about this business?" Marvin asked.

"What business?"

"This fucking cop business."

"What do you hate?"

"I hate how they make it look so easy on TV. In thirty minutes — an hour, tops — the private eye or the TV cop gets a case, asks a couple questions, takes a break to pee during a half-dozen commercials for some kind of after-shave, and comes back to solve the crime. It's easy on TV."

Hank didn't say anything. He was thinking of his daughter, wherever she was tonight. He remembered how she used to love to watch snow fall when she was a kid.

He remembered the first time she stepped outside to touch the snow. She must have been three years old. It was a Saturday morning, and he was in the kitchen making breakfast, some pancakes, and she was sitting just across from him, still in her pink and white Minnie Mouse pajamas, looking out the window at all that whiteness spreading across the lawn and swirling in the air. He turned to get something out of the refrigerator, and he heard the back door open.

When he turned around again, she was gone.

He moved quickly to the door and opened it, and there she stood in the middle of the yard. It was like she didn't know yet that snow was wet and cold, or maybe how cold and wet it was didn't matter at all to her. She stood in the backyard, stood in all that white swirling snow, and stretched out both her hands to catch the falling flakes.

Nothing mattered to her but the wonder of it.

There was some miracle in that snow that she wanted to touch. She was like that back then, and sometimes she was still like that now, or at least she had been until the last few months — out there opening her hands, letting the world with all its miracles settle gently on her palms. He hoped that wherever she was right now, that was still the way it was for her. That was what he hoped for, almost as much as he hoped she'd wind up back home soon and safe. If he were a guy who got down on his knees to pray, that's what he would be praying for. Better that than the other shit he could picture.

Marvin poked Hank with the neck of the Jack Daniel's bottle. "Your turn, Hank, and then we got to get back to work. The half-minute detergent commercial is almost over, and the fuckers watching this freaking TV cop show are getting ready for us to figure everything out in the next ten minutes."

Hank took the bottle. Felt the burn going down again, too fast. Always too fast. He wanted to slow it down, but he couldn't. So he drank and drank and drank till there was nothing in the bottle but emptiness and a memory of what had been there burning his throat.

It was late already. He had to sleep.

Tomorrow he'd follow the leads he had, no matter how shit-ass they were. He'd go talk to the Blackstone Rangers. And if that didn't work, he'd try to track down the fruity dealer who lived with his mother — the guy that Ernesto had mentioned — if Ernesto and Joe Dubchek got him the guy's name.

He'd try pretty much anything at this point.

CHAPTER 36

HANK SAT AT his kitchen table waiting for Hazel to come home. She was off somewhere…bingo, maybe? Over at one of her friends? She hadn't left much of a note—just something about how she'd be home soon. He'd been sitting there for most of an hour now.

The coffee cup in his hands was already cold. He really didn't want to drink the stuff anyway, black and old, reheated and muddy. And it wasn't just that it tasted like crap; it was hard enough these days to sleep without drinking coffee at night, so why bother if it was burnt?

Hank hadn't always been like that. He remembered back when he was a kid living near the end of the Logan Square Elevated. All night long, the trains rumbled in and rumbled out, their steel wheels scraping endlessly against the metal rails. A hell of a racket, but he slept right through it, usually. Yeah, the noise gave him stupid dreams about subway tunnels and frogs, dark mazes and coffins full of lost screeching babies, but still he could sleep through it.

Even in the war, it was like that. He never had trouble sleeping at the front, not in Normandy after the landings, not in the Ardennes Forest that final winter of the war. He would just put his head down, cover himself with a poncho, and he was out—and then most of the time it was hard to wake him up, even when everyone else was already up and firing their weapons around him.

But it wasn't like that now. Being a cop, living on a cop's schedule, worrying through a cop's worries — the body in the alley, the guy who wouldn't stop beating his wife, the priest raping altar boys, the altar boy who maybe ended his life to escape the Father and his father and maybe didn't... that stuff kept repeating itself in his head like an all-night bad-news radio station he couldn't turn off. With all that, Hank was surprised when he could catch more than a couple of hours of sleep at a stretch.

A lot of nights, he slept for an hour or so and then he was up until dawn. Someone once told him that Leonardo da Vinci, the guy who painted *The Last Supper* and the *Mona Lisa*, slept that way, and that's how all the great geniuses slept. He didn't believe it.

Most mornings, Hazel would wake up at around six and find him smoking a cigarette on the back porch, staring out at the tomato plants in the spring and summer, their empty cages in the fall, or the snow covering everything in the winter. She'd shake her head and put her hand on his shoulder and give him a kiss.

It was hard to believe his sleep could get any worse than it already was, but it was worse now. Since Margaret had gone missing, any little thing would stir him awake — the light from a streetlamp, the wind rubbing against the windows, a car crunching slowly over the crackly ice on the street outside his house. He knew why this was: His sleeping self was the eternal optimist, always figuring that any little thing was the sure sign that Margaret had come home, was just about to walk in the door. Hank's sleeping self was more a stranger to his waking mind every day.

Hank lifted the cup and took another sip of the bad coffee and thought some more about Margaret — the good little girl she had been, the good big girl he'd thought she still was. Last fall was when it all started falling apart. The summer before that was the kind of summer they'd always had. Weekdays, Margaret would play games like Monopoly or Clue or Sorry on somebody's front porch with her friends from the neighborhood, or she and a girlfriend would ride their bikes over to Portage Park or the other park they liked, the one just south of Wrightwood whose name he could never remember. They would play tennis or just lie around on a picnic blanket reading whatever they were reading — some novel by Charles Dickens or George Eliot, or maybe a recent one like *Valley of the Dolls* or *Exodus*. Hank didn't always approve of what his daughter was reading that summer, but he'd always figured reading couldn't get her into trouble.

Hank heard a noise behind him, the front door opening, and he turned around. "Hazel?"

"Yes, it's me. I'll be right there . . . just hanging up my coat."

Hank was a little disappointed. He loved his wife, but she wasn't the one he most wanted to hear coming through the front door right now. He picked up his cup of burnt coffee, walked over to the sink, and poured it out; then he opened a cupboard and took out a quart bottle of Jack Daniel's and a couple of small tumblers. He brought them to the table and poured Hazel and himself a couple of fingers. He drank his down fast and poured himself another. At least it wouldn't keep him up.

Hazel came in and sat down across from him. She touched the rim of her glass, circling her palm around it.

"Where you been, Hazel? Bingo? I almost started without you."

"Yeah, I went to bingo over at St. Ferdinand's Parish."

"That usually ends around nine."

"Yeah . . . I stayed after. I wanted to talk to Father Williams."

"How come?"

"You know how come. I wanted to talk to him about Margaret. I wanted him to pray with me."

She didn't say anything for a while. After a moment or two, she picked up her glass and took a sip of the Jack Daniel's.

Hank looked at her and shrugged. "How did the praying go?"

She looked at him, a long look, the kind of look a woman gives a man when she knows he's hurting and she knows she can't help.

Hank took a long drink and poured himself another.

Hazel reached for his right hand and gently turned it clockwise.

"Hank, there's blood on your sleeve," she said.

"Yeah, Marvin and me, we've been out looking for Margaret. We questioned a couple of guys down near Division Street. One was a dope dealer, and the other was a snitch in a Puerto Rican gang, the Latin Scorpions."

Hazel waited for him to say more, but he didn't.

"Did you get anything from them about Margaret?"

"Maybe a little...not much. Most of it was 'maybe this, maybe that.' 100% bullshit. Maybe. Probably. We left the snitch trying to piece together a name or two of other people we can talk to. I hope he does."

Hazel shook her head, like she could see that Hank didn't feel very hopeful. She let go of his hand and picked up her glass. She finished her Jack Daniel's and put the glass down on the table.

"Why don't you pray with me?" she asked.

"I can't pray. You know I can't pray. I can't see the point. I mean, what's the point if I don't believe there's a point?"

"Pray with me."

Hank shook his head and finished off his drink.

"Pray with me for Margaret," Hazel said again.

He shook his head one more time, sighed, and then got on his knees.

Hazel knelt next to him.

CHAPTER 37

BEFORE TAKING THE first step down into the basement, Marvin stopped and read the sign: THERESA'S LOUNGE. LIVE ENTERTAINMENT EVERY NIGHT. JUNIOR WELLS AND HIS BOYS.

He turned around and said to Hank, "Too bad we got nothing from Ernesto yet, but you know, I think I'm going to like this place. I bet these Blackstone Rangers know the funkiest places to hang out in the whole South Side."

Hank didn't say anything.

Even before he opened the door to the bar and stepped in, he knew this place was going to smoke him. There were bars all over Chicago, in white neighborhoods and black ones and Hispanic ones, in Polack neighborhoods and Italian neighborhoods. If Brooklyn was the City of Churches, then Chicago was the City of Bars. On every corner and in the middle of every block, you could go down some steps or up some steps and find yourself in a place where you could buy yourself a beer and a shot if you had the money. And if you didn't have the money, you could always sit there on a bench against the back wall, praying that some friend or buddy you hadn't yet met would show up and offer you just a little one, maybe a shot of vodka or a half glass of Schlitz, the beer that made Milwaukee famous.

Hank had been in more than his share of bars, but this one was different. Opening the front door, Hank knew it right away, sure as shooting.

It was way too busy for a Monday night. Working men were the guys you mostly saw in Chicago's corner bars and basement bars, and most working men couldn't afford to hang out much in the middle of the week — maybe a quick beer and a shot on the way home, but not a real evening out, no matter how good the bar was. But on this Monday night, Theresa's Lounge was jumping; this wasn't a bar for people who made their money in factories and offices.

Electric thunder ripped off a guitar and stopped him dead, tried to push him right back up the steps. He felt like he was struggling against a blues storm. A long bar crowded with sitting and standing singles and couples ran along one side of the place. Booths and tables took up the other. Everybody seemed to be jiving steady to the beat. In the back, way way in the back, there were some more tables and a bandstand.

And that's where the blues was popping.

A short, fat black man in a red wool cap with a yellow puffball on top was killing his harmonica, grinding his face into it and twisting his body like a snake, twisting tighter and tighter as the mouth organ's notes got shriller and shriller like some kind of raggedy insect was screaming in ecstatic moans about the end of the world.

Next to the guy with the harp, a tall skinny black man in a blood-red t-shirt was rocking gently over his guitar, slower and slower as he smacked those steel strings harder and harder. It was the ultimate blues riff, carrying the crowd where it wanted to go. People nodded their heads and humped their shoulders and gyrated their asses. A young woman, just a kid in a long winter coat with a pint bottle of something, was dancing slowly on her own in front of the band. The guys on the bandstand seemed not to notice her at all or care what the hell she was doing. Every once in a while, she would jerk her head back and let out some kind of moan or yell that Hank couldn't hear. Maybe it was in time to the music and maybe it wasn't. Hank couldn't tell. She didn't seem to be drunk, and she didn't seem to be sober. She was where God meant all of us to be.

Marvin nodded his head and pointed his finger at the girl. "High on life," he said. "You betcha."

The guy with the harmonica put down his harp just then, held it tight to his chest, and shouted out a lick from some blues song, some holler, that went all the way down to Dixie and even further than that, down to the Delta, down to Parchman Farm, down to the wet brown mud of the black Mississippi. He shouted out, "Say, old man, what kind of woman is this? I said, Say, old man, what kind of woman is this?!" And then he shouted it all again, asked it in a blues growl that tied him to the plantation fields and the whips that broke the soul of the South and damned their white masters sure as Jesus was standing on the levee calling for the flood.

And there it was again, he was shouting it out like sin was on vacation: "Say, old old man, tell me, what kind of woman is this? I said, What kind of woman, yes, what kind of woman is this?!"

Marvin came up behind Hank. There was a bottle of Bud in his right hand and a bottle of Pabst in his left. "I don't know what kind of woman it is either," he said, laughing, "but she sure must do it fine." He gestured at the woman in front of the bandstand who was doing her slow jerking solo, and started bobbing his head in time with her short bobs and slippery steps.

"Come on, we got a man to meet," Hank said, taking the Pabst and walking over to an empty booth near the door. He sat down, and Marvin followed.

After a couple of minutes, a waiter came over, a tall, dark-black kid with an Afro the size of a beach ball. He started wiping the brown Formica table with big looping circles, just barely avoiding the detectives' beer bottles. He didn't say anything at first, just scrubbed with his dirty rag, scrubbed hard. When he was done, he looked first at Hank and then at Marvin, and said, "What you want?" He didn't say it with a smile or an even an ounce of interest. He said it like he was talking to the trash cans out back still full of last night's empties and puke. He said it like he didn't give a damn about what Hank and Marvin wanted.

Marvin sat up straight and grinned the biggest grin he could, and he looked at the kid in the Afro and said, "What the fuck is this? Is this service? Is this what I'm going to tip you for when you get done doing whatever the fuck you think you're doing here?"

The kid in the Afro stood there. He didn't say anything at first. He just stood there, stood straight as the cross on Calvary Hill the morning after, his black face getting blacker and blacker as his rage started building. Between the dim light and the sweat on his face, he looked almost purple, metallic, like something from nowhere, from outer space or maybe beyond outer space. Suddenly, he threw his scrub rag in Marvin's face and said, "Fuck you, you fuckin' white man, coming into this place like you was Jesus born of virgins. Stay on your own side of town, don't go fuckin' with us. I ain't serving any white man." He said that and he walked right out of Theresa's Lounge.

Marvin kept smiling as he watched him go, then he turned back to Hank. "That soul brother is going to be a cold, cold brother. He should have at least put a coat on over his apron if he was going out into that snow."

Hank took a swallow of his beer and looked around. The band was still ripping. A smiling black man in a brown business suit and a yellow tie was coming toward their booth. Sliding and shuffling and grooving to the music, he had a quart bottle of something in his left hand.

"Now what?" Marvin said. "I think I'm getting more good company than I can stand."

The man in the brown suit put the bottle and three shot glasses down on the table and said, "You white boys mind a black man sitting down to supper with you-all?"

Marvin grinned. "Not if you-all bring the turkey and the grits."

The man rolled his head back and laughed a laugh that went all the way back to creation and beyond, back to Jehovah laughing his own first big laugh at the frisky antics of Adam and his rib-mate.

"O my brother, my brother," the black man said at the end of that laugh, "you have seen the gift and the glory and have definitely entered into solemn union with the giver. Let me pour you both some of this Dewar's White Label, which is no great shakes when it comes to scotch but is the best this poorly stocked basement has to offer, and a sight better than the watered down piss you're drinking at the moment."

He picked up the bottle and started to pour.

They weren't the usual ounce-and-a-half shot glasses; they looked a little bigger, at least two ounces. Hank could see the point — maybe the music wasn't the only reason why Theresa's Lounge was hopping on a Monday night.

Hank and Marvin's new friend filled the shot-plus glasses to the top and then some, letting the Dewar's flow over, spilling just a little over the table the kid with the Afro had just scrubbed. Then, still standing next to the booth, he took one of the shot glasses and downed it clean. He looked down at Hank and Marvin. "Didn't your mama never tell you it's not good to drink alone? Bottoms up, white boys."

Marvin said, "Yes, sir," picked up his glass, and threw it back. Hank followed him.

The man poured out three more shots. "Now, I did you boys a favor, and it's your turn to do me one. You know what I mean. You got to invite me to sit down with you-all, like we was neighbors and brothers, you see — brothers in the next life at least, if not in this one."

Marvin threw his shot glass back again. "My friend, we would both love to have you take a seat beside us because you are clearly one fiercely friendly son of a bitch, but we're waiting for someone — a member of a social club of some sort known as the Blackstone Rangers."

"The Blackstone Rangers? That's one tough group of motherfuckers, yes sir," their friend said, nodding his head wisely. "And who do you think I might be? A country preacher looking to inspire you to a life of virtue? The Black Messiah, perhaps?" And he laughed again, laughed that creation-cracking laugh.

Hank looked at him. "In that case, have a seat."

Marvin scooted toward the wall, and the man in the suit sat down next to him. "Now that we're brothers, lapping up the juice of life together, maybe you can tell me what you want from my Blackstone Ranger brothers."

Hank leaned forward. The band was shaking through another

number. The skinny guitar player had his eyes closed and was singing, wondering what his baby was doing tonight. Was she kneeling by her couch praying for some five-dollar miracle? Was she standing in her bedroom looking at the howling moon? Was she sleeping with the young boy who lived down the street and grooved like the ocean spinning away its dreams? The electricity Hank had felt in the earlier songs was gone. This one was about the quiet moments just before a woman broke her man's heart into a million pieces.

Hank looked back at the man sitting across from him. "We're here on an investigation — about a dog who died in a bad way."

"You talking about that dog on the North Side? That golden retriever? I read about it in the paper, the *Sun-Times*. Terrible. Just terrible. Do that to a dog? Crucifying it? Jesus, I wouldn't do that to a *cat* — or even a white man."

"Yeah," Hank said. "We're looking into who did it and what happened to the people who were with the dog before it died. Couple white kids. Male and female."

"Hmm...so this isn't really about that dog," the man smiled as he leaned back and pushed up the brim of his pork pie hat. "You-all don't give a fuck about that poor dog, that golden retriever with his whole golden, doggy life in front of him. You're just worried about some white-ass mother-fucking rich kids from Downers Grove or Darien, or maybe the North suburbs like Skokie or Evanston. Even if that dog could sing the blues like that skinny guy on the stage there, you wouldn't be interested in him the way you're interested in those white folk. And now you tell me what's so special about these here whities. Why you all the way down here in Woodlawn looking for them when you should be uptown, sleeping in your white sheets and dreaming about whatever the fuck white people dream about?"

Hank threw back a shot — his third. The Dewar's was doing its stuff. He felt like talking, felt like being neighborly.

"We're not looking for both of the kids. Just one — the girl. The guy's just some loser, a piece of trash who thinks he's a big-deal dealer, but he's just an asshole. It's the girl we want."

The man in the suit nodded his head, looked to the right and then to the left, ran his tongue over his lips, nodded his head some more. "I know you, Mister Detective. You want to fuck this girl. Huh? Fuck her? I know you. She's just some piece of white ass you got a schoolboy crush on. Let me ask you, your momma know about this?"

Hank wanted to take the bottle off the table and smash it across the guy's face, blind him if he could. Instead, Hank kept his cool, leaned back, and shook his head no.

"She's my daughter. Her name is Margaret," Hank said slowly. "I just want to see her home again. Back from wherever she is right now."

The Blackstone Ranger narrowed his eyes, stared at Hank for a moment, then turned to Marvin beside him. "You believe this shit? I bet you want a piece of her too."

Almost instantly, Marvin's Colt .45 was out and pressed against the man's left side, aimed just where his heart ought to be.

The skinny guitar player on the bandstand finished the last note of his song with a hard downward sweep on the steel strings of his electric guitar, then started taking the guitar strap off. It was time for the band to take a break.

"I don't want to fuck anybody but you, sugar pie," Marvin said. "But my friend's telling the truth. We're looking for his daughter. You know anything about her, about Margaret? She's a nice kid, and she's in some kind of trouble. I don't understand how she got into this mess between your gang and that North Side spic gang, the Latin Scorpions, and this golden retriever somebody crucified. But we sure do want to get her back. You got anything to tell us?"

The black man in the brown suit and yellow tie stared at Marvin, then he looked across the table at Hank again. "Is this the way this is going to be? I come out here on a cold winter's night with a bottle of Dewar's and friendship and good will in my heart, and all you do is press a gun against my tender ribs? Like my momma used to say, 'A mouth full of gimme and a hand full of much obliged.' That's all you are, white boys. I'm leaving."

He put his hands on the table and started to push himself up. He didn't get far, though.

Hank put his hand on the black man's hand. "Wait," he said quietly. "This can play out two ways. You can sit back down, and we can talk. Or I can grab this bottle of Dewar's you brought to my partner and me, and I can smash it across your face. The bottle won't break, but the scotch will pour all over you and your beautiful brown suit and your clean yellow tie, and then you'll tumble backwards over the seat, right into the booth behind you where a nice young couple are sitting enjoying a platter of French fries with lots of ketchup. Grease and ketchup stains are hard to get out."

The man in the suit shook Hank's hand off his hand and smiled. "You know what I like about you white-boy cops? When you want to, you can talk so plain that you can be easily understood by even the dumbest motherfucker regardless of race, creed, or fucking color."

Hank nodded.

"So talk."

"Good, I will," Hank said. "Sit down."

The man did, and Hank poured him another shot of scotch.

"Now let me tell you plainly and truthfully," Hank said. "We don't give a fuck about you and your gang and whatever is going on between you and the Latin Scorpions. We don't care about this stupid junkie Willy Reichard who somehow got himself caught between your boys and those Puerto Ricans. And we don't care about this dog, this dead golden retriever. You can crucify as many mutts as you want — it won't make any difference to me or my partner. You understand?"

The Blackstone Ranger picked up his shot glass and threw the Dewar's back. "Yeah, I get it. You just be interested in the chick, your daughter."

"Yeah," Hank said. "Just my daughter."

"Unfortunately, I got nothing for you then. You just wasted your precious time and mine coming down here to Woodlawn. When we got to that fool Willy's place, there was only that stinking dog, howling and growling at us like we be some kind of bears or squirrels or I don't know what the fuck. You ever notice how lots of dogs don't like the black man? They see him like some kind of thing that ain't human, ain't to be trusted. White man's dogs got the white man's prejudice."

Marvin nodded. "Yeah, I've seen it."

"Well, I'm sick of that shit. I got no choice but to put up with it from white *folk*, but not from any damn dog even if it's got pretty blond hair."

Hank picked up the bottle, looked at the bottom. There was about three or four ounces left sitting there. He poured Marvin and the man in the suit and himself a short shot each and put the empty bottle down.

"Thank you for your cooperation," Hank said and threw the shot back.

After drinking his own shot, the Blackstone Ranger in the brown suit stood up and said, "I do hope you find your daughter. I'd go back to those Latin Scorpions. They're assholes and are not to be trusted around women — especially around young girls."

"Thanks," Hank said. "That's real good to know."

"Yeah," the man said. "Good luck." He got up and walked out of Theresa's basement lounge just as the skinny guitar player got back on the bandstand and started tuning up his guitar.

Marvin lit a cigarette. "You know, I kind of like this place. I just wish it wasn't all the way down here on the South Side. I hate the drive."

He passed the pack of smokes to Hank then. Hank lit one up and took a drag.

The guitar player did a riff that was more jazz than blues. Hank recognized it. It was a slow piece — a song he liked, "Blue Moon". Not jittery or over-electrified, just the sound of quiet longing mixed with a touch of despair. The harmonica player came out of some back room and walked up to the microphone. He took it in both hands, and he started singing about how the moon saw him standing there without any kind of dream in his heart, without any kind of love of his own.

A couple got up from their seats at the bar and walked to where the band was playing. The woman took the guy's hand in hers and gently pressed into him. He pulled her even closer and they were dancing slow, a dance that seemed like it would never end.

Hank watched them. He liked to see people dancing. Old people, young people — it didn't matter. He figured everyone liked to watch people dance. There was some kind of magic in the mix of music and love, words and bodies touching without any kind of pushing or pulling, bodies just being there.

Blue Moon.

Blue Moon.

Blue Moon.

Marvin said, "I think we're done here. We met the guy from the Blackstone Rangers. He gave us what the Latin Scorpion guy Ernesto gave us: shit. Time we get going home."

"Yeah," Hank said. "Let's first have another drink and listen to the rest of this set. They're doing a nice job on this."

Marvin took another little drink and started singing, "Blue moon, you knew just what I was there for. You heard me saying a prayer for someone I really could care for...."

CHAPTER 38

HANK SLOWED DOWN and pulled the Ford to the curb. Darkness and silence filled the street; the only sound was the slow crush of hard snow beneath his tires. Finally, there was the soft rub of his front right tire against the curb.

The sound woke Marvin up, and he looked around. "What the hell is this? This ain't home."

Hank didn't say anything. Most of the lights were out in the three-story brownstone apartment buildings lining Dorchester Street, and snow continued to fall, coming down heavy again.

But Hank had no trouble recognizing the place.

He remembered what it was like the first time he and Marvin were here. It was hot back then, early summer back in the days before the world started believing in air conditioning like it believed in Jesus. He and Marvin in their sport coats, sweating like nobody's business, stood there at the door knocking, waiting for the guy they already figured was probably a killer to answer it, knowing that when he did, anything could happen.

"What are we doing here?" Marvin said, shaking Hank back into the present.

"Reminiscing, I guess. It's been a while since you and I played judge and executioner. I wanted to see how I felt about it."

"You don't know how you feel about it? I know how I feel about it. I feel fucking great about it. That guy was an asshole, a motherfucker, and what we did to him was what should have been done to him, in spades, long before he started murdering people."

"In spades…?" Hank asked, stepping out of the car. The wind pushed the fresh snow hard. Falling, it covered the old snow, making it feel dry, crunchy underfoot. He could hear it and feel it in every step as he crossed the sidewalk, until he stood in front of the building.

He remembered everything about that case, from the first dead body to the last. He remembered twenty years of victims, innocent and not-so-innocent people left to bleed out on dirty floors or filthy mattresses, carefully cut up and stuffed into suitcases like packed meat, mutilated to inspire fear or carefully arranged as if to show some kind of weird love, or just dumped in a random ditch somewhere. He remembered the killers he and Marvin had sent to jail, but even more he remembered the ones he and Marvin couldn't send to jail — the ones who got away until they did something stupid, and the few, like this guy, who didn't get away.

Hank put his right hand out, palm up, and watched the flakes falling on his skin and melting slowly.

Then Marvin came up and stood beside him.

"Hank, fuck this. What's the point of this shit, coming here? You know as well as I do that we did the right thing when we did what we did. We shot that bastard dead and buried him in the woods in Wisconsin so deep that not even Jesus, when he comes back to Earth in a cloud of Technicolor glory, will be able to figure out what the hell we did with the body. We did what we had to do."

Hank nodded and didn't say anything for a moment. When he did speak, he said, "Yeah, we did the right thing. The only thing we could do...but that still doesn't make me feel good about it."

"He was a killer who didn't give a shit about who he killed."

"Yeah, yeah, I know. He was evil. He enjoyed the killing. We stopped him, and we had to stop him. There was nobody else."

"That's right. So what's the beef? Why are we standing here in the cold and snow staring at his old building, thinking about what we did to him?"

"I don't know why. Maybe I just wanted to think about him for a moment and remember him and also remember that we put a stop to him. That we did something good that stopped him from doing more killing. Or maybe it's not that. Maybe I needed to remind myself that I can be almost as much of a bastard as he was, almost as bad as he was, killing someone like it was simple and easy and unimportant."

Marvin grabbed Hank's arm. "Hank, you're talking stupid talk. This guy kills a bunch of innocent people and you and I stop him. There's no question here about anything."

"No question?"

"You're just feeling like shit because of your daughter. You're feeling sad and lonely and afraid and maybe even guilty for some crazy reason, and you're having trouble not taking some of that out on the jerks we have to spend most of our time dealing with, that's all. I've known you twenty years now, and I know for a fact you're a better guy than most, sure as fuck better than me." Marvin smiled. "Come on, let's get out of here. Get some food, some sleep. Then tomorrow we got to get back to work. These stupid gang leads aren't getting us any closer to Margaret."

Hank turned to his partner. "Give me a couple of minutes. You go ahead, back to the car."

Marvin shook his head, turned around, and walked back through the falling snow.

Hank watched him go, then faced the building again. He didn't know what it was that was bugging him. It had been a little more than ten years since he and Marvin killed this killer, shot him in the head and buried him in that grave in the woods, but there was never a day that Hank didn't think about how wrong that had been, and never a day when he didn't answer himself back that he would do it again if that's what it took to stop a murderer.

His thoughts drifted back to Tommy Sawa. Why was it, Hank wondered, that there was always some asshole ready to kill a kid or rape him or just beat him stupid in return for his love and goodness? Why?

Then Hank wondered about Margaret. He wondered who had shaken her loose from her family, from the kid dreams she had growing up, from the grown-up dreams she'd been starting to live out, from the life he'd thought she was living. He looked up at the first-floor windows of what had once been a killer's apartment. It was dark. Silent. There were no answers there — just an ordinary place now, with ordinary people living in it. Hank knew that it made no sense to come here and ask the questions he was asking.

He put his palm out again and watched the snow settle on it. First it fell softly, slowly, like winter was pretending to be something it wasn't. Then it fell faster and faster, till the snow stopped melting as it landed and started sticking to his palm, covering it like a blanket.

He watched it pile up and wondered what it meant.

Chapter 39

HANK LOOKED OUT the window of his office in the Shakespeare Substation on California Avenue. Looking west out toward Logan Square and Pulaski Road, and beyond that to Oak Park beyond the city limits, everything was snow — a soft, fluffy, cold mattress of snow, on the rooftops and on the trees, in the streets and in the alleys.

And the snow was still falling. Weeks of it already, since before that day when Sister Mary Philomena came knocking on his door to tell him about Father Ted and what he had done to Tommy Sawa the altar boy.

Hank suddenly thought of the great flood, the one they talked about in the Bible. Forty days and nights of thunder and rain, and what was left of the world fit into a boat that was 300 cubits by 50 cubits by 30 cubits. He wasn't much good at math, didn't know a cubit from a cruller, but he remembered one time when he was in fourth grade listening to a priest spell it all out during a sermon. He told the boys and girls and their parents that in modern units the Ark was 520 feet long by 86 feet wide by 52 feet high. Hank remembered thinking that it wasn't really much of a boat to hold that many animals and food for all of them.

Hank guessed that falling rain was worse than falling snow. That rain killed everyone and everything, the good and the bad, except for the Noah family and their livestock. This snow here in Chicago was piled three or four feet high in spots, lower but icy in the streets and on the sidewalks, but not many people had died from it so far. There were the usual number of heart attacks and snow-related accidents plus the murder of a nun and the death of a schoolboy, but nothing like what the flood brought to Noah's world.

The wind outside started picking up; he could hear it coming through the cracks around the window casing. The windows in this old police station were crap. He could hear the cold wind, and he could feel it blowing in, too. He might as well just have screens up for all the good the windows did.

A soft knock on the door startled him, and he pivoted around to face it.

A woman in a dark blue coat with some kind of fur collar stood there in the doorway.

He didn't recognize her at first, and said, "Yes? Can I help you?"

Standing there for a moment, the woman seemed surprised by the question. Then, in a Polish accent, she said, "Detective?"

That's when Hank remembered her: Tommy Sawa's mother. He stood up.

"Please, come in," he said, gesturing for her to sit in the metal chair across from his own.

"I don't mean to take up your time, Detective, but I need to tell you something. My husband, Bruno, didn't want me to come. He thought I was being stupid, but I knew I had to come and tell you this, even if you won't listen or you tell me I am being a foolish woman."

She stopped for a moment and looked at him.

Hank could feel the strength in her. Mrs. Sawa wasn't someone who could be easily stopped when she felt she had to keep going, and he had no intention of trying.

She nodded her head once and continued. "I want to tell you this: He didn't kill Sister Mary Philomena, my Tommy, and he didn't kill himself. I know this. I remember the way he looked at me when he told me what he heard about Sister Mary Philomena's death. I don't know how to say it — my English isn't so good. But when he told me about the sister's death, he told it like he got hit with a shovel. The words came out slow, like they weren't words he ever thought would come out of his mouth. Like they were in some other language, one he would never understand no matter how long he practiced it. I've known liars, Detective, just like you have. I spent three years in a concentration camp for women, Ravensbrück in Germany."

She stopped speaking again. Hank thought he knew what she would say next.

"The guards there would tell me anything just to get me to smile at them or give them something. You know what I mean by this, to give them *something*? I don't have to tell you what the war was like, what those guards were like."

Hank nodded.

"They lied to me, and to the other women. Every day they lied. And mister, when you hear enough lies, you know when you hear the truth — and what I heard from my Tommy that day was the truth."

Hank didn't move, kept his voice even, said only the minimum he had to so she'd keep talking. "What did he say?"

"Tommy said he didn't know anything about what happened to that poor Sister Mary Philomena down in the basement until he heard it from the other kids. He saw her the day before in the hallway of the school, just like usual, and the next morning the kids were saying she was dead."

She stopped again, and Hank looked at her. She wasn't crying, just nodding her head slowly as she spoke. She was the kind of person he didn't see often. She was talking about her dead son, dead only a week now, and she wasn't crying. Sure, she had cried back when he and Marvin questioned her, right after they found Tommy's body in the closet, but she seemed beyond crying now. Maybe whatever happened to her in the concentration camp had prepared her, steeled her, for any terrible thing to happen, even the death of her only son.

"Detective, that's what I know. I know he didn't kill her, no matter what the police say. It wasn't in him to do it. If it was in him, I would have seen it in him when we talked about the sister's death. And another thing: If he didn't kill her, why would he kill himself?"

Hank had seen this before, a mother arguing that her son or her husband hadn't done some bad thing that she couldn't imagine him doing. He knew what he had to say, the thing he always said to mothers and daughters and wives, women who couldn't believe the murders and robberies, the kidnappings and brutalities the people closest to them had been accused of doing.

"Mrs. Sawa, thank you for coming in and talking to me about this. I know it's hard for you — your son Tommy, a good boy, being accused of killing the sister and then taking his own life. You've given me a lot to think about, and as soon as you leave, I'll talk to my partner, Detective Bondarowicz, and we'll see how what you've told us can help us to understand what happened to the sister and to Tommy."

"You don't believe me. You think it's all bullshit. I'm no fool, I can see that you think I'm just a mother who thinks her son couldn't do anything wrong. Let me tell you something. Tommy didn't kill the sister, and he didn't kill himself. You want to know how I know he didn't kill himself? I'll tell you. When I came home and found him hanging in that closet, the door was closed, and there was no chair in that closet, no stool, nothing to climb on, nothing he could pull himself up with. That's right — the door of the closet was closed all the way, shut tight, and that step-stool was outside it on the floor. You think about that. How did he lift himself up to put his neck in that rope if he had no ladder or chair? He couldn't pull himself up with his hands — Tommy was never strong enough to climb on the monkey bars in the playground. He had to use that stool, but then how did the stool get outside the closet while the door was closed? And if the door was open when he kicked it out, how did he close it while he was hanging there dying? There's no doorknob on the inside, no hook, nothing for him to hold!"

Tommy's mother gave Hank a hard look and then nodded as she stood up.

"You think about that," she said. "You just think about that again. You think about how my Tommy could stand on a stool, put a rope around his neck, then kick the stool right through a closed closet door into the middle of the room."

CHAPTER 40

HANK THOUGHT about it.

Sitting at his desk, looking out the window, he thought about what Tommy Sawa's mother said about the closet and the step-stool. Outside, the sun was just a dirty glow peeking from behind gray clouds as the wind shoved them across the sky. There wouldn't be any kind of let-up on the bad weather today.

He picked up the phone and called Marvin, asked him to come over and help him think about it some more.

—⁘—

Marvin sat down in the same chair Mrs. Sawa had sat in. "What's up?"

Hank told him.

Marvin shook his head and said, "Shit." He said it slowly and quietly, a sort of whisper. Then he took out his pack of Chesterfields and lit one. He shook the wooden match a couple of times till the flame was out.

"You know," Marvin said, "women are always coming up with these stories, these bullshit theories about how innocent their hubbies and their kiddies are. The patrolman who was the first guy on the scene saw the room and the closet. I remember him taking out his notepad and reading it straight, just like a boy scout."

"And what did he say?"

"You know as well as I do what he said."

"What was that?"

"Fuck," Marvin said.

"Come on, what did he say?"

"He said that when he got there the closet door was partly closed, and the stool was outside the closet."

"Yeah," Hank said, "that's what we saw too. But if you remember, he also said that *she* discovered the body when *she* opened the closet door — it's down in the file that way, too. So there's nobody to testify about that closet door except for Mrs. Sawa, and at least her story's consistent."

Marvin took a drag on his cigarette and let the smoke out slowly. "What are you gonna make of it? That the kid didn't kill himself because the stool was outside the closet and he was inside the closet with the door closed?"

"It's one way of looking at it."

Marvin shrugged and took another drag. "You know as well as I do that this kind of evidence is pretty much bullshit. Somebody remembers a door being open, and somebody else remembers the door being closed. Did the kid kick the stool when he hanged himself, and did he kick it all the way out of the closet into the middle of the room? Did he miraculously kick it right through a closed door? Maybe yes, maybe no. He was an altar boy — maybe miracles were normal for him. And if he didn't kick that stool out of the closet when he hanged himself, how did it get out? Are we saying somebody hanged the kid, killed him, and then dragged the stool out of the closet on his way out? The whole thing is just maybe yes, maybe no. One lawyer would argue one way; the other one would argue the other way."

Hank took one of Marvin's cigarettes out of his pack and lit it, took a drag, kept it in, let it out. He liked smoking. Liked it as much as watching the Cubs on TV or barbequing pork chops on the grill in his backyard. He remembered the first time he'd smoked: he snuck one of his dad's cigarettes, a Lucky Strike. Smoked it in the basement, just inside the door of the coal shed. He remembered worrying that his dad would find out when he got home from work, smell the cigarette smoke lingering in the basement. But he didn't.

Hank looked at Marvin.

Marvin looked back at him. "So where do we go if the kid didn't kill himself?"

"Why're you always asking me questions you already know the answers to?"

"Why?" Marvin leaned closer. "You know why. It's my job. I get paid for asking useless questions, except for now when I'm suspended and I'm doing it as a volunteer out of the goodness of my heart. Didn't you ever watch *Dragnet?* 'Just the facts, ma'am.' Besides, useless questions take your mind off Margaret."

"Nothing takes my mind off Margaret."

"Yeah, but we can pretend they do."

Hank stood up and walked over to his file cabinet, pulled out the autopsy report on Tommy Sawa, and handed it to Marvin. "You read it when it came out, right?"

"Yeah, I read it."

"Read it again."

Marvin shrugged and tossed the file on Hank's desk. "I don't have to."

Hank didn't pick it up. He didn't have to, either. He knew what the report said. The differences between a suicidal hanging and a homicidal hanging aren't that hard to spot. Usually, a homicidal hanging shows some kind of evidence of a struggle: bruises on the body where the killer raised the victim up to the noose, or where the killer and the victim struggled before the hanging. A suicide didn't usually show those sorts of bruises — just the bruises and cuts where the ligature, the noose, strangled the victim. And then there was blood and skin under the fingernails of the homicide victim. Unless the victim was somehow made unconscious before the hanging — which also normally left some kind of evidence, like drugs, opiates, excessive alcohol in the body, or a blow to the head — he probably fought like all hell to keep himself from being strung up, and there would be tiny bits of the killer under the victim's nails. All that stuff was pretty much a sure sign, and none of those sure signs appeared on the corpse of little Tommy Sawa. Not a bruise, not a shred of skin or a speck of blood, not one single little indication of a struggle.

The kid was clean.

Hank opened the file, flipped through a few pages, and then he closed it and put it back in the file cabinet.

"So where do we go, chief?" Marvin asked as he pressed his cigarette butt out in Hank's ashtray.

Hank shook his head and looked out the window. The snow was coming down again, the wind swirling it hard and fast. It was hard to see the roofs of the garages across the alley in back of the station, and it was harder to see the trees beyond them. Everything was a fucking winter wonderland waiting for Old Saint Nick and his goddamn reindeers to cut short their vacation and come around again.

Hank swiveled around in his chair to face his partner. "You know what I think?"

"Yeah," Marvin said, "I think I know what you think."

"I think it's time to go see Father Ted Bachleda again and ask him what he thinks about all this."

CHAPTER 41

MRS. POPOWSKI SHOWED them into the rectory's reception room and pointed at the couches with a grunt. Hank knew the housekeeper hadn't been too happy to see them the first time they came to the rectory. She seemed less happy now.

Marvin grabbed her hand like he was going to kiss it and said, "Smile, honey, you might be on Candid Camera."

She frowned, jerked her hand loose from his, and huffed off to get Father Ted.

Marvin watched her leave, and then he turned to Hank. "She sure ain't no fun. That's probably why the priests are always cozying up to the little schoolboys. And girls too, I guess."

Hank took off his fedora and said, "Marvin, some day your bullshit is going to get you into trouble."

"It already has — I'm suspended, remember? I could have been a captain of detectives ten years ago if I wasn't such an asshole. You too, for that matter."

Hank nodded and looked up.

Father Ted entered the room from the corridor opposite the front door, wearing a floor-length black cassock. He was walking fast and seemed pissed off, his lips pressed tight, his eyes intent, searching. He didn't sit down.

"Really, I don't get it," the priest said, "why you detectives are here again. It can't be about that poor boy Tommy Sawa. I thought that investigation was closed. What's this about?"

Hank said, "We're just tracking down some loose ends, Father. Dotting the i's and crossing the t's, that kind of stuff. We hope you've got a few minutes to spare for some questions — just a couple, really."

"I don't. According to what I heard from your lieutenant, everything that had to be done has been done. And if that's true, I don't see the point of this interview."

"The point?" Marvin said. "The point is that we have a couple of questions we want to ask, and when you answer them you can go back to watching *Gomer Pyle* or whatever you do when you're alone."

Father Ted pointedly ignored Marvin and addressed Hank. "I'm not answering any questions. I'm sick of this, you two tracking me down and badgering me with false accusations and disgusting insinuations. I'm done with you. If you have questions, present them to the Archdiocese's lawyers, and if they think it necessary, they'll pass them on to me."

The priest turned around quickly and left, his cassock swirling.

"Well, that didn't go as well as I thought it would," Marvin said. "And I didn't lay a finger on him this time. So much for the rewards of virtue."

Hank said, "It's not over yet. Come on."

He took off after the priest, with Marvin close behind.

They caught up to Father Ted at the bottom of the stairs leading to the third floor.

The priest turned around, an exasperated look on his face.

Marvin walked up to him. "Father, one question. Then we'll leave you alone."

Shaking his head no, the priest said it again: "No questions!"

"Listen, Father," Hank said. "Sister Mary Philomena saw you with Tommy Sawa, and then she's dead. Then Tommy Sawa's dead. You need to talk to us, tell us what you were doing with the boy."

"What do you mean she saw me with Tommy?" Father Ted asked, then stopped for a moment. "…I'm not talking to you," he reminded them as he turned and started rushing up the stairs.

Hank leaned forward and quickly grabbed the hem of the priest's cassock with his hand. Father Ted tripped, lurched forward, and tumbled into the stairs. His face smashed into one of the steps and then smashed into another as he slipped down the stairway and came to rest on the landing.

Hank said, "Oh, shit."

Blood was pouring from the priest's nose and mouth. He seemed confused, stunned. He shook his head and then shouted, "Help! Help me!" His cries filled the stairwell.

Hank leaned forward to help the priest up, get him back onto his feet, but Father Ted didn't want any help from the detectives. He pulled back from Hank and called out for help again.

Somewhere Hank could hear a door opening and footsteps running toward them.

He tried again, pulled Father Ted up and tried to steady him on his feet — then Mrs. Popowski rushed into the stairwell, waving her arms and shouting something in enraged Polish that Hank was probably better off not understanding. Hank put his hands up, palms out, to stop her, but she surged straight at him.

CHAPTER 42

HANK CAME TO in a hospital bed.

A monitor stood next to him keeping track of his vitals. He watched the dials for a moment, listened to their beeps, and tried to make sense of what they were all trying to tell him. He couldn't. The noise was just noise, and his vision was blurry. The letters and numbers and words on the machine looked like hieroglyphics and scratches. Two plus two wasn't equaling anything at the moment.

Marvin was sitting on a chair at the foot of the bed, reading a comic book. If Hank closed one eye, he could see a duck in a Superman suit on the cover.

"I'm back," Hank said.

"Where from?" Marvin replied.

"You tell me. The last thing I remember was the housekeeper at the rectory rushing toward me and cursing me out in Polish or something even worse. I've seen women that pissed-off before, but only at you." Hank stopped talking. His hand went to his forehead and felt a cotton bandage. "What's this?"

"She fucked you up, fucked you up bad, partner."

"Yeah, I guess."

"I think you must have broke some ancient Polack rule about not beating up priests, because that housekeeper came at you like you were Satan or his evil twin brother. She rushed straight at you and smashed into your chest and then really worked you over. She tackled you like you were a third stringer for the Chicago Bears, sent you flying down the stairs with her on top of you, beating your face and calling you every damn thing in the Big Book of Polack Curses."

"Holy shit."

"She probably said that too — but in Polish, and with lots of feeling."

"Is she okay?"

"Oh yeah, definitely. You two tumbled down a flight of stairs together, but you broke her fall. I always tell people my partner's a nice guy."

"Well, I'm glad she's okay. And what about me?"

"You? Well, not so good," Marvin said and smiled. "They think you have a concussion, but that's not the worst of it. The worst of it is that you and I have both been suspended indefinitely."

"Indefinitely? That's not good."

"Yeah, the guy in charge of all the good little Catholics in Chicago, Cardinal Cody, called in some favors. He told the Powers that Be that you're an asshole, and you've been harassing his best priests. Like all shit, it flowed downhill, and it didn't take long to get down to Lieutenant O'Herlihy."

"How long have I been out?"

"They brought you here about two hours ago. You were pretty far out of it when they brought you in, and as far as I could tell this is the first time you woke up, except for maybe a little mumbling once or twice."

Hank raised both his hands to his head and felt the bandage. His head was throbbing now. He wasn't sure if this was something new, or if it had been throbbing the whole time and he just hadn't been awake enough to notice. Everything seemed confused. Blurry.

"Does Hazel know I'm here?" Hank asked.

"Oh yeah. She knows. She's here in fact — just stepped out for a cup of coffee. She'll be back in a minute."

"What did O'Herlihy say?"

"If you have to ask that, you're really fucked up."

"Come on."

"He's not happy."

"What else?"

Marvin shrugged and put the comic book down on a table. "He's worried about the reaction from the Cardinal and the rest of the Catholic big shots. It looks to O'Herlihy and everyone else except your beloved partner and maybe Hazel like you're on some kind of crazy vendetta, tailing this priest, trying to fuck him up. I told O'Herlihy the thing today was an accident, that you were just trying to stop the guy so you could ask him a couple questions, but O'Herlihy didn't buy it. You really put the whammy on the guy this time — when you grabbed Father Ted and tripped him on those stairs, he came down hard on his face, had to take five stitches. He ain't gonna be the pretty boy he always was. You know, that kind of stuff — beating up priests — doesn't sit well with Captain Feltt either. He doesn't see the point of it. You could have asked me about it first. I'm an expert."

"Yeah, I can guess what they're all saying. There doesn't seem to be much point to what we did. The way they've got it, the kid who killed the nun is dead, and there doesn't seem to be much of a connection between the priest and the nun and the altar boy. Case closed."

"Even with your blurry eyes, you see it pretty clearly, partner."

"Yeah." Hank winced. The pain in his head was growing worse now. It felt almost like there was a crack in his skull, a crack that was getting wider and wider. He closed his eyes and wished Hazel were there in the hospital room with him.

When he opened them a moment later, she was there, just coming in. He gave her the best smile he could.

Hazel said, "Oh, Hank," and she walked up to him and gave him a careful hug.

He smiled some more. It felt good to smile. Really good.

"Did Marvin tell you?" Hank said. "We're suspended indefinitely."

"Yes, I heard," Hazel said. "Without pay."

"Marvin didn't tell me that."

"I didn't want to worry you," Marvin said and smiled.

Hazel sat down on the foot of the bed and said to Hank, "Is that okay? Do you have enough room?"

"Sure. It's fine. Any news about Margaret?"

Hazel put her right hand on the bed, smoothed the white sheet, pulled it even smoother. Hank could see she was holding something back, probably wondering what she could tell him in his condition.

"Really, honey," he said, "I'm feeling better than I look. You don't have to worry about me. What have you heard?"

"Hazel, he's not kidding," Marvin added. "His doc was in here just a couple minutes ago, said it was no big deal, the concussion. He wasn't using that part of his body anyway."

"See, I'm almost 99% better than I was a couple hours ago," Hank said. "What have you heard?"

Hazel looked at Marvin. He nodded, and she started, "I've been talking to Carolyn, Maureen's mom. I had a short day at work today, and I went over there for coffee after I got home — before I got word about what happened to you. Carolyn's worried about Margaret, too. She's been calling, stopping by, even — and she's been talking to Maureen about her."

"Yeah? What did she find out?"

Hazel shook her head. "Maureen told her the same stuff you found out, the stuff Margaret never told us. Both of the girls have gotten themselves mixed up with these drug dealers. It started pretty innocently. The guys were selling small amounts of marijuana, what they call nickel bags, to their friends and classmates, but recently they've upped the stakes, trying to make a real business out of it. And there's this new drug called LSD, and these boys have been selling that too."

Hank nodded. "Yeah, that's what we found out too. Last week Marv and I were in the apartment of one of the guys she was hanging out with, and we went through his stuff. We found LSD in his icebox, lots of it, maybe two thousand bucks' worth."

"Carolyn told me something else. The girls, Maureen and Margaret both, were helping these boys, these dealers, distribute their drugs."

"Shit," Marvin said. "Are you kidding?"

Hank gave his partner a look. "Let her talk."

Hazel stood up from the bed. "Maureen told her mom they were carrying LSD around for the dealers. But Maureen made it sound like it was no big deal. She said that the girls were just what they call 'mules'. They would carry the LSD from one place to another. She said they carried the drugs in shopping bags sometimes, and in their purses other times. The dealers told them they would be safe, since no one would think it was strange for girls to be carrying shopping bags and purses around. And the dealers told them that since they weren't involved in any exchange of money for the drugs, they weren't really guilty of any crime."

Hank shook his head. The pain came back immediately, and he wished he hadn't done it. "Honey, that's pretty much bullshit about them not being guilty. These guys were feeding them a line. If you carry drugs, you're dealing drugs, money or no money. You're part of the operation. We're talking about jail time."

"Three to five years," Marvin added. "Maybe more. This ain't good news."

"Why would they do it?" Hazel asked.

"The excitement? The money?" Hank said and shrugged.

"But Carolyn said that Maureen told her they were just mules, that they weren't involved in the money part."

"That might have been a story Maureen told her parents because she didn't want them to worry. I don't know."

"And what would Margaret need money for?" Hazel said. "She's nineteen, lives at home, takes public transportation to her classes. She doesn't have a car, never asked for one, doesn't seem to want to buy a lot of stuff. I never hear her talking about wanting things — fancy clothing, jewelry, a TV, a hi-fi set. I never heard her talking like that. Did you?"

Hank put his right hand up on his forehead, pressed it just above his eye. The pain was still there, stronger now. He closed his eyes. He thought about one night in the Ardennes, that last winter of the war. It was cold and dark and getting colder and darker, and he stood up and looked out of his log shelter and a sniper's bullet hit his helmet and knocked him back down. His head rang and rang back then, and there was pain for a long moment, and then it stopped. It wasn't like that now. The pain was there, and it wasn't going anywhere. It just seemed to be building up, getting worse.

"You okay, Hank?" Hazel asked.

"I feel like shit."

"Maybe we should just stop. Talk tomorrow, after the doctor sees you again."

"No, that's okay. It comes and goes. Now it's going. I can feel it getting better."

"Okay, if you say so," Hazel said. "Anyway, there's really not much more that I heard from Carolyn. She mentioned another dealer that Maureen heard about, somebody other than this Willy character. This one is an older guy, maybe in his late thirties or early forties, who supplies guys like Willy and his friends. Maureen didn't have his name or address, but she said he lived with his mother. Isn't that odd for a drug dealer? He's somewhere up on the North Side, near Lake Michigan. Maureen said they talked about this guy like he knows all kinds of things, so she thought maybe he'd know something about where Margaret is."

Marvin cocked his head and said, "A dealer who lives with his mother? We heard something about a guy like that from one of the jerks we were questioning, one of the small-time hoods who knows Willy Reichard."

"Yeah," Hank added. "We were about to try to find him and talk to him when we had this other stuff about Tommy Sawa and Father Ted drop in our laps. Now that we've been suspended, I guess we don't have anything better to do, so we might as well check out these leads even if they're probably bullshit. Maybe this guy knows something. And if he doesn't, maybe his mother does."

"Not tonight, Hank," Hazel said as she stepped closer to him and pressed her hand gently against his cheek, feeling for fever.

Hank nodded. "You're right. Not tonight. But definitely tomorrow."

"Yeah," Marvin chimed in. "Definitely tomorrow, if we can get the docs to let you out of here. We'll search this dealer out and give him hell."

CHAPTER 43

IT WAS DEFINITELY not tomorrow; the doctors kept Hank under observation all night Tuesday, all day Wednesday, and Wednesday night too. He wasn't feeling up to fighting them and didn't have a badge to flash, and Hazel was on their side.

In the meantime, Marvin got busy trying to track down the address of the mama's-boy dealer; Ramirez was no further help, and without a name to work with it took a little time. He asked around, talked to some North Side detectives and patrolmen he knew, called in a few favors. He figured that there couldn't be a whole hell of a lot of guys pushing psychedelic whiz-bangs who were living with their mothers on or near Wilson Avenue, and it turned out he was right. It took almost forty-eight hours to track it down, but Marvin had an address for one Mr. Russ Kight a couple of hours before it was time to pick up his partner Thursday morning. That almost-forty-eight hours was enough time for Hank to start feeling a little better.

But not much better. In fact, Hank still felt pretty crappy.

His head was still throbbing, and his equilibrium was for shit. Getting out of the hospital that morning was hard, and even sitting in the car finishing a couple of cigarettes wasn't easy. Hank hoped he could get some balance back before he walked up to the third floor and knocked on the drug guy's door.

He looked up at the building.

"What do you think, man?" Marvin asked. "You think two cops who've got their badges temporarily stuck in someone's desk drawer are gonna get a warm welcome from Mr. Kight the Drug Dealer?"

"Only one way to find out," Hank said. "Knock on his door and see what happens."

Marvin chuckled. "You're sounding more like me every day. But seriously — you ready to try hiking to the top?"

Hank didn't say anything. It was a good question.

Kight's building was pretty much what he'd expected. Marvin's research had led them to a corner building, three stories tall with twelve apartments, on the corner of Wilson and Clifton. A nice corner once, but the neighborhood had seen better days. The trash can in front of the place was filled to overflowing with all kinds of shit, and a bum was pushing a shopping cart loaded with bulging trash bags past Hank and Marvin's unmarked police car. There was a leash attached to the bum's cart, and a mutt trailed behind. The dog looked a lot better fed and better dressed than the bum did.

Hank took a drag on his cigarette and looked down the street. He had been up this way before, plenty of times over the years, and the street had never regained the glamor he remembered from the 1940s and early 50s. East of the building, just past the Wilson Avenue El station, there was a burlesque place, Chez Mademoiselle's. It looked dark and tired this early in the day, but it was still open. A big, starry-rainbow sign hanging above the door said the place never closed. For a moment, Hank imagined some old, tired stripper twirling her star-spangled bra to the grind of "A Pretty Girl is Like a Melody", so slow the guys in the audience were falling asleep over their hard-ons.

Just next to the El station there was a bowling alley. That place was closed.

Hank scratched underneath the bandage on his forehead and said, "I guess you can see a stripper any time of day or night, but you can't bowl around the clock, even here on Wilson."

"Hank, my friend," Marvin said, "I'm happy to see that banging your head on a staircase hasn't interfered with your Holmesian powers of observation and detection."

"What the fuck are you talking about?"

"Or your legendary shit sense of humor."

Hank looked at his partner. "Come on. Let's go see what Mr. Kight is doing this morning."

"You sure you can manage the stairs?"

"If I fall down again and bang my head on a dozen of them, I'll let you know. Any idea if Russ Kight has a housekeeper?"

Marvin laughed and pushed open the car door. "Watch the ice as you get out of the car — it's melting a little today, and it's slippery. Okay, it's show time!"

Kight's apartment was a long way off from the top of the dark stairs, the last door on a long corridor. A skylight gave Marvin all the light he needed to read the names on the doors.

He nodded to Hank as he came up to the landing. "You need a hand, buddy?"

"Fuck you," Hank answered, and stopped for a moment to catch his breath. The climb was even harder than he'd thought it would be. Between his lost sense of balance and the headache bouncing around his cranium, he felt like a cross between Jimmy Stewart in *Vertigo* and Boris Karloff in *Frankenstein*.

Marvin could see it, too. "Really, man — you okay? You look like shit. Old, beat-up shit, in fact."

"Yeah, I'm okay. Just never ask me to climb a flight of stairs again."

"Okay, gotcha. You sure you're ready for this?"

"For what?"

Marvin looked at Hank and squinted. "Huh?"

"Just funning you. I'm ready, Freddy."

Marvin said, "One little concussion and he's stealing my lines. Okay then." He knocked on the door.

After a moment, it opened about three inches, as far as the chain on the other side would let it.

Marvin took a step toward the door. "Hey, you Mr. Russ Kight? We're detectives with the Chicago Police Department, and we got a few questions for you."

"Certainly, gentlemen, let me open the door."

Marvin gave Hank a wink as Mr. Kight closed the door and slid the chain off. Any cop knew this was the tricky moment, when you could expect some kind of action if action was going to happen. The guy on the other side of the door knew they were cops, knew there wasn't much chance of their being here for his benefit, and knew that this was his best chance to flee or come out with guns blazing.

Neither happened. The door opened and a short, skinny, red-headed guy in a dark-blue sport coat stood there with a smile. "Come on in, gentlemen. I can't imagine what you might need from me, but I'm happy to help the Chicago Police Department in any way I can."

Hank could see that the living room was to the left of the door, but Kight didn't lead them there. Instead, he took them down a hallway toward the back of the apartment.

Somewhere behind him, Hank could hear a country tune playing on a radio, Frankie Laine singing about finding love south of the border, down Mexico way. Hank had heard the song more times than he could count, and he still liked it.

He let Marvin follow Kight down the hallway to the right, while Hank stepped into the living room to take a quick look around. There were homemade wooden bookcases from floor to ceiling along the walls and more bookcases back to back in the center of the room. It looked like a library. He shook his head and caught up to Kight and Marvin. This was one strange place. The hallway was stacked with boxes and boxes and more boxes, about five feet high.

Kight finally led them into what must have been the dining room, but there was no dining room table and no cupboard filled with fancy plates and saucers. Instead, there was a card table and four chairs, and yet more boxes lining the walls.

Kight stopped at the card table and offered them chairs. Hank was thankful to sit down. The vertigo was harder on him than he'd thought it would be.

Marvin stood near the table and looked around. "Mr. Kight, before we start, let me ask you — what's in all of these boxes? You must have at least a couple hundred of them."

"Certainly," Kight said, resting his hand gently on a stack of boxes leaning up against the wall. "In fact, I've got 254 boxes altogether in this apartment at the moment. And what's in them? Well, I'm a dealer."

Marvin shook his head when he heard that, and sat down at the card table next to Hank. "You're telling us you're a dealer? You're kidding, right?"

"No, I'm not kidding. I'm a dealer. The boxes contain stuff I sell: old books, mostly novels, and old comic books and old magazines."

"You mean old like Shakespeare old?"

"No, mostly they're relatively recent books — first editions, mystery novels, science fiction novels, westerns. What you'd call low-brow books, stuff like Mickey Spillane's Mike Hammer novels or Edgar Rice Burroughs' Tarzan stories or Robert Heinlein's science fiction books. And of course comic books aren't exactly high culture either — but there are people who like to buy that kind of stuff, and I like collecting it and selling it."

"Heinlein, huh?" Hank asked.

"Yes, and Asimov, and lots of others. I've got a beautiful set of the Anthony Boucher *Treasury of Great Science Fiction* somewhere, if you're interested."

"You make a living off this stuff?"

"Sort of. I've got a daytime job, of course — I'm a pressman at Ace Printers. But the comics and the books help. It started as a hobby. I was looking for the stuff I liked, and then I discovered that people were willing to pay me for the things I'd found. For instance, I found a copy of an old *Astounding* magazine with a John W. Campbell story from before he became the editor. I paid a dime for it and I should be able to sell it for a couple bucks."

Marvin looked around. "And that's what's in all these boxes? Old books and magazines and comic books?"

"Yep."

"So if I got up and opened up a box, I might find a Mickey Mouse comic book about him chasing ghosts across the top of the Empire State Building in the middle of a blizzard?"

"I don't know if I've got that particular issue, but I'm sure I have at least one that's like it."

Marvin laughed, then he stood up and walked over to one of

the stacks of boxes lining the walls. "Mind if I open a box, Mr. Kight?"

"Not at all. *Mi casa, su casa.*"

Still chuckling, Marvin lifted the top box from a stack of five and set it on the floor. Then he opened the next box, the one it had been sitting on. "Would you look at that!"

Kight smiled. "What did you find?"

"Detective Comics No. 27! It's one that I bought when I was a kid. It's got Batman in it — I think it was his first appearance, when he was still *The* Batman!" Marvin turned a page, studied one of the images of Batman. Then he turned another page and looked at the illustrations there.

After a moment, he said, "These pictures look like shit — I didn't remember how bad the artwork was."

"Yeah," Kight said. "You're right about that, but that comic book is worth about fifty dollars. You remembered right — it is the first appearance of Batman, and major character debut issues are rare and valuable."

"Holy collectible kid stuff, Batman — fifty bucks!" Marvin gently placed the comic book back into the box.

Kight smiled and said, "I'm glad you gentlemen are getting a chance to learn something about collecting comics, but didn't you say you had some questions for me? I'll bet they weren't about Batman's first appearance."

Hank shook his head slowly. There was no pain this time. He heard a noise behind him, and he turned. An old woman in a gray bathrobe stood in the doorway that led to the living room.

"Russell?" She was looking down at the floor, and she continued in a slow whisper, "I think you forgot my water. Didn't you say you were going to get me some water? I'm thirsty, honey, and I need a drink. Just some water."

"Sorry, Mom, I was heading just now to the kitchen to get you a glass when these gentlemen knocked on the door. They're police detectives, and they have some questions."

"Police detectives? What do they want here?"

"Sorry, ma'am," Hank said, "just some routine questions for your son. There's no problem here. We'll finish up soon."

"Russell, can you get me some water first?"

"Sure, Mom," Kight said. He looked at Hank, and Hank nodded back.

"Sorry about that, officers," Kight said when he returned. "She's kind of sickly, and absent-minded. She's not always too clear-headed. When she wants something, she wants something — you know how it is."

"No problem, Mr. Kight, we understand," Marvin said. "We shouldn't be taking up your time like we are."

Kight shrugged and smiled. "So what I can I do for you fellows?"

Hank looked at the boxes, and then he looked at Kight. "We're involved in a missing persons investigation. Do you know two young men, Helmuth Muller and Richard Houser?"

"Oh, sure, of course I do. They're both comic collectors. I've sold them books and bought books from them. That's weird that they'd be missing. Are they missing?"

Hank ignored his question. "And do you also know Willy Reichard?"

"Sure, Willy Reichard. I know Rick Houser and Helmuth better. They're pretty serious about comics, much more so than Willy...but sure, I know all of them. Willy came over about a month ago, and I sold him a Dell Comics *Prince Valiant*, a comic strip reprint from the 1930s. We talked about Dell a lot when he came over, and the reprints they used to put out."

"Well, Willy Reichard is the focus of our missing persons investigation. He's disappeared with a young woman, and there's some concern about the two of them."

"No kidding? That's so strange...honestly, I haven't seen much of him lately. He used to come over with Rick and Helmuth, maybe once a week. We'd drink cokes, talk about comics, even play some cards, but Willy's been coming over less and less."

Marvin walked over to some of the cardboard boxes stacked up near the windows. "You mind if I look through some more of these boxes? I'll be super careful. I love these old books."

"Sure, detective, no problem," Kight said. "If you see something you like, I'll give you a good price."

Marvin smiled, walked over to a box, and opened it up. "Thanks. Now, what were you saying about Willy?"

"Oh, yeah, I think he's getting into the hippie scene. He's been letting his hair grow long and trying very hard to grow a beard. And the last time I saw him, he was wearing a tie-dyed shirt and bell-bottom pants. I think that was when he came over to buy that *Prince Valiant*."

Hank looked over at Marvin, who had just closed up the second box and was opening another.

"You have much to do with the hippie scene, Mr. Kight?" Hank asked.

"No. I see it around me some, in the young kids who come around to buy books from me, but I'm 39. I've got a sickly mother and a nine-to-five job. Besides, I don't look good in bell-bottoms, and I'd rather listen to Johnny Cash or Merle Haggard than the Rolling Stones or the Dave Clark Five. You know Merle Haggard? His version of 'I'm Walking the Floor Over You'? Better than Ernest Tubb's. Me, I don't much care for most of the new music, rock and roll, the Beatles or the Byrds. There's no edge to it. Too much puppy love."

Marvin was taking comic books out of a second box and stacking them on the floor. He pulled one out of a plastic bag and held the book to the light. "Mmmm, I like this. *Captain Marvel!* I remember this guy. What the hell happened to him? He survive the war?"

Kight shrugged. "He survived the real war but not the Cold War. Superman and DC Comics sued him and put him out of business."

"You're kidding!"

"Nope. It happened."

Marvin turned some pages slowly, staring at the superhero in red, his chiseled chin, the luxurious cape flowing over his shoulders. "I didn't remember him being this well dressed. He makes Superman look like a wrestler in a circus sideshow."

Marvin handed the book to Hank.

Hank looked at the cover. He remembered the comic. He hadn't ever bought it, but he knew it. His kid brother was a fan of Captain Marvel, all that Shazam stuff. Hank handed the comic back to Marvin and turned to Kight.

"How about drugs?" Hank asked. "You ever see any of that kind of stuff?"

"Drugs? What do you mean?"

"I mean like non-pharmaceutical drugs, recreational drugs."

"I get you now. Drugs? Not much…some. And nothing heavy. No heroin, no cocaine, no LSD. Most of the kids are too young to be thinking about any kind of drugs at all, but not those three. Willy and Helmuth came here high on grass one time. There was a girl with them too. They said they wanted to show her some of my old *Fawcett's Funny Animals* comics — you guys remember those? I pulled some out. They all looked at one and started laughing at Hoppy the Marvel Bunny, who was pretty much the star character of that series. They couldn't stop laughing, in fact, and that's when I asked them if they were drunk. I thought they might've been, but Helmuth insisted they weren't drunk. He said what they had was better than beer, better than wine or whiskey. He said he was feeling hoppy, just like the Marvel Bunny. He kept saying that for a minute or two and laughing about being hopped up. Then Willy said they had smoked some 'really good weed'. Asked me if I wanted some. I said no and threw both of them out, along with the girl. I was afraid they would start drooling on my comic books."

"You remember anything about the girl who was with them?"

"Oh yeah, sure I do. I don't get many girls up here. Pretty much all the collectors are guys, you know. This girl with Willy and Helmuth was a kid, younger than them both. They're what? Around twenty-two? Maybe twenty-four? She was probably eighteen or nineteen — what the kids call a teenybopper, a girl who likes to hang around older guys she thinks are cool or something. She was wearing an Ike jacket. You know, the khaki kind that stops at the waist? But it was probably her dad's or her boyfriend's, so it looked kind of boxy on her, too big in the shoulders."

"Do you remember anything else about her? It sounds like she might be the girl we're looking for."

Kight pushed his chair back and sat up straight. He lifted his chin and closed his eyes. He looked like he was trying to remember, playing the scene back to himself and trying to find something he'd missed. Marvin watched him for a moment and then went back to going through the box he was searching.

Hank didn't take his eyes off Kight.

After a couple minutes, Kight leaned forward and smiled and said to Hank, "You know, I think I get what you're doing. You're talking to me to distract me while your partner goes through my boxes like a house on fire. I bet he's looking for dope. I bet you gentlemen think I'm some kind of drug dealer."

Hank nodded. "I think you got us figured out pretty good, Mr. Kight. You can save us a lot of bother by telling us whether you are or you aren't. It helps us the most if you tell us you are, since we'd be ready to believe you without having to go through another 250 boxes, and your freezer, and everything else around here just to prove you were lying."

Kight looked at Hank and smiled, and then the smile got broader and Kight started laughing.

"I can absolutely guarantee you that I'm not a drug dealer. I'll even call my poor old mother in here to verify that."

"No need to disturb your mother again, Mr. Kight. My partner here will just go through a couple dozen more boxes, and that should give us the evidence we need. If he comes up dry, we can leave the last 200 for another time — it'll give him something to look forward to on a rainy day. Meanwhile, can you tell us anything more about the girl who came here with Reichard and Muller that day?"

"I can't remember the girl's name, but I do recall something that Willy said to her at one point. It was when they were reading the

Hoppy the Marvel Bunny comics, and Willy and Helmuth were laughing. Willy said to the girl, 'You're no fun. I should've brought Maureen instead.' And the girl in the Ike jacket said, 'Screw you.' That's it. That's all I remember about her."

Hank knew this was getting close to things he actually needed to know. "Did they seem close? This girl who wasn't any fun and Willy?"

"I don't think so. He didn't seem to be looking at her or paying any kind of special attention to her. You know how it is when young people first start getting together, dating and such, you see something between them. You can feel a sort of warmth between them, a connection. The way they look at each other, the way they listen to each other — sometimes it's really intense, sometimes it's subtle, but there's always *something*. You know what I'm talking about. With Willy and this girl, I wasn't getting anything like that. The connection between her and Willy didn't seem that different from the connection Willy had with Helmuth...in fact, not even that close. The girl didn't seem like much of a pal of theirs. Really, I'm not sure what she was even doing with them."

Kight stopped then and looked at Hank. "What do you guys really want? You're not acting like you really care whether I'm selling marijuana or LSD or anything like that — it's more like you just want something to hold over me."

Marvin looked up from an issue of some comic book called *Weird Science* and said, "You're right. We don't give a rat's ass whether or not you're dealing." Saying this, he sighed and put the comic book back into its box.

Hank said, "My partner's right. This really is a missing persons investigation. We want to find the girl and Willy. But mainly the girl. She's what this is all about."

"Well, you really don't need to work so hard, then. I told you when I let you in that I was happy to help, and I was telling the truth. I can't tell you anything else about the girl, since I met her just that one time. But maybe I can help you with Willy Reichard. I know a couple of things about him."

"Yeah?" Hank said and leaned forward at the table.

"Yeah. There's this woman he dated for a while, maybe a year ago. She was a couple years older than he was. She was hot stuff. Very attractive — movie-star attractive. In fact, she was like a Miss Kansas or Miss Missouri in the Miss America Pageant a couple years back. Something like that . . . way above Willy's class, I thought."

Hank looked at Kight like he was spinning a story. "Really?"

"Really. Willy was always talking about her, and her being Miss Kansas or Miss Missouri of 1963, bragging all the time about how much attention she was paying him. He could be a real asshole sometimes — it was all about how big a deal he was because he was dating this beauty queen. Anyway, I remember her name. It was unusual, like it should be the name of an actress, a star of the silver screen. It was Margo Watts."

"Margo Watts."

"Yeah, that's it. She lived down someplace along the lakefront, Sheridan Road, south of here, just north of Belmont. He would brag about that too — the swanky place she lived. Anyway, they broke up — probably she dumped him, although that's not the way Willy told it. Still, if he was in trouble and needed some help, she's someone he might go to. Someone who lives where she lives must have some money, or friends, or maybe both."

Hank stood up and shook the comic book dealer's hand. "Thanks, Mr. Kight. You've been a big help."

"My pleasure. I hope you find the girl you're looking for. But Willy?" Kight paused. "If he's lost, I wouldn't bother finding him. He's pretty much just an asshole."

Chapter 44

IT WASN'T HARD to find an address for Margo Watts, and like Russ Kight had told them, her apartment was right on Sheridan just a block north of Belmont. It was a five-story apartment building with a doorman outside and a canopy covering the stretch from the doorway to the street. The place came as advertised: swanky.

Hank got the feeling that this building would probably have felt more comfortable being on the Upper East Side of Manhattan, but here it was stuck in Chicago, providing domestic comfort to the almost-rich and the used-to-be-famous.

Nobody living there had to worry about wind or snow or much else, he figured.

The east side of the building, the side facing Lake Michigan, had balconies for each apartment, and every balcony was covered with an awning. Hank imagined what they would all look like in the spring after all the dirty snow finally melted. The ladies and gents living here would open their doors and step out onto their balconies and look out at the lake and live in some fairy world neither he nor anybody he knew could imagine, drinking pink or orange cocktails and listening to some smooth jazz left over from the party the night before.

Hank looked at Marvin, who nodded and said, "Oh yeah, this is where they live, the rich people. A swanky place for a swanky lady and her swanky friends."

It wasn't much trouble getting by the doorman. He was happy with his job, and he knew that messing with the cops wasn't a great strategy for holding on to it. So he was friendly and helpful and informative: he told them that Miss Watts lived on the fifth floor and that the elevator was right over there, and he even let them know that she was at home and alone, for a change.

The elevator was a slow crawl up to the fifth floor, and Marvin kept yammering.

"I'm looking forward to this. You know, here we are, two suspended cops who've been dealing with a lot of shit recently, between the kid-raping priest and the dead nun and the good boy who couldn't take it anymore and his charming father and drug dealers and spic gangsters and black gangsters who have great bars with excellent music but no information. We're overdue for something different already. This should be swell, a Miss America babe to question, probably a view of the lake…maybe she'll have some kind of fancy, super-sophisticated martinis she'll mix up for us."

Hank heard without really listening.

He was thinking of his daughter Margaret and all the bad things she might have fallen into. He'd been dealing with bad people and the way they brought misery down on themselves and the folks around them for most of his life, and he knew what could happen to a kid like his daughter if she fell into their company. Drugs, prostitution, all kinds of crime…stupid, sloppy, dirty crime. And it wasn't always the obvious ones who were the worst. He remembered what happened to the kid sister of one of the patrolmen down at the Lakeview Station a couple years ago. She was about Margaret's age, maybe a little older. She started going with some creep from Skokie who she met at school, Roosevelt University. At first he seemed like a nice, sweet kid, but then they found him with her body in a state park in the woods north of Oshkosh, Wisconsin. He was sitting in front of a tent tending the campfire. She was in the tent behind him, cut deep as anything from between her breasts down to her vagina. When the sheriff there asked him why he did it, the guy didn't hesitate. He said, "She wanted to tempt me to sin, but I kept her clean for Jesus."

***

Marvin's mouth stopped when the elevator did, and he was the first one at Margo Watts's door. He turned to Hank. "You okay?"

"Yeah…I was just thinking about Zebrowski's sister."

"The one they found cut up in Oshkosh?"

"Yeah."

"What the fuck you thinking about that for?"

"What else should I be thinking about? I've got a daughter out there somewhere."

Marvin shook his head. "Hank, you ain't no fun anymore, brother."

"Knock on the fucking door, Marv."

Marvin gave the door a couple light raps. There was no answer, and then he knocked again, harder, like he meant it this time. He turned to Hank, smiled, and said, "I love knocking on doors like a cop does."

Hank was about to tell him to stop being Bozo the Clown when the lock clicked and the door began opening, slowly, on a blonde in a lacy sky-blue bathrobe.

She was tall, built like one of those German girls Hank was always running into at the end of the war — a real Valkyrie, big boobs but everything else lean muscle. The lacy bathrobe was sort of on and sort of off; Hank could see her tits plainly and catch flashes of her pink bikini panties. The room behind her was dark. Somewhere in it, Hank could hear a record player playing, Tony Bennett telling him about autumn leaves drifting by his window, drifting past in reds and golds, and about how it reminded him about some summer kisses he remembered on sunburned lips a long time ago. It was nice.

Marvin was the first to say anything. "Miss Watts, we're police officers. I'm Detective Bondarowicz, and this is my partner Detective Purcell. We're pursuing a missing persons investigation, and we're wondering if we can come in and ask you a few questions."

Standing there, she said, "Shit," and then she thought for a couple of seconds and added, "No." She started to close the door, but Marvin blocked it with his foot.

"Really, ma'am, we've just got a few questions, and then we'll leave you alone. Really, five minutes. That's all we're asking."

Margo Watts said, "No," again, but more softly, and leaned the weight of her body against the door.

Marvin responded by leaning his own body against hers, only the two inches of steel door between them. "Are you going to help me?" he asked his partner.

Hank smiled. "I don't think you need any help from me, partner. I don't think there's much fight in Miss Kansas this afternoon. She's drunk or stoned or both."

Marvin snapped the door toward him, and then just as quickly pushed it back toward Margo Watts. She wasn't expecting that at all, and she landed hard on her bottom, five feet into the apartment.

"You jerks…you fucking jerks…you fucking jerk cops, I'll sue you both!" she shouted as Hank walked past Marvin into the apartment.

"I apologize for my partner, ma'am," Hank said, extending his hand to the blonde on the floor. "He's not good with doors."

She wouldn't take Hank's hand. She slapped it away and continued screaming at them, "You cops are just hoods. You call yourselves 'police officers'? Hoods…the way you break in, knock me on my ass…fucking hoods! I may be from Kansas, but I know hoods."

"Ma'am, we do apologize," Hank said. "We've just got some questions, and then we'll get out of your hair." The way she was shouting, he wanted to add that she didn't sound like she was in Kansas anymore, but he decided that it wasn't the best thing to say to get the interview moving more smoothly. He hoped Marvin didn't come up with the same idea on his own.

"My hair? What are you talking about? It's my ass. You broke my fucking ass, you assholes!"

Hank looked over at Marvin, and his partner shrugged. Hank gave him a nod and Marvin stepped over and got behind Margo Watts. As Hank extended his two hands to grab hers, Marvin lifted her from the back.

"Thugs and hoods, thugs and hoods, thugs and hoods," she kept repeating as Hank and Marvin steadied her on her feet and then walked her over to a light-blue plastic-covered couch.

Seated, she pulled her bathrobe tight around her and said, "I want a drink. Where's my drink? Where's your drink? Why the fuck am I the only one not drinking?"

Marvin said, "Good question. I was wondering that, too. I'll go into the kitchen and get us all something. What are you drinking, ma'am?"

"Vodka…straight up or on the rocks, but there aren't any rocks, so I'll take it rockless."

"Yes, ma'am," he said as he started toward the kitchen.

"And don't call me 'ma'am', you asshole!"

"Yes, ma'am," Marvin said, and kept heading where he was heading.

Hank looked around. The place was dark as a cave. He started walking around the living room flicking on lights.

He stopped across the room from Margo. Clearly, she wasn't in any great need of another drink. Her eyes were rolling as she tried to focus, and she kept pulling on her bathrobe like there was a lot more lace to draw tight around her than there was.

"Mind if I look around?" he said.

"Suit yourself, you fucking hood, you fucking thug."

Hank followed Marvin into the kitchen. Everything was brand spanking new and up to date, like something out of a General Electric Progressland newsreel or the "Glories of Today" exhibit at the World's Fair in New York that he'd read about. All the appliances were done up in a light brown sort of copperish finish — the refrigerator, the stove, and even the dishwasher — nothing like the plain white enameled ones he'd been seeing in kitchens since he was a kid growing up in Logan Square. He walked over to the refrigerator and opened the door.

He didn't know what he was expecting to see, so he wasn't surprised when he saw it. Next to a quart of Borden's buttermilk there was a glass jar with a bunch of plastic bags rolled up inside it; they looked just like the ones they'd found in Willy's freezer. Like Willy's, these had little red squares of blotter paper in them and were labeled "Red Dog". But this wasn't a big haul of acid...maybe a hundred bucks' worth. This wasn't a dealer's supply. Maybe a present from an admirer?

Hank said, "Huh."

Marvin finishing pouring vodka halfway up a third cocktail glass and looked up. "What are you 'huh'-ing about?"

"Dope. LSD. There must be some kind of plague going on. Every time we turn around we run into an icebox with acid in it. And this is the same kind that Willy Reichard had in his ice cream cartons."

"Let me see that," Marvin said.

Hank handed the jar to Marvin.

Marvin opened it and took out one of the little packets of LSD. "You want one?"

"What, are you kidding? I thought you said that stuff gives you a bad trip every time, a real pain in the ass."

"Maybe this time will be different," Marvin said, shoving the packet into his pocket.

"Let's go talk to Miss Kansas of 1953."

"I thought she was Miss Missouri of 1963."

"Whatever."

<center>~~~</center>

When Hank and Marvin got back to the living room, Margo Watts was still slumped on the couch. Hank had to look twice. With her sky-blue bathrobe, she sort of blended into the thing — almost like she and the couch were one, some kind of weird symbiosis of satin and vinyl.

Marvin handed her one of the glasses of vodka and sat down across from her. Hank watched his partner take a sip of the vodka and wince. It was good stuff, Smirnoff's, but Marvin seemed to be having a hard time with it. Maybe it was too early in the day, or too late in the day, or Marvin had just discovered that warm vodka was the one form of booze he didn't like. Who knew?

Hank put his glass down on the coffee table but didn't sit down. He didn't want to sit. He'd had enough sitting and waiting; he wanted to get moving, doing something to find his daughter. He looked at Margo Watts. Her eyes weren't rolling now, and she wasn't pulling on her bathrobe. Maybe the vodka was sobering her up. He had known that to happen.

"We found the LSD in your refrigerator, Miss Watts," Hank said.

"Oh shit," she replied. She lifted the glass of vodka to her face and pressed it against her forehead, but there were no rocks to cool her head.

"Yeah, shit," Marvin said. "You want to tell us about it?"

"Wait a minute," Margo said, leaning forward, "I don't know what the fuck you're doing here. You break into my apartment, you knock me down, you go through my refrigerator, and now you're asking me questions like I'm the one who did something wrong."

Marvin smiled. "We're confused, too. We're sitting here having a drink together, a nice healthy drink I was kind enough to make for you, and you won't stop bitching about me and Hank doing this and that. Where's the gratitude?"

"Gratitude?" she screamed. "Fuck gratitude, I'm calling the cops!" She started to stand, and then she couldn't, falling back on the blue couch again and bouncing interestingly as she hit.

"Miss Watts," Hank said, "what my partner means to say is that we still have a couple of short questions for you. We're not here to arrest you or hassle you. We just need to know a little about one of your friends, Willy Reichard."

"That son of a bitch!"

"Oh, you do know him?" Marvin asked.

"Oh yes, I know that motherfucking son of a bitch."

Hank stepped over to the record player and turned Tony Bennett off. "Yeah, he's the one. Willy Reichard. We're looking for him. He may be traveling with a young girl, pageboy hair, about nineteen years old."

"She the hippie bitch in the Eisenhower jacket?"

Hank held himself back. He was afraid of what he would say or do if he didn't.

Marvin must have sensed this, because he immediately said, "Yeah, she wears an Ike jacket. That's the one. Where did you see her?"

"That prick Willy brought her here a couple times. He was always bringing girls over after I dumped him. Wanted to show me he didn't need me, or something. I didn't give a fuck. Yeah, she was one of them. Pukey little tramp, always looking down her nose at me like she thought she was better than me. I should have kicked her ass out of here the first time he brought her, kicked his ass out too, but I didn't. Instead, I said, 'Come on in, sweet child, and make yourself at home.' I acted like I was the fucking den mother to the whole show. Stupid. Stupid. Stupid. And what did she and that asshole Willy do? You can guess what they did. They went into my goddamn bedroom and fucked on my good yellow sheets until they were covered with so much blood I had to fucking throw them away. And you think that either of them offered to pay me for them, or even say they were sorry? That little whore came here to spill her fucking blood all over my bed, and they didn't even say, 'Pardon us, Margo, we didn't know losing her virginity would be that messy!'"

Margo Watts lifted the vodka to her mouth again and downed it all, downed it quick like she knew there was more in the kitchen, like she knew that her visitors would get her more if she wasn't sober enough to lift herself up and carry herself there to fix it up on her own.

Then she looked at Hank, and her eyes were rolling again, and her words started coming out of her mouth like they had to compete with a tongue that was getting fat and wobbly as it took in more vodka like a sponge. "You aren't drinking, soldier," she said, trying to keep her head steady. "How come you aren't having any fun here? Just standing around like you got a train to catch or a movie to see. What the fuck is that all about? We're supposed to be having a little party here!"

Hank knew what she wanted him to say, knew what she might even want him and Marvin to do.

And Hank knew what he wanted to do. He wanted to take his gun out and kill Margo Watts. Plain as that. No words, no arguments, no discussion. No mincing around. No rolling eyes, no fucking sloppy tongue, no head weaving here and there. That's what he wanted to do — shoot her dead for saying what he'd heard her say and would always hear her say, even after she was dead and gone from the bullet he wanted to put into her fucking brain.

But he didn't do it.

Instead, he took off his hat, held it in his right hand, and bounced it against his leg. That's all he did...that, and ask her one last question, the important one.

"Do you know where Willy and this girl are now?"

Miss Kansas of Whenever didn't hesitate, but she didn't answer the question either. "Say, are you going to drink that vodka your little friend here brought you? If you ain't gonna, I sure will."

Hank handed her his glass of vodka and asked his final question again. "Do you know where Willy and this girl are?"

"Say, is Willy in trouble with you cops? God, I hope so. Selling dope, trying to be a big shot, bragging about the little whores he's running with…I hope he's in trouble, trouble big as an H-Bomb!"

Hank held himself, steadied himself. And then he asked his one last question one last time: *"Do you know where Willy Reichard and the girl in the Ike jacket are?"*

"I don't know where *she* is, the little tramp, but I know where *he* is. Whenever he gets in trouble in town, he lights out for the territories, his secret hideaway."

"Where would that be?"

"The territories? You aren't a big Mark Twain fan, are you? Never read *Huckleberry Finn?*"

"No, ma'am, I'm not a big reader, Miss Watts."

"Christ," she said and took another sip of her vodka. "There's a place northwest of town, over by Crystal Lake. Willy goes there when things get fucked up and funky here. Maybe he's there now. Maybe his little girlfriend is there with him. Or maybe he's got a different one already. I don't give a fuck. Fuck his girlfriends."

Hank put his hat back on and reached inside his sport coat for his memo pad and a ballpoint pen. "Who lives there? How do they know Willy?"

Margo Watts reached over and picked up her drink again.

"How do I know how Willy knows them? You think I'm his goddamn mother? You're as stupid as he is. It's just a place he hangs out. Hippies live there, or someone who likes hippies, maybe takes them in off the street and gives them some food and a fucking bath. I don't know and I don't care."

"I understand, Miss Watts. Could you tell us where this place is, exactly, up in Crystal Lake, ma'am?"

"Only if your fucking partner gets me another drink, and only if you stop calling me 'ma'am.'"

CHAPTER 45

IT TOOK HANK and Marvin almost two hours to get to Crystal Lake. It wasn't far, only 44 miles, and most of the trip was on Interstate 90, but the weather was shit for driving. Hank wanted to push the Ford V8 cop special to the limit, but the roads wouldn't cooperate. A January thaw had hit hard earlier in the day, and by evening the melting ice and snow had turned a lot of the roads into swamps and creeks. Even where the highway was clear of icy water and snowy ruts, Hank still couldn't push it like he wanted to.

He looked at Marvin. His partner's eyes were closed, and he was sleeping. The guy was just too much. Give him a couple of shots of Cutty Sark or Johnnie Walker Red, or even warm vodka in a pinch, and he was good to go. Every day was a beautiful day, the best day of his life. Every broad was Raquel Welch. Every meal was filet mignon with a baked potato on the side covered with sour cream and chives. The guy just never grew up. So even though the traffic was a problem, Marvin wasn't letting it be his problem.

There were still a lot of people trying to get home, and the roads, especially once you got off the interstate, were a terror. Barrington Road and Algonquin Road and Pyott were still pretty much the cow paths they'd been forty and fifty years ago: two lanes, dark and curvy, not built for the kind of fast cars Detroit was churning out now or the huge population growth the drug and gang and race problems in Chicago were creating here in the suburbs. Folks with any money in their pocket were trying to get away from Chicago as fast as they could, and the real-estate boom west and northwest of the city was pouring a river of gold into the pockets of the developers. Fuck them. They were getting richer and richer and laughing at the roads their brothers and sisters from Chicago were trying to navigate. Maybe in fifty years these roads would be updated to handle the daily exodus and the nightly return, but right now they were pretty much shit.

But Hank didn't want to think about real-estate developers or roads or traffic.

He wanted to think about Margaret, his daughter, and what he would say to her once he found her. If he found her.

He wanted to tell her that she was nineteen and that fucking around with drug dealers wasn't smart at that age or any other age. He wanted to tell her that he knew where that kind of stuff led — he'd seen it more than he wanted to remember, the drugs and the stupid fucking. He'd been a cop for a lot of years, and he'd seen a lot of girls who hooked up with bad boys, thugs and guys who wanted to be thugs. He wasn't sure why it happened. Maybe there was some kind of evolutionary defect in human beings that made people who were innocent and loving and kind and intelligent enough about everything else want to turn away from all that and search out the ones who were none of those things. He had seen it with good girls and he had seen it with good boys — something made them want to turn to someone they ought to know wasn't good for them. Sometimes they got hurt, hurt bad, but came out of it still good and maybe a little smarter. And sometimes they decided that being one of the assholes was more fun after all, and turned their back on everything they used to be.

Hank figured that's the way Tommy Sawa was being seen now by the cops and the newspapers. Yeah, the nuns liked him, and his mom and dad — when his dad wasn't pissed at him for some stupid reason or no real reason at all — sang his praises, and his friends wept at his funeral like they really were grieving. But the way the story was spinning, there was something else going on in good little eleven-year-old Tommy. Something turned him away from everything he knew was right and good and holy, and turned him to the ugly, like ugly was the new Jesus, turned him into a little nun-killer whose suicide, closing himself in a closet and hanging himself in the darkness, was understood as the last, desperate act of his former, better self. At least that's the way the cops were reading Tommy's story. They weren't pointing fingers at the priest, Father Ted, not at all. He didn't figure into any of their narratives — Tommy had just gone bad, and nobody was interested in how or why or who. The Cardinal had Father Ted's back, the police and the DA had marked the case closed, and everyone was happy.

Tommy was gone, dead and gone. And the newspapers and everybody else was saying it – the case was closed.

And Margaret?

Hank wanted to press his foot down on the gas pedal, race through this sludge and ice and snow like some kind of cowboy hero or medieval knight, get to Crystal Lake now, right now, right this second.

Even though he knew he was too late.

A lot of what he feared would happen to his daughter probably already had happened to her. He knew it: the Margaret he'd known all these years was gone and wasn't coming back. He didn't want to think about it.

And he also didn't want to think about what he was going to do when he got to the house in Crystal Lake. Judge and jury and executioner? Again? He was remembering too much. And then Hank remembered further back, to the war. There was stuff there too that he didn't want to think about.

But it was always there to be remembered, like some kind of bad smell that just wouldn't go away no matter how many red roses you set up on your tables and credenzas, no matter how much and how hard you scrubbed the whole house down with vinegar. It was a scent that was with you from the start of your day and would still be with you at the end of your life.

He remembered the killing he saw and the killing he did. Right now he remembered the time he came upon three of his buddies, guys from his platoon, in a field outside a village east of Arnhem. Their hands were tied behind their backs and their feet were bound with rags. The Krauts had slit their throats. Hank remembered standing there in that field, a gray day, some dead cows scattered around. He couldn't stop looking at the cuts, those strange wounds that almost looked like smiles. They were long, but they weren't very deep. He knew what that was about. The Krauts who did it wanted his friends to die slow, wanted them to be screaming and weeping for help for the five or ten minutes it took them to bleed out.

He remembered what he did that night. He led his squad to a farmhouse a couple fields over from where he'd found the bodies. There were some Germans inside. He didn't know if they were the guys who did it or not. It didn't matter, not really. He knew what mattered.

What mattered was that he wanted to kill someone, and he wanted to kill them slow.

That's the way he felt tonight. The daughter he loved wasn't dead, but he knew for a fact that she'd never be the same, that something in her, something he'd loved, would never come back. And he wanted to kill whoever was to blame for that. He wanted it bad, even though he knew it wouldn't do Margaret or Hazel or him any good. It wouldn't do anybody any good, but that didn't seem to matter too much.

───≈───

An hour later, when Hank finally pulled over to the curb at the address Margo Watts had given them, he cut the engine and watched his wipers play with the drizzle for a moment. They would sweep it away, and then some more drizzle would be there again, and then they would sweep it again. He shook his head. Everything was telling him he had screwed up his life and that nothing he or anybody else could do would change things. The rain and snow would just keep falling and falling. The shit would keep dropping from the sky.

Marvin stirred. "This the place, Cisco?"

Hank looked around, took his time answering. "Yeah, Pancho, looks like it."

"You know, Hank, this isn't anything like what I expected to find at this address."

"Yeah? What did you expect?"

"I expected one of those new ranch houses I'm always seeing pictures of in the Sunday *Trib*. You know the ones I mean — big sprawling red-brick haciendas."

"Maybe it's like that on the inside."

"What does that mean? How can it be like that on the inside if the outside looks like a big old farmhouse? You stoned, man? You taking some of that dope we found at Margo Watts's?"

"No, just talking. It's probably just one of the old houses that the tornadoes missed and the developers haven't gotten around to knocking down yet."

"It looks like one of the houses you used to see in all those Mickey Rooney movies before the war. You remember them — the Andy Hardy movies?"

Hank remembered Mickey Rooney and his movies with Judy Garland and his movies without Judy Garland, but he didn't feel like talking about them or waiting any longer for Marvin to finish talking about them. He opened the car door, put on his hat, and started walking through the drizzle toward the house. Even though it was pretty late, the inside of the house was lit up like a snow palace, on all three floors.

Maybe they were having a party, Hank thought.

He beat Marvin to the front porch, and he rang the bell.

He couldn't hear any voices, no movement either. If there was a party, it was the quiet kind, kind of like an elegant afternoon tea. He stepped over to the window next to the door.

"See anything, Hank?" Marvin asked as he reached the porch and knocked the wet snow off his shoes.

"Yeah...two people sitting on a couch watching some shit on TV. *The Tonight Show* with Johnny Carson, I think. But they must be stone deaf, because I rang the bell a bunch of times and they didn't move."

Marvin looked in and then said, "Let me try." He walked back over to the front door and rang the bell one more time.

Again Hank heard the clear, musical rising and falling sound of the chimes ringing inside, but he still didn't see any kind of movement from the couple watching TV. Even after Marvin gave the door a half dozen hard police-style knocks, there was nothing.

Hank leaned closer to the window. "I don't think the folks in there are alive, Marvin."

"What?"

"I think they're dummies — you know, mannequins. Take another look."

Marvin stepped over to Hank, and the two stood at the window staring in. Still nothing moving except on the TV.

Hank couldn't hear what Johnny Carson was saying in his monologue, but Hank could see him suddenly raise his left arm over his head and nod his head with his tongue sticking out of his mouth and a stupid grin on his face. The camera then swung around to the audience. Some people were throwing their heads back and laughing with their mouths wide open, other folks were applauding and smiling. The couple on the couch in front of the TV didn't move, didn't even twitch.

Marvin shook his head. "I think you called it, Hank. These folks are dummies. This is some weird shit."

Hank heard a noise to his right then, and he turned quickly in that direction.

A young-looking, shirtless, long-haired hippie in blue bib overalls was slowly walking toward them. As the guy got close to the dim little pool of light on the porch, Hank could see that he had a smile on his face and a shotgun cradled in his arms.

His revolver was out and pointed at the hippie's head before Hank had time to think about it. Marvin was right there with him.

Hank spoke first. "We're cops, motherfucker. Put the gun down right now, or you're dead."

The hippie smiled, all the while staring at Hank with big eyes. "Listen," he said, "I don't mean you guys any harm. I respect the pigs as much as I respect the sun coming up and the moon going down. I just want to know what you're doing here poking around my front porch and looking into my window like it's some kind of giant TV set. You sure don't look like Santa's elves, so there must be some other reason for showing up here on my front porch. Maybe you just like Johnny Carson, and your TV's on the blink?"

With his pistol still aimed at the kid's head, Hank studied him. He didn't seem to be worried about having two pistols pointing at him, two nervous fingers on two triggers. The kid seemed calm, almost like this was some kind of jokey exchange he had memorized and rehearsed and loved to perform in front of an audience — the way he held his shotgun like it was a stage prop and maybe not a weapon he'd ever learned to use, the silly repartee about elves and Johnny Carson, all of that shit. The kid was playing a part.

Still holding his shotgun, the hippie kid smiled some more and said in a slow drawl, "Gentlemen, I do believe we may have a miscommunication here."

Hank didn't know where this was going, but he looked the kid in the eye and said, "Let me ask you a question before I shoot you."

The kid smiled again and said, "There are no questions if there are no answers."

"What the fuck are you talking about?" Marvin said.

The kid kept smiling. "Your hearing needs some clearing, pig. I said, there's no questions if there's no answers, but if you don't like that I can say that there are no answers if there are no questions — just as east is west and west is east, as well as left and right. Dig?"

Pistol still pointed at the hippie, Marvin said, "Oh, I get it. You're drunk or high, maybe both."

The hippie kid bowed low. When he righted himself, he said, "You want to see my gun? It's a Duesenberg, but I call it a doozy."

Marvin kept his pistol aimed but got out of his shooting crouch. "You got to tell me, what the hell's a Duesenberg? You're too young to remember the car, and I never heard of a Duesenberg shotgun."

The hippie gave a giggle, which grew into a laughing fit.

Hank walked up to him quickly and grabbed the shotgun away. He handed the weapon to Marvin.

Marvin cracked it. "It's empty. No shells."

The kid was still laughing.

Hank walked up to him again and gave him a solid punch in the stomach. The hippie doubled over, wrapped his arms around his belly, and crumpled backwards into the wall. He landed on his ass.

"What'd you do that for?" the kid gasped.

"I wanted to get your attention, kid, and I hope now I got it. Like I said, we're cops, and we're here because we're looking for someone. We don't have time to play around with you today. I'm going to ask you a question, and you're going to give me a straight answer, or I will fuck you up bad. Got it?"

The hippie didn't give them any kind of jiving answer this time. He just nodded at Hank.

"Okay, I'm going to ask you a question," Hank said slowly, "and you're going to give me an answer."

The kid didn't say anything, didn't nod his head, nothing. Hank pulled back his foot and kicked him in the side, and then he did it again. The hippie didn't cry out, but Hank could see he was hurting.

He sat there crumbled against the wall and pressed his arms even tighter around his body.

"Look at me," Hank growled.

The hippie turned his face up to Hank and said, "Yeah...okay. I'm looking."

"We're looking for a girl. Her name is Margaret Purcell. She's supposed to be traveling with a guy named Willy Reichard. You know anything about either of them?"

The hippie didn't answer. Hank could see he was in pain, trying to make himself smaller and smaller, pressing himself into a package that he hoped would be too small for Hank to kick again. Hank took a step back and looked at Marvin.

Marvin gave him a nod and stepped forward. Smiling, he said, "There's only one way you're going to win here."

The hippie looked at Marvin and slowly uncurled a little. "I'm Willy Reichard. Maggie's inside, upstairs."

"Anybody else in the house?" Hank asked.

Willy shook his head. "No. The guy who owns it mostly lives with his girlfriend over in Woodstock."

That was what Hank wanted, but it wasn't enough. He stepped forward, pushed Marvin aside, grabbed Willy Reichard by the throat with both hands and dragged him up off the floor.

"Hey, Hank, ease up...come on, Hank. Stop," Marvin said.

Hank didn't stop.

He rammed Willy's head against the wall, and then he did it again, holding the kid upright so he couldn't curl back up into a ball.

Reichard shouted, "Please, please, I told you what you want. Don't hit me."

Hank grabbed Willy's overalls and drove his other fist into

the hippie's face. From five feet away, Marvin heard the bones in the kid's face turn to mush. He rushed forward to try to pull his partner back.

Hank turned and shoved Marvin across the porch and into the snow, and then went back to the work of killing his daughter's hippie lover. He drove his fist into the guy's face again, and there was almost no resistance. What bones had been there doing the job of keeping the kid's face looking like itself were gone. Pounding his face felt like punching a plastic bag full of ground beef, and Hank did it again and then again.

He finally stopped and watched the kid slowly come unglued from the wall. Willy Reichard sank to the floor of the porch beneath the weight of his battered head.

Hank wiped his bloodied hands together and looked at the kid — the jello, the mush, the dark oozing mess that was his face. Beyond the shapeless blob of his nose, there were no visible eyes in his face, no cheekbones, no smile, no stupid wisecracks.

Hank didn't know how he felt about all this. He didn't feel any better about Margaret. Didn't really feel any better about anything. He wondered if he should kick Reichard again.

He decided not to. That would be even more stupid than coming out here looking for his daughter had been. Hank knew that whatever he did today, Margaret was gone and would always be gone until she decided not to be gone anymore. This kid, this hippie, this asshole bleeding from his mouth and eyes and nose had no say in any of that, and really hadn't had much say in Margaret's leaving in the first place. If she was ready to run off with some jerk who was never going to amount to anything good, she was going to find a jerk to do it with — Willy Reichard was nothing special, just an ordinary drug-dealing asshole who got unlucky enough to get picked by a cop's daughter to be her first big mistake.

Hank took a couple of steps back, just to see if anything interesting was going on inside the house. In the living room beyond the big picture window, the mannequins were still watching TV, enjoying it just as much as before. Now some tall skinny singer with a beard and long hair was playing a guitar, and then he wasn't — he was just standing there and bowing and everyone was applauding. The audience was applauding, and Johnny Carson was applauding, and Ed McMahon was applauding harder than anyone, applauding like it was all he did to keep a steady supply of Alpo on his plate.

Hank walked back to Willy Reichard, knelt down, and started going through his pockets. When he found a ring of keys, he stopped and went over to the front door.

Marvin was there. "You had enough of that?"

"Yeah," Hank said, "I had enough. Too much."

"Good."

"Call the local cops and get them to come out here and take care of this hippie asshole. Tell them he pulled a shotgun on us and I had to struggle to disarm him. He needs some medical attention."

"Okay," Marvin said and leaned into Hank. "You sure you're okay?"

"Yeah, I'm okay. Peachy."

———————

The house was still sort of decorated for Christmas. An aluminum tree with pink ornaments and blue lights stood in the corner of the dining room. A crèche sat on a credenza in the opposite corner.

Marvin walked over to the TV in the next room. He looked at the mannequins for a second and turned the sound down. "I hate it when the sound's so loud you can't hear yourself snore," he said. "Those dummies are gonna damage their hearing like that."

Hank said, "You okay waiting for the cops with Willy?"

"Oh sure, I'll keep an eye on him. It doesn't look like he'll want to talk much. It's a shame...I wanted to ask him about what the fuck these dummies were doing here watching TV in the first place." He paused for a second. "You know, before you go upstairs to look for Margaret, you should probably find a towel or something and wipe the blood off your hands."

Hank looked down at his hands. His right hand was a mess, broken skin and more blood than he'd realized, most of it Willy Reichard's. He walked over to the crèche on the credenza and used the ratty old white cotton blanket the crèche sat on as a towel to clean his hands. His right hand was still bleeding some, so he tore a strip from the blanket and wrapped his hand with it. Then he went upstairs to look for his daughter.

It was a big house. A wide wooden staircase led to the second floor, and there were four bedrooms there. He found Margaret in the third one he checked.

The room was dark, but he had no trouble seeing his daughter. Light from the corridor filtered in, and more light reflected off the snow outside, washing the room in a soft purple clarity.

She was dressed, sleeping in the bed under a quilted comforter.

He sat down next to her.

"Honey, it's me. Dad."

She didn't wake, didn't move. Lying there, she was once again the child she had been. Her hair, the softness of her smile, the stillness of her breathing. Hank could almost fool himself into believing that she was still the baby he remembered from so long ago. He wanted to tell her a story about a little girl just like her, also named Margaret, standing on a beach near dawn with all the blueness of all the blue skies in the world coming out to see her smile. He wanted to sing her one of the songs he sang her so long ago, "San Antonio Rose" or "Give My Regards to Broadway". She loved those songs, but her favorite of all was "Buffalo Gals". For some reason, she always thought of herself as the Buffalo Gal, the one dancing with the holes in her stocking and her knees a-knocking and her toes gently rocking by the light of the moon. She always wanted him to sing it one more time, again and again.

He reached for her shoulder with his left hand, the one that wasn't bleeding, and he let it rest there, and he started singing softly about the Buffalo Gal.

He knew she would wake eventually, and when she woke, he figured she wouldn't be happy about him thinking of her when she was a kid, just a baby in pink pajamas covered with yellow giraffes, and he was right.

Her eyes opened in the snow-tinged darkness, and she was frightened.

"Where's Willy?" she cried. "You hurt him. I know you hurt him."

Hank didn't know what to say. She was right — he had hurt Willy, hurt him bad, as bad as he could without killing him.

Margaret pushed Hank's hand off her shoulder, then struggled out of the comforter and stood up.

"Get away from me!" she shouted at him. "I've got to find Willy."

"Honey," Hank started, trying to calm her, "Willy's okay. Don't worry about Willy. Marvin's taking care of him."

"Oh God," she said, "*Marvin's* taking care of him? Marvin's a killer!"

She grabbed a winter coat from the floor and started for the door.

Hank reached for her. "Honey, just relax, really. Marvin's not going to hurt him."

She jerked her arm loose and screamed, "Get away from me!" She rushed down the stairs then, taking them two at a time. Hank followed her as fast as he could.

When Margaret got to the first floor, she looked around and ran into the living room. The mannequins sat still on the couch, still watching Johnny Carson and *The Tonight Show.* Johnny was talking to a pretty brunette who seemed to be very happy about something.

Hank got to the bottom of the stairs while Margaret was still in the living room looking for Willy Reichard. "Margaret, you've got to listen, honey, please."

She wasn't listening. She walked quickly into the kitchen and then slammed the kitchen door shut as she hustled back into the living room.

And then she stopped there and looked out over the heads of the mannequins and through the big window behind them.

Hank didn't have to turn to the window to see what she was looking at. A blue light rotated through the falling snow, washing everything in the room with its blueness, coloring the room inside and the drifting and swirling snow outside with its icy glare.

A Crystal Lake police car stood in front of the house, its rooftop light rotating and splashing its blueness everywhere.

Margaret spun around and ran for the door, shouting over and over, "Willy, Willy!"

Hank followed.

On the front porch, Willy was still propped against the wall, his body still crumpled into a sack of pain, his head bent into his chest, blood still dripping onto his shirtless chest and bib overalls. He wasn't moving.

Marvin stood a couple of feet away from Willy, keeping one eye on him and another eye on the two patrolmen walking up the drive.

Margaret rushed to Willy and knelt down beside him. She touched his bleeding face and then turned to Marvin and said in a whisper of tears, "You did this, you killer. You did this. You killed him! You killed him! You killed Willy."

Marvin shook his head and said, "Maggie...."

Hank reached them then. "Honey, Willy's not dead. He's okay. He's just — "

"Just what? Beaten? Unconscious? Dying? Fucked up? Marvin did it!"

Hank told her the truth. "Margaret, it wasn't Marvin. I did it." And then he stopped telling the truth and gave her the official version: "Willy came at us with a shotgun. Out of the dark. I had to stop him. I had to."

"You did this?"

Hank looked at the hippie boy again. Willy was starting to come around. He lifted his head up and then slowly dropped it forward again.

"I did it."

"*Why?* Willy's not a killer. He never hurt me or anybody else."

"We didn't know that. When he came at us holding that shotgun, we didn't even know he was Willy."

She turned to Willy, took a yellow handkerchief out of the pocket of her coat and pressed it against his bleeding cheek.

The first of the Crystal Lake patrolmen stepped onto the porch. "We got a call that two Chicago detectives needed backup. It looks like you've got it pretty much under control. Is this the kid you had to disarm?"

Hank turned to them and nodded.

"Yeah," Marvin said. "This is the kid. He came at us with a shotgun in his hands. He seemed hopped up on some kind of dope. Possibly LSD. We didn't have an easy time subduing him — he's going to need some TLC at the local hospital, I think."

"We'll take him there," the patrolman said. "Who's the girl?"

"My daughter," Hank answered.

"Fuck. Don't tell me — she's the hippie's girlfriend?"

"Yeah, looks that way."

"She's going back with you?"

"Yeah," Hank said.

Margaret turned away from Willy and faced her father. "No, I'm not. I'm staying with him."

Hank looked at her. Yes, she was the little girl he used to sing "Buffalo Gal" to at bedtime, and she also wasn't that little girl. She was a nineteen-year-old college girl with some kind of crazy connection to this beat-up asshole drug dealer. So what was he supposed to do? Yank her up by her arm and drag her into his police car, with her struggling and wailing all the way? Was he supposed to bawl her out in his gruff dad voice? *Wait till I get you home, young lady! Wait till your mother sees what you've done!*

Hank looked at Marvin. Marvin did what he always did when he was faced with a tough question with no clear answer: He shrugged and looked like he needed to go to the can real bad.

The patrolman lifted his hands to Hank in a pleading sort of *what the fuck am I supposed to do?* gesture and said, "It's your call. I got to get this kid to the hospital. He looks like he's hurt pretty bad. Maybe worse than he looks, and he looks bad enough."

Hank looked at his daughter again and then faced the patrolman. "Can she go with you to the hospital? In your squad car?"

"Sure, easy as pie."

"Great. We'll follow you there."

CHAPTER 46

HANK SAT AT the kitchen table. His hands — with their scarred, scabbed backs and smooth palms — were wrapped around his coffee mug. They pushed it in slow, small circles across the grayish-white Formica surface.

He looked out the kitchen window to the backyard. It was still dark out. He doubted there would be much of a sunrise this morning, but he figured it would start getting light soon, probably a little after seven. The radio on the kitchen counter was playing some kind of rock and roll. A group was singing a song about all the leaves being brown and the sky being gray. Hank didn't know who they were, but it seemed like a perfect song for a winter's day like today.

In Margaret's bedroom, Hazel was trying to get her daughter to sleep. They had been home for a while now. Willy Reichard had gone straight into the emergency room at Good Shepherd Hospital in Barrington, and the docs and nurses there patched him up pretty good. Hank had figured that's what would happen. Most of the time the scrapes and bruises and cuts you get in a fistfight — even a hard one — look worse than they are. Hank tried to tell Margaret that while they waited in the hospital reception room for Willy to get out of the ER and Hazel to show up. Hank had called his wife as soon as they got here, and she made it to the hospital in just over an hour.

Hank was glad she came. Margaret wouldn't talk to him, wouldn't look at him, blamed him for everything. She was mostly right, of course. Hank had beat the shit out of Willy the Dealer, beat the shit out of him to the tune of twenty or thirty stitches across his face. Hazel took some of the heat off Hank. She tried to explain to Margaret why her dad felt he had to do what he did. Margaret cried for a long time. But she pulled herself together and listened to her mom when Hazel told her she needed to come back home and get some rest, that there was nothing left for her to do right now at the hospital and she had to take care of herself because Willy would need her to care for him later.

So they had come home and Hazel was putting Margaret to bed.

Hank let go of the coffee mug and looked at his hands. The knuckles were swollen and there were plenty of cuts and scrapes — he'd hurt the kid the way the kid deserved, and his hands showed it. At first Hank had wanted to kill Willy Reichard for what he'd done to Margaret, dragging her from her home, but in the end he knew it didn't make any sense. Margaret was a strong-willed kid, smart and sharp and tough. She wasn't the kind of girl who got dragged from one place to another. She made her own decisions. Always had. It was one of the things that made Hank so proud of her.

So why did he beat the boy so bad? Why had he wanted to kill him?

Hank lifted his hands closer to his face, extended his fingers, looked at them. He guessed he knew the real reason he'd wanted to kill Willy, and it didn't have a lot to do with his daughter.

He looked up then and saw Hazel.

She was standing in the doorway to the kitchen. She was looking at his hands now, the same as he had been.

"Do you want some more coffee?" she asked.

"Sure," Hank said and lifted his mug to her.

She took it and walked over to the stove, filled his mug, and returned the coffee pot to the stove.

"Thanks," he said. "Are you going to sit down?"

"I don't think so. I don't want to sit down. Not yet, at least. I want you to explain to me why you did all that to that boy." Hazel leaned back against the counter.

"Do we really have to do this? It's been a long night."

She shrugged. "Hank, talk. We need to talk. Please."

Hank drank the coffee. It was barely warm at all. "I wanted to kill that kid, that hippie drug dealer."

"Why? I mean, I was upset too. A couple of weeks went by and we didn't hear from Margaret. But I didn't want to kill him. I just wanted Margaret back."

Hank looked across the room at his wife. He wasn't sure how to answer her question. Did she really want to know why he beat the kid the way he did, or was she just talking to fill the silence? His uncertainty stopped him. He'd been married to Hazel for almost twenty-two years. There were things about his job he told her about and things he didn't tell her about, things he would never tell her about. And he'd always assumed that she knew there were things like that, and he'd also assumed that she agreed she was better off not knowing about those things. She was a smart woman, and she knew enough about the business he was in to know that there were things she didn't want to know.

But now she was asking him about one of those things.

He nodded and said, "Okay."

Hazel stood there by the counter for a moment. Then she nodded her head, walked over to the table, and sat down across from him.

"I've been a cop for more than twenty years, and before that I was in the army in Germany. You know all that.... One of the things I've learned is that most of the real assholes, the ones that do the seriously bad stuff, the stuff that you and I hate to even know about, get off scot-free. It's not like in the movies where the bad people get punished no matter how rich they are or what kind of powerful friends they have. Take that kid Tommy Sawa, the altar boy they say killed Sister Mary Philomena. Maybe you think he did it, or maybe you think he didn't, but he's dead either way. Let's say he did it. Let's say he deserved to die, even though he was only eleven. So now he's dead. Score one for the side of righteousness and justice. But what about the asshole who drove him to kill the nun? The priest who seduced the boy, turned him, twisted him into thinking that killing a nun and then killing himself was his only choice?"

Hazel shook her head slowly and whispered, "Hank."

"Let me finish. Just let me finish. You wanted to talk about this, so let me talk."

Hank picked up his mug again and put it down without drinking any more of the coffee. He looked at Hazel sitting across from him. He wondered for a moment if he should take her hands, and decided not to.

"The priest, Father Ted Bachleda," Hank said, "is out there tonight, probably sitting in a bar downtown — maybe at the Palmer House, maybe somewhere else just as glitzy — drinking a fancy twenty-dollar bottle of wine with a couple of his fellow priests who've got the same kind of hard-on for little altar boys as he does. Nobody is going to stop any of these priests. I've been hearing about this kind of stuff for as long as I've been a cop, and I can tell you that neither the Police Superintendent nor Mayor Daley nor Cardinal John Cody is ever going to bother doing anything about any of this. It's the same thing with these drugs. Willy Reichard is dealing drugs, and he looks like some kind of small-time dealer, selling a nickel bag or a dime bag to his friends, but you didn't see what I saw. He's an asshole who thinks his shit doesn't stink. He thinks nothing is ever going to happen to him, so he can do whatever the fuck he wants. If he thinks he can make more money selling harder drugs that can actually kill people, that's fine with him. He can sell drugs, he can seduce our daughter, he can run rings around the Blackstone Rangers, and he can party with the Latin Scorpions. None of that matters because nobody is going to stop him. That's what he thinks. Well, he's wrong, Hazel. I'm going to stop him. I'm going to stop him from selling drugs, stop him from ruining people's lives."

"Hank, that's not how the law works — you know that. You can't try to stop this stuff on your own. There are procedures that you have to follow. You make it sound like the Wild West, a world without any law except who draws a gun faster."

"That's exactly what it is. I don't know yet if Reichard will ever spend time in jail, but I know for a fact that he's going to be carrying some scars for a long, long time. And every time he smiles or frowns, he'll feel it and remember the pounding I gave him. And maybe that will stop him from being an asshole somewhere down the line."

"And what about Margaret? What are you going to do about her?"

Hank looked at Hazel, and didn't say anything.

"Hank, what are you going to do about our daughter?"

"I don't know."

"You going to beat her, too, until she stays home? Is that it? Is that what you'll do?"

"I don't know."

CHAPTER 47

A SUSPENDED COP is not a cop: no badge, no power of arrest, no job. Hank Purcell knew very well that he wasn't supposed to be anywhere inside the Shakespeare Substation, at least not anywhere past the reception counter downstairs. So he owed Jimmy O'Kaine, the desk sergeant, for letting him sneak up here to his office. He didn't want to be stuck at home right now, with Hazel and Margaret and his mess of a life.

Sitting at his desk, Hank leaned back and looked at his hands. Some of his fingernails were cracked, and some were okay. But it was the knuckles that had him staring. They were scarred pretty bad. A thin, fading scab ran across the side of his left hand, and another ran along the top of his right hand. There were plenty of fresh scabs too. He had hurt Willy pretty bad, bad enough to mess his hippie-boy face up and bad enough to leave yet more scars on Hank's hands that would be there for the rest of his life.

But really, his hands didn't look that much different today than they did twenty-three years ago when he was Willy's age, a twenty-four-year-old kid in the army, hunkered down in the Ardennes, waiting for Hitler to send his stormtroopers into the forest where he waited in the cold, wrapped in rags and snow. All that was missing now was the shivering. He didn't shiver anymore. That was good.

Hank turned his hands over then and looked at his palms.

They looked like they belonged on somebody else's hands. There were no fading scars on that side, no healing scabs, and he couldn't see his broken nails from that angle. Hank's palms were pretty much the way they were when he was a kid, a teenager during the Great Depression. He remembered the night he sat on a park bench with his first girlfriend, and she told him she was going to read his palms and tell him what his life would be like. He didn't laugh. He said, "Sure, go ahead." He still believed in that kind of stuff, or maybe he just didn't not believe in it yet, or maybe he just thought being agreeable might help him get lucky.

So she took his right palm and told him stuff — the kind of bullshit kids tell other kids all the time, about how he was going to go on adventures to Madagascar and meet kings dressed as beggars and beggars dressed as kings, and how one day a princess would look at his palm just like she was looking at it right then, and the princess would bend down slowly and kiss it just like she was doing.

But none of that happened, and that night on the park bench was about as lucky as he got with her, and she was long gone and almost forgotten. Now Hank was a middle-aged cop looking at his own palms, still the palms they were so long ago, wondering what they had to tell him.

Were his hands a metaphor?

He remembered the teacher he had in third grade, the one with the funny name, Sister Mary Gummarius. She taught her class about metaphors, and used as her example a poem called "Trees" by a guy with a strange name for a guy — Joyce Kilmer. Sister Gummarius said that a metaphor looked like one thing but meant something different, something bigger, braver, brighter. A tree was never simply a tree. It was a miracle and a gift from God.

Hank still remembered the poem and all of that stuff that Sister Gummarius told him about metaphors; and he looked at his hands, the palms and then what was opposite the palms, and he wondered what it all meant, the scars and the scabs and the broken fingernails and the palms that were still the palms of his youth.

That's when Marvin walked in. Maybe Jimmy O'Kaine had done him the same favor, or maybe Hank's partner in suspension had just walked in like he belonged there and nobody wanted to buy themselves trouble by telling him otherwise.

"What the fuck are you doing?" Marvin asked. "Planning on getting a manicure? Maybe getting your fingernails painted pansy purple?"

Hank looked at Marvin, nodded his head, and said, "Yeah, I want mine to match yours."

"What a sweet thought."

The phone rang then. Since he wasn't supposed to be here, Hank didn't figure a phone call at his desk was likely to be anything good; even at the best of times, police detectives didn't get a lot of phone calls from people wanting to tell them happy news. This time he figured it would be Lieutenant O'Herlihy calling to fire him for good if he was sitting there at his desk ready to answer the phone.

He picked it up anyway. It wasn't O'Herlihy.

He listened for a minute, nodded, and said, "Sure, I understand. The boathouse at Fullerton Beach. One o'clock."

"What's up?" Marvin said.

"That was Father Ted Bachleda. He wants to meet me at Fullerton Beach."

"No shit?"

"No shit," Hank replied. "And he doesn't want you tagging along."

"Well, I'll not surprised he doesn't want to see me. He's probably afraid I'm going to whip his ass even worse than you did."

Hank nodded. "You're probably right. I don't think you made much of a friend there."

Marvin smiled. "Well, then, you better get your nails done pronto for your pansy pal the priest."

CHAPTER 48

HANK PULLED HIS hat down over his ears and tried to sink into his warm black wool overcoat.

It wasn't that cold outside, at least not cold like it had been the last few weeks.

The January thaw had started Thursday morning and kept up through the whole weekend into today; if it lasted two or three more days, almost all the snow and ice that had fallen from the sky over the last few weeks and made itself at home in Chicago would be gone. All that would be left would be a fake spring and some scattered mounds of dirty snow in dark alleys, old snow smeared with coal dust and dog piss and shit. That would be it, except for memories of a merry Christmas that wasn't really very merry for most people. And then winter would come back hard and stay around for a while.

But right now, even that fake spring hadn't quite made it to Chicago, and might never get here before the crappy weather returned.

Standing outside the boathouse at Fullerton Beach, looking south toward Lake Shore Drive and the Loop, Hank felt the wind coming off the lake. Maybe somewhere in the suburbs, the January thaw was like a movie trailer for spring, but here on this slick icy sidewalk, he felt the wind coming down from Canada. Sandwiched between the lake and the still-frozen city, it was still winter, and the January thaw was nothing but a fairy tale you told your kids, if they were young enough to believe it.

Hank looked at the gray sky over Lake Michigan, and at the lake itself. There were layers of ice, a shelf of ice, extending from the beach into the lake for a city block or so. The ice would probably still be there even if this thaw ran for another week. He would have expected the warming to bring some walkers and loungers out here, people looking to catch a few rays of sun while they could, but that wasn't happening. He guessed there just wasn't enough of that lucky old sun.

He looked at his watch again and wondered where Father Ted was. He was supposed to have been here twenty minutes ago, at 1:00 PM. Was the priest jerking him around, calling him and setting this meeting up and then hiding in his car and watching Hank freeze his balls off? Probably not. Father Ted never struck him as a joker of that type. A fucking pedophile for sure, but not a joker.

Hank wondered what the priest was going to tell him when he did show up. Was he going to jabber on about how he wasn't really guilty? That he had been set up by the Evil Altar Boy Tommy Sawa? That nothing was the way it looked? That Sister Mary Philomena had made the whole thing up out of some kind of crazy celibate sexual frustration?

Or was Hank finally going to hear the truth? That the priest himself, Father Ted Bachleda, seduced the altar boy, killed the sister who saw what happened, then killed Tommy Sawa to make it look like the poor kid was a little Judas hanging himself out of remorse?

Hank didn't know what to expect; but he looked up at that moment and saw the priest making his way across the parking lot behind the boathouse, and he figured he'd know pretty soon what was on Father Ted's mind.

⟳

"Sorry I'm late," the priest said, extending his right hand to Hank.

Hank didn't take it, didn't shake it. He looked at the wound along the right side of the priest's face. The stitches were still fresh, still raw. Hank's eyes must have lingered there too long. The priest hesitated for a moment and then touched his face with his gloved hand. He smiled then and said, "I forgive you for this."

"Thanks for the forgiveness — but I would do it again today. Twice."

"Nonetheless. I forgive you and your partner, and I want to tell you that I've already made arrangements to have the suspension lifted for both of you. I can't be certain of the timing, but I would suggest you not make any leisure plans for tomorrow. Once word comes down from the Cardinal, things in Chicago happen quickly."

Hank looked at the priest for a moment and then nodded. "So what's this about?"

"Jesus H. Christ," the priest said, shivering a little and looking around at the gray clouds and the ice and snow still packing the sidewalks and the beaches. "I wasn't expecting it to be this windy out here. I figured the thaw would have made it as far as the lakeshore by now."

Hank didn't smile or shake his head or purse his lips. He wasn't interested in chit-chatting with the priest about the weather or anything else. Hank didn't give him any more time to admire the view. "Father, you must have something on your mind. So tell me already. Let's not waste time on bullshit."

"I think you've been spending too much time with your partner. You're starting to sound like him."

Hank wanted to say, "Fuck you," but instead he said, "So talk. I'm listening."

The priest shrugged and said, "Anyway, thanks for coming without Detective Bondarowicz. He always makes it harder."

Hank gave no response.

Father Ted said, "Mind if we stroll on the sidewalk toward North Avenue Beach while we talk?"

Again, Hank didn't say anything, and the priest didn't wait for an answer. He started walking the curving, ice-covered sidewalk trail that headed down toward North Avenue Beach.

Hank nodded at the priest's back and began following him along the path.

The priest had taken only a half-dozen steps when he started talking. "Maybe you won't believe me, but I'm going to tell you the truth — what I witnessed and what I learned. I know your partner thinks I'm guilty, and I'm pretty sure you think so as well. You believe I killed Sister Mary Philomena and then killed Tommy Sawa, all because I was doing something obscene with Tommy and she caught me at it."

"Yeah, that's pretty much the way we figure it."

"I've never done anything improper with Tommy Sawa, or any other boy, or any girl, or even with an adult. When I became a priest I took a vow of celibacy, and I take that vow seriously."

"So why did the sister come to me and tell me she saw you abusing Tommy?" Hank asked. "Are you calling Sister Mary Philomena a liar?"

"No, I'm certain that Mary Philomena told you the absolute truth about what she saw, but she reached the wrong conclusion about what Tommy and I were actually doing. If she had ever spoken to me about what happened, the misunderstanding would have been cleared up...it's just a shame that we never had a chance to have that talk. I never had anything to fear from the sister, and I never felt anything other than sorrow at her death."

Hank shrugged and pressed his hands deeper into the pockets of his long wool coat. The wind off the lake was picking up. He wasn't feeling any of the January thaw anymore; he was cold and getting colder.

"Father, you're telling me you take your celibacy seriously. Why should I believe you? Why shouldn't I just call your whole story bullshit? Because it's convenient for me to believe you? Because it would get me in line with the rest of the city of Chicago? The case is officially closed already, and whether I believe your story or not, I have to get it all out of my head and move on to the next miserable piece of shit I have to deal with as a dumbass cop in Murdertown. Right? So I'm still not sure why you're telling me this. Why do you give a damn what I think? Are you afraid that Marvin and I are going to come looking for you some dark night and beat the crap out of you, or worse?"

"You can believe that I keep to my vows or not. I can't prove it — how can anyone prove something like that? Only God knows the full truth. He is my Judge, and yours. But I haven't finished my story, and by the end I don't think you'll have such a hard time believing me."

"So go on, then. It's cold out."

"Sister Mary Philomena thought she saw me fondling Tommy Sawa. 'Fondling' is the wrong word, I guess — too soft. It suggests an act of charity or kindness or fondness that's never really there when an adult does to a child what she thought I was doing. An act like that deserves a harder word, an uglier word, one that doesn't suggest loving or tenderness. When an adult, especially an adult who is supposed to represent the love and power of God, does such things to a child, it is evil."

"You're going to have to lay it out straighter than that for me, Father. I don't have the time or the patience to ponder words and ideas and inner motives like you do. What are you trying to tell me?"

"First, I'll tell you the easy part — not that even the easy part is easy," the priest said. "Tommy Sawa came to me for comfort and counsel. He had been abused. He knew that it was wrong, but he was such a good, obedient child, and he never wanted to rebel against the people he had always been told were put in authority over him by God. I was able to get him to explain to me what was done to him, what he was made to do. It was terribly painful for him to tell me these things, and if this is what Mary Philomena saw, I'm not surprised that she thought I was the abuser. And even when Tommy had explained what happened, I couldn't persuade him to tell me who did these things to him. I knew it was a man, and I suspected that it might be his father simply because there weren't any other obvious suspects — but I had no real evidence, nothing I could use to find who did it and make him stop."

Father Ted looked like a weight was bearing him down. He sat down on a bench along the sidewalk. There was no ice on the bench.

"Dear Jesus, I just want to confess."

Hank sat down too.

The wooden bench was cold, and Hank shoved his hands deeper into his pockets and pressed his arms closer to his body. He wanted some warmth. He was tired of all this walking through the ice and looking at the snow, feeling the wind always clawing at his face. He was tired of all that, and tired of listening to this priest spinning his story.

But a confession? Sure, why not? That was what Hank had been hoping for.

Hank leaned back on the bench and looked Father Ted straight in the eyes. "If it's a crime, that's the kind of confession I deal with all the time. If it's a sin —"

"It's a sin."

"Then I can listen, but you know I can't give you a penance or absolve you of anything. If you want to confess to the most half-assed priest in Chicago anyway, go right ahead."

Father Ted looked older now than when Hank first met him. He had just started out at Saint Fidelis Parish then — the young priest that the kids identified with, the one they liked to hang out with, the one with cool, longish hair who knew the words to the Top 40. The guy sitting across the bench from Hank today looked like any other guy approaching middle age who just wanted to go home and sit in front of a TV and watch *Bonanza* or some other aging guy pretending to be drinking highballs and crooning on *The Dean Martin Show*.

Father Ted looked down at his hands. "My sin is a sin of omission, rather than a sin of commission."

"Just confess. If I'm your confessor, I'll tell you what kind of sin it is." Hank could tell the priest needed to spill whatever was on his conscience, and he figured that if Father Ted wanted a gentle confessor, he'd have chosen someone else for the job.

Father Ted looked up at Hank, then back down. "My sin is that I knew someone was molesting Tommy Sawa, and I didn't tell you when I should have — when you first came to the rectory to accuse me of abusing the boy."

"So you knew about it before Sister Mary Philomena was killed?"

"As I said, I knew someone was abusing Tommy. I didn't know who it was at that point, but I do know now."

The wind was coming off Lake Michigan harder now. The January thaw was ending before it had really started.

Hank took his right hand out of his pocket, gestured palm-up to the priest, and said, "Tell me, already."

"It was the pastor, Father Thomas Plaszek."

Hank didn't say anything for a moment, and then he shook his head a couple of times and said, "Are you fucking with me? That old man? He can barely get himself out of a chair without help. You're telling me that he assaulted Tommy Sawa?"

"Yes. That's right. Father Thomas started with him even before I arrived at Saint Fidelis. I don't know how long it was going on. Maybe from when Tommy was six, or even five. I don't know, but it was going on all the time I was there, until Tommy died."

Hank didn't shake his head. Didn't shrug. Didn't say anything.

It didn't make sense. Why would an old priest, an old tired priest like Father Thomas, still be craving a young boy, or a young girl for that matter? Hank had seen a lot of sexual assault during his twenty years on the police force — kids with kids, parents with their own kids, men with girls and men with boys. There were blitz assaults that came fast out of nowhere, and long-term, slow-growing assaults where the perpetrator gradually seduced his victim, and then there was everything in between. The perps were strangers and friends and relatives and teachers and babysitters. He'd even known women to do it. But there were always some common factors. And one of them was that the people who did it tended to be younger, forty years old down to kids who were barely teenagers. Old guys, guys like Pastor

Thomas, normally weren't involved. Their sex drive seemed to be pretty much kaput by then, Madeira wine or no.

Hank told Father Ted as much, and waited for his response.

He didn't have to wait long.

"Detective, I don't know a lot about police work, but I do know something about sex. A lot of my time is taken up administering the Sacrament of Penance, and sex is what most of the people who come to confession talk about. One of the things I've learned is that sex isn't always about penetration and erections, or even about desire or lust. Sometimes it's about other things — the need to control, to have power over a weaker person…sometimes even the need to be cruel, the need to hurt. At least at the end, that's what I believe it was with Father Thomas, what was driving him."

Hank looked at the priest sitting across from him on the cold bench and thought for a moment about how strange it was to be talking about sex, about what sex is and isn't and might be, with a man who was a professed virgin and had taken a sacred oath to remain that way. The world was a crazy place, and most people fit right in. Hank shrugged and said, "Let me ask you a different question. What makes you think Father Thomas was the guy abusing Tommy Sawa?"

Father Ted took his gloves off, looked at his hands, shook his head. "I'm not supposed to tell you. I took an oath to God when I became a priest, swearing that I would never tell such things. It's called the Seal of the Confessional, and I know you know about it as a policeman and as a Catholic. It's my absolute duty as a priest to keep the things I hear in the confessional a secret. The earthly punishment is excommunication, but I'm going to tell you anyway. Father Thomas came to me in confession. Told me about his sins.

Told me about what he did. He did it with Tommy and he did it with other boys too, boys who are still boys and boys who haven't been children for twenty and thirty years. He told me about the boys, about what he did to them, and what he made them do to him."

"What did he say he did with the boys?"

Father Ted put his head in his hands and started weeping.

Chapter 49

THE JANUARY THAW hadn't lasted long, but Hank Purcell wasn't surprised. He was born in Chicago and had lived there all his life except for the years when he was in the army trying to kill as many Germans as he could. And what he knew about Chicago was that nothing good lasted long here, especially not good weather.

A couple hours after Hank shook the weeping priest's hand and started driving his Ford west toward Halsted, the cold wind off the lake was already dumping another heavy snowfall on the city. By the time he got to Tony's Little Italy, a bar and restaurant on Harrison Street he and Marvin liked, Chicago was once again looking like a winter wonderland. All the city's dirty piles of slowly melting snow that had been covered with coal dust and worse crap were now drifted clean by the new white stuff fluffing out of the darkening sky that would look pretty until the next time the dogs came around. It made him want to sing like Dean Martin sang — "Sleigh bells ring/ Are you listening/In the lane/Snow is glistening/A beautiful sight/ We're happy tonight…" — but he didn't.

Pulling up to Tony's, Hank didn't see Marvin's broken-down Plymouth anywhere, but that was okay. He didn't expect his partner to be there right on time waiting with bated breath to hear what Father Ted had told Hank that he didn't want Marvin to hear. Marvin was pretty much always late or absent or indifferent, except when there was somebody to fuck over. Then he was wide awake and ready for anything. He liked that part plenty — enough to be punctual, more or less.

Hank locked the car and walked into Tony's. Whether you were freezing your ass off in January or sweating it off in the middle of July, the place was always the same. There were strings and strings and more strings of blue and green holiday lights tacked up along the ceiling and around the enormous mirror behind the bar. And in the corner in the back, there was always the broken-down plastic Santa statue that Tony had picked up somewhere, probably at the flea market on Maxwell Street.

It was always Christmas at Tony's Little Italy. Maybe that's why Hank liked it.

Tony's mom, Annie, was behind the bar drying a glass when she saw Hank. She smiled and spread her arms out wide, and her eyes said to Hank exactly what he needed to hear.

He walked up to her and took the hug she gave him, and held on to her and held on to her some more, until he saw Tony come out of the back.

"Hank," Tony said, laughing, "what kind of hug is that? You stay away from her for couple of months, and then you show up, and you just give my mom a little boy-scout hug? Let me show you a hug!"

And Tony walked up fast to Hank and wrapped his arms around him and lifted him a foot off the sawdust that covered the barroom floor. "That's the way, *paisano!*"

Hank held onto Tony for a long moment, even after Tony set him down.

Letting go finally, he said to Tony and his mom, "It's good to be here."

Smiling, Annie picked up another wet beer stein and started drying it. "So how's the missus and your daughter — Hazel and Margaret? I miss you all, but I miss them two the most."

"You know how it is. The city's getting bigger and bigger and filling up with so many cars, it's hard to get down here from Austin and Narragansett unless you got a couple, three hours of traveling time. I wish I could have brought them. They both love this place. I'll tell you what — maybe you can fix me up a jar of your red sauce and some of Tony's bread to take home, and I'll pass it on to the girls?"

Annie smiled again. "Sure, I can do that. You get Tony to give you some red wine, and I'll take care of the sauce."

Hank watched her go off to the back of the bar where the kitchen was, and then he turned to the bar and Tony. "I'll take that glass of red…a big glass, a really big glass."

"You got it," Tony said, and started pouring. "Where's your *scooch y guch* pal, Detective First-Class Marvin?"

"Marvin? He should be here pretty soon. We're wrapping up a case and we both figure this is the best place in the city to do it."

Tony pushed a half-pint glass of red wine across the bar. "You're using this as sort of your office away from your office? Is that right? Getting away from the chief? I get it. You know me, I won't breathe a word."

Hank was trying to think of something light and funny to say about cop work when he heard the door behind him open and let in a blast of cold air and snowflakes. He turned to face it.

What he saw immediately was Marvin's back. His partner was pretending to close the saloon door against a tsunami of snow and wind. It would push him back a foot or so into the bar, and then he would almost manage to push the door closed and shut the blizzard out. Over and over he struggled, like Charlie Chaplin in the old silent movie about prospectors up in Alaska. Then, switching to his best W. C. Fields imitation, Marvin shouted, "Suffering succotash, ladies and gentlemen! Please discombobulate yourselves and lend me a generous hand. The fucking wind is trying to break in, and it ain't a fit night out for man nor beast!"

Tony threw his head back and started laughing and clapping. Hank smiled too, and then he walked over to Marvin and pretended to help him push the door closed — and after a great struggle, actually closed it.

"You guys..." Tony said, "You guys are just like Bud Abbott and Lou Costello! Maybe better. You make me laugh every time you come here. I'm kind of glad you don't come here more often. I mean, I wouldn't get any work done, and besides, I don't like to laugh *that* much."

And then Tony laughed some more. And so did Marvin and Hank.

Marvin took his wool cap off and unwound the scarf from around his head. "Jesus," he said as he started peeling off his gloves, "I feel like a stripper up north of the Arctic Circle. When's this shit end?"

"I got just the thing," Tony said, walking over to Marvin and handing him a glass of Jack Daniel's.

"Ah yes, a warming glass of straight sunshine made from the sweet and holy nectars grown only in the land of cotton where old times are never forgotten," Marvin-as-W. C. Fields said, and threw it back.

Tony laughed some more and said, "Why don't you fellows grab that middle table. It's quiet there, and warm besides. A good place to work, to do some police business. I'll put on some music and get you a refill."

Tony walked over to the carnival-bright Wurlitzer jukebox in the corner, put in some quarters, and punched some buttons. After a couple clicks, Billie Holiday's whiskey-soaked voice came drifting slowly from the speakers. She was singing a song Hank knew. It was the one about somebody loving somebody else and how it was no good unless they loved you all the way. Yeah, that's what it was, "All the Way". He wondered for a moment about Tommy Sawa and the old priest. All the way? The kid was dead and the nun who tried to protect him was dead too, left on that basement floor like it was a slaughterhouse. Two good people dead so some old fucker could go all the way, his way.

Marvin carried his drink over to the middle table and sat down. Hank followed him.

As he walked with his red wine in his hand, Billie Holiday was asking him, "Who knows where the road will lead us?" And her answer was there too. "Only a fool would say."

Hank thought about that for a moment, and then he thought about what the point of all the singing was, all the words she was spinning out in a voice that felt like it had been wrung out and hung out to dry. It was the answer only a fool would say: "It's no good unless he loves you all the way."

Hank guessed he was the fool Lady Day was singing about, a man who loved his wife and his daughter. He sat down and looked at Marvin — another fool, a different kind of fool.

Marvin lifted his glass of Jack, sniffed its sweetness, and threw it back.

"Oh yes, oh yes, that's fine, Tony," he said. "Keep 'em coming."

"Coming right up, Detective," Tony said, and brought another glass of Jack over for Marvin.

Hank watched Tony go back to the bar, and then he picked up his glass of wine and drank some. He remembered years ago when he was trying to stop smoking…he was always talking about cutting back, cutting back for Margaret, cutting back for Hazel. It never worked. Now it was the same with the wine and the whiskey. He was always trying to ease up on the booze, drink a little less, stay a little more sober for Margaret and Hazel, and he never seemed to manage it.

Marvin was smiling and staring at him. "Before you tell me what the padre was afraid to say in my august presence, I got some good news: You and I are back in business! The city dropped the suspension for both of us."

"I figured that was coming soon — Father Ted said something about how it was in the works. Before it gets too late, remind me to call Hazel and tell her. She'll be glad to have me out of her hair."

"So talk, Hank — what did the padre tell you that he didn't want to share with me around?"

Hank didn't hesitate. "He told me he didn't do it. He didn't kill Sister Mary Philomena, and he's not responsible for what happened to Tommy Sawa."

"What the fuck are you talking about?"

"According to Father Ted, the old priest, Father Thomas, was raping the altar boy."

"What the fuck?"

"Yeah — the old priest, the pastor."

Marvin slapped his drink down on the table, spilling half of the Jack Daniel's that was left. "Yeah, yeah, I heard you — the old guy. But what the fuck? This is bullshit. You telling me that an old man who could barely stand up was raping Tommy? What the fuck kind of crazy story is that?"

"Yeah, he was raping Tommy, and he confessed it to Father Ted."

Marvin shook his head, and Hank went on with the rest of what Father Ted had told him, about how Father Thomas managed to convince Tommy Sawa that he was somehow the guilty one instead of the victim, got him so twisted up that he got his hands on a cheap knife and followed Sister Mary Philomena down to the basement and killed her after she learned about what he thought was his sin. About how Tommy confessed the murder to the rapist who was still his priest, his intercessor with God. And about how Father Thomas talked the kid into committing suicide to save his soul.

Marvin looked at Hank like he had just discovered that his partner was some kind of idiot. "Father Ted is just telling you this crazy shit to get himself off the hook. You can't tell me you believe this crap!"

Hank shrugged and put his scarred, scabbed hands on the table. He looked at them and then he looked back up at Marvin. "I think we can believe him," he said.

"Why?"

Hank didn't answer for a moment. He was remembering where all this started, the time not long after Christmas when Sister Mary Philomena came to his house out of the snow to tell him about Tommy. It had been good to see her. Talk to her. She brought something — some feeling — to him that he needed, that he'd been missing for a long time.

Hank finally nodded his head and tried to answer his partner's question. "Bachleda said that the old priest, Father Thomas, confessed it all to him — what he did and what it was like — and it didn't start with Tommy Sawa. There were others."

"Fuck."

"Yeah, fuck. The way Father Ted told it, it sounded like the old priest was proud of the way he'd hurt the boy. It made me sick to hear it."

Hank looked at Marvin. His partner was staring at him. It was a look that Hank didn't see often on Marvin's face. Marvin was serious, angry. Hank could see his partner's lower jaw slowly grinding back and forth. Marvin looked away, toward the bar, and said to Tony in a slow, quiet voice. "Another round for me and my pal here, please."

On the Wurlitzer, Billie Holiday had finished singing about the love that was going to go all the way and now it was Frank Sinatra. Hank recognized the song; Old Blues Eyes was singing something that had been a big hit a couple years ago, telling them about the summer wind and the autumn wind and the winter wind, and how it didn't matter what kind of wind it was, the loneliness never stopped. It just went on and on.

And then the drinks were on the table, and Marvin was throwing back his Jack and gesturing for another for him and for Hank.

Hank drank half his red down.

"Hank, let me ask you this. How do we know that Father Thomas did this stuff Bachleda said he did, that it wasn't just Father Ted shifting the shit over to the old priest?"

"Like I said, Tommy wasn't the only one. The old priest told Father Ted that there were other altar boys he used like he used Tommy, and they're not dead."

"We got to talk to Father Thomas."

"That's just it, Marvin. We can't talk to the old guy. He's gone."

"What, he's dead too now? Shit. How come nobody told us?"

"Not dead — just gone."

"Gone? Gone where?"

"Just gone. You know how they handle it with these priests who get into any kind of trouble, especially trouble involving kids. The priests just disappear — they get reassigned, sent to Ecuador or Ghana or Timbuktu, all the way to hell and beyond, to some lost parish where Father Thomas becomes Father Tadeusz or Father Tuomo or Father Timoteus. Or they stop being priests altogether, and start new lives with different names, different addresses, different everything, no work to do but they never go hungry. You remember that priest at Holy Name Cathedral, the one the cops at State Street Station were after a couple of years ago? He was the one with that 'rent-a-boy' scheme. Remember?"

"Yeah, I remember that asshole. He found these immigrant boys from broken or lost families, and he took them in, gave them a home, got them into school. Then he organized a little business renting them out to other assholes around town, priests and ordinary perverts, anyone with some money to spend on sex with little boys."

"And you remember what happened to him?"

"…He disappeared."

"Yeah," Hank said. "Father Thomas is gone like that. Nobody's going to be asking him any questions. At least not any questions about altar boys in Saint Fidelis Parish."

Hank didn't say anything more for a while, and neither did Marvin.

They sat with their drinks, listening to the jukebox selling its songs. Old Blue Eyes gave way to a woman singer Hank didn't recognize. She sounded colored, but he wasn't sure — sort of like Billie Holiday but with a sharper, tougher edge. There was nothing "down home" about her as she sang about how she was feeling good and there was a new day coming, a new dawn. She sounded tough, hard, pushy, a proud black woman demanding respect. He liked what he heard, and he wished it were true. A new day, a new dawn for her and for everyone, one without priests hurting children and getting them to kill themselves, one without good women getting murdered in basements.

Marvin took up the last of his Jack Daniel's, threw it back like he knew there was more coming somewhere down the road, and said to Hank, "You think the lady singing here on the jukebox is right? You think there's a new day coming?"

Hank looked at Marvin, then he picked up his glass of red wine and finished it. Before he could tell Marvin what he thought about new days and new dawns and how fish and rivers and blossoms knew how he felt about what the new day coming would be like, Marvin started laughing.

He started laughing and laughed some more, and he didn't stop. Not for a long time.

CHAPTER 50

HANK STOOD STUCK at the front door of his bungalow fumbling with his key ring.

Winter was back. He was living in a world of snow, wind, ice, and cold again — the Ardennes without the beautiful scenery and the Kraut snipers to keep things interesting. The thaw — like every good thing — had come to an end. Despite what the woman on Tony's Wurlitzer was singing about, it didn't look to Hank like there was any kind of new day coming any time soon.

He was drunk and he knew it, knew it as sure as he knew it was too cold to be outside. He had had too much wine, and then after that he had had too much Jack Daniel's, and why not?

He and Marvin had been celebrating the end of a case that would never really be closed because the guy who had done the terrible things he had done was never going to be caught or charged, or even publicly identified. When you fail like he and Marvin had failed, there was only one thing to do: celebrate the failure. Celebrate it like the Fourth of July and New Year's and Mickey Mouse's fucking birthday rolled into one.

He wondered what he was still doing outside the front door of his house. He didn't know why the lock was still locked. The key was there in his gloved hand and the lock was there in his wooden door, and he couldn't figure out how to bridge the gap from one to the other.

He wished he could. The wind whipped at his back and pushed at his front, and the snow swirled ice around his face and into his eyes. The drinks he drank at Tony's Little Italy were starting to wear off, just enough for him to feel the cold as his gloved hand fumbled some more with the key and the lock. He wondered how drunk he was. Too drunk, evidently, for this lock and this key.

The key finally found its way into the lock, and Hank turned it, pushed the door open, and rushed himself in so he wouldn't get too much snow on the living room carpet.

He was closing the door behind him as Hazel came in from the kitchen.

She didn't look cross or annoyed or even peeved. She just looked tired. "Hank, it's almost midnight. You've got a work day tomorrow."

"Yeah, a work day. Didn't get much of a vacation after all. Got to be down there by 8:00 AM. No problem — I'll be sober enough by 6:00."

"You've been drinking?"

"Yeah, me and Marvin," Hank said as he tried to get out of his long wool coat. "Can't you tell? We were celebrating fucking up another case."

"Looks like it was quite a celebration. Let me help you with your coat."

"Yeah, quite a case, quite a fuckup — so it needed quite a celebration."

Hank took off his hat and his scarf while Hazel unbuttoned his long wool coat.

He smiled at her.

She didn't smile back.

She stowed the coat and the hat and the scarf in the closet next to the front door, then turned back to Hank. "Margaret heard about Willy, about what happened to him."

Hank knew this was coming. "How'd she take it?"

"How'd she take it? She's nineteen and her boyfriend's going to jail. How do you think she took it?"

Hank shrugged. "It's for her own good."

"Well, she took it hard. She found out early this evening. Her friend Maureen called. I don't know how Maureen heard about it, but she did, and she told Margaret, and Margaret started crying on the phone. I heard her from the kitchen, and I came into the living room here, and Margaret was saying 'Oh, no' over and over again and crying, big sobs."

Hank walked into the kitchen and stopped at the sink. He took a tall glass with a picture of Wonder Woman from the drying rack and filled it with warm water. He liked to drink warm water in winter. It was something he remembered his dad doing on cold days during the Depression when there was no money to heat their apartment.

Hazel stood in the doorway between the kitchen and the living room. She looked at Hank and asked, "Did you know about Willy?"

Hank nodded. "I knew."

"As soon as he was discharged from the hospital, they arrested him. He's down in Cook County lockup now. Maureen told Margaret that he might get as many as ten years in jail."

"That's about right. Assault with a deadly weapon, plus his drug dealing. Ten, twelve years was what I figured."

"And you knew?"

"Yes, I knew. O'Herlihy and I talked about the charges a couple days ago, while Willy was still in the hospital — Friday afternoon, I guess it was."

"You didn't tell me? You discussed it with your boss, and you didn't tell me?"

"O'Herlihy knew I had a personal interest in the case, and he asked my advice. I gave it to him."

"And you didn't tell me?"

"I figured you'd try to get me to put in a good word for him because you knew it would hurt Margaret if he got put away."

Hank filled his glass with warm water again. He didn't want to be hung over in the morning when he had to get back to work. The water would help. It always did.

Hazel shook her head. "You knew it would hurt Margaret, but you still did it."

"Yeah, I did, and I'd do it again. Willy's a deadbeat, an asshole, a druggie, a dealer, and probably a thief, too. And it sounds like he had sex with a bunch of minors — from what people told us about him, a lot of his girlfriends were fifteen, sixteen years old. That's rape. That's what the law would call it, statutory rape, even if the girls were willing. Ten years sounds about right for a guy like him — he could go down a lot longer if we had some of his teenybopper ex-girlfriends to testify. He'll be getting out of prison when he's about 34 and Margaret's about 29. They can sort it all out then."

"There had to be better ways to handle this. She's a kid. She's taking it hard."

"Taking it hard? Yeah, but sooner or later it would be harder if they stayed together. The guy's a piece of shit."

"Ten years. Think about what that means to a kid like Margaret. *Ten years*, Hank."

"I'm not sorry. I want that asshole away from her. I don't care what Margaret feels about him. I don't care at all."

Hazel stared at Hank, then she shook her head and stared at him some more.

Hank looked back at her.

"I'm done," she said, and turned away from him. "I'm going to bed."

Hank put his glass down and watched her leave.

He'd known it was going to end this way — Margaret crying up in her room, Hazel pissed-off and walking away from him. But he couldn't see any other option. Nothing good was going to come of Margaret having anything to do with Willy. He was a criminal, and if a good long time in jail didn't straighten him out, he'd probably always be one. Maybe a bunch of years in lock-up would save him, maybe not. But Hank figured — or maybe just hoped — that at least it would give Margaret something else to think about. He didn't see his daughter turning out to be the kind of woman who would wait eight or nine or ten years for her boyfriend to get out of the pen.

He pulled open a drawer and took out a pack of Hazel's smokes. He lit one of the Luckies with a wooden kitchen match, drew in a deep lungful of smoke, and held it there as he pushed open the back door to the porch.

It was uncovered and empty except for the snow that was starting to pile up again.

The stuff was coming down slow, but the flakes were large and wet. He figured the January thaw had released a lot of moisture into the air, and it was riding the snowflakes back down again. If it kept up like this, there would be another eight inches on the ground by morning.

He took a drag on his cigarette. Then he lifted his chin and let the light-blue smoke come out slowly. He watched the flakes swirl through the smoke. Winter sure did have its miracles, he thought.

He wondered if the old priest was watching all of this from some back porch somewhere in one of the western suburbs, the rich ones. Darien, Downers Grove, Naperville? Or maybe by now he wasn't anywhere so close to Saint Fidelis Parish and its little altar boys and its grown-up altar boys. Maybe he was in Bolivia or Columbia or Brazil. Some warm, tropical Garden of Eden with palm trees and sweet nights. Those were nice places, places you couldn't get to from here, not unless you had some money or some connections.

The old priest had the connections and the luck.

He rapes a boy, gets the poor kid feeling so guilty and defiled that he panics and kills a good nun. Then he talks the kid into killing himself — somehow, after all that was done to him, the kid still believes that priests know what's right and what's wrong and can tell you how to get to heaven. And the old bastard gets away with it, gets a new life, maybe a new name, maybe even a new little altar boy.

Hank took what was left of the cigarette out of his mouth, looked at it for a second, and then flicked it hard into the sky, into the flakes falling slowly from heaven like angels.

Tomorrow was a work day.

Epilogue

Nights in the winter in the snow, the old man would kneel in front of the church, weeping until the priest came out and told him to move on.

The old man did as he was told. He was a good Catholic, a good boy, and he always did what the fathers asked him to do.

He struggled off his knees and turned toward home.

And then the priest went back into the dark church and found a pew near the confessionals and prayed for his own soul.

Author's Note

I went to a Catholic grade school in Chicago called St. Fidelis. It was part of a parish that included an enormous and beautiful church, a rectory where the five priests lived, and a convent where the 20 or so nuns lived. I started going to this school when I was 6 years old in 1954, and left when I was 14. When I graduated, the school was probably at its peak, with about 800 students. It was the center of my world as a child; even when school was out, a day didn't go by when I didn't pass the school or see the nuns or priests who taught and ministered there.

In all the time I was at St. Fidelis, I believed what the priests and the nuns said to me and to the other students. They were special people God had chosen to do His good work. There seemed to be a holiness surrounding them, and when I saw the priests saying Mass in church or listening to confessions or patting one of my friends on his shoulder, I believed what they had told me. At such moments they were not just Father Francis or Father Ed or Father Leonard or Father Chester or Father Anthony. They were in some way almost like God. And sometimes I could even sense this in the way the light formed around them and the way their voices spoke the words intended for me to hear and the way these priests stood with their arms stretched out as if they too had been nailed to the cross.

I felt this holiness about them, and I wanted to share it. This desire stayed with me as I started attending a Catholic high school,

St. Patrick's. For a time there, I dreamt of becoming a priest myself, and sometimes I even talked to a priest there about whether or not I had a true vocation for the priesthood — but what stopped me was always the same feeling, a feeling that I was not good enough morally to embody the spirit of God, even if only for a moment; a feeling that I was too much in this world and not enough in the holy world where the priests and nuns lived.

I felt this way about my parish and its priests and its sisters for a long time, as I went off to college and grad school and started a family and became a university professor.

It must have been in the mid-1980s when my view of St. Fidelis and priests and nuns changed. I had been living and teaching in south-central Illinois, and rarely came up to Chicago anymore, but one day an old friend there contacted me and we made arrangements to get together for dinner. As we ate, I started talking about St. Fidelis and the priests and nuns we had both known. I talked about how much they had taught me and how my education there had made me the person I am. After a while, my friend started laughing; and when he stopped he told me about what the priests and the nuns had taught him. He told me about the priest who sexually abused him, and the nuns who knew but covered it up. One of those nuns even married one of the priests to try to help him control his pedophilia.

In the years following that dinner, I learned that this old friend wasn't the only one who was abused at our home parish. Other friends who had been students there told me that St. Fidelis had an extensive history of pedophilia — three of the five parish priests were accused of abusing young parishioners. Some of my friends who were approached by these priests were lucky enough to fight off their advances, and some weren't. In either case, the experience of assault and sexual abuse was something that haunted them; they still carry this burden today, almost 60 years later. As you can imagine, it's not something they are comfortable talking about.

And what happened to the priests? What happened is what typically happens to such priests. They were never tried, never brought to justice, never publicly disgraced. Instead, they were simply moved from one parish to another until they quietly disappeared from the list of priests in the Archdiocese of Chicago. Two of their names have, however, appeared on another list, the list of accused sexually-abusive Chicago priests. That list at present contains over 150 names. What surprises me is that the list is so short — in fact, the name of one of my parish priests who was abusive still doesn't appear on it.

I didn't write about any of this for a long time. I was mainly writing about my parents and their experiences in the war, how they were taken to the concentration camps and what their lives were like there. It wasn't until after I wrote my fourth book about my parents that I started thinking about St. Fidelis and what it was like growing up in that area of Chicago. Thinking about my childhood, I wrote *Suitcase Charlie*, a novel based in part on the fear I felt growing up at a time when dead children were being found in Chicago's city parks. When I started writing *Little Altar Boy* in 2014, it was a different kind of fear that inspired me. It wasn't a fear I knew personally. It was a fear that I sensed in my friends who — 30 and 40 and 50 years after being sexually abused — still lived with their fear and hurt.

That fear is still experienced by my friends and the other abused students at St. Fidelis, and abuse survivors at hundreds and thousands of other parishes around the world. It never goes away.

ACKNOWLEDGMENTS

I want to thank those friends of mine who shared with me their stories of being abused by their priests. I know how difficult it is to share these stories. When things like this happen to us, we are generally too young to realize what is happening or to understand why it's happening. We blame ourselves, we feel guilty, we feel somehow that we are the ones who brought this terrible thing into the world. Often, our response is to hide what has happened to us, to turn to silence. It takes courage to tell these stories, and I want to thank my friends for their courage.

I also want to thank those who helped me with their professional expertise. Richard Banaszkiewicz and Bill Savage, two retired Chicago police officers, patiently helped me understand the workings of the Chicago Police Department. They answered my questions when I had questions, and they told me when I didn't have questions why I should have questions. Thanks also to Steve Radlauer for sharing his knowledge of the jargon used by drug users and dealers in the 1960s, and to Daniella Levy for perfecting the Spanish, both Marvin's and the real stuff.

I would like to thank all my writing friends in the Hill City Writers Group for endlessly reading through my manuscript and reminding me where the commas and the clues needed to go.

Finally, I want to thank Don Radlauer and Yael Shahar of Kasva Press for their encouragement and their patience. My books would be just files on my computer without them.

About the Author

Born in a refugee camp in Germany after World War II, John Guzlowski came to America with his family as a Displaced Person in 1951. His parents had been Polish slave laborers in Nazi Germany during the war. Growing up in "Murdertown" — the tough immigrant neighborhoods around Humboldt Park in Chicago — he met hardware-store clerks with Auschwitz tattoos on their wrists, Polish cavalry officers who still mourned their dead horses, and women who had walked from Siberia to Iran to escape the Russians. In much of his work, Guzlowski remembers and honors the experiences and ultimate strength of these voiceless survivors.

An acclaimed poet, Guzlowski is also a respected teacher, literary critic, and author of both fiction and nonfiction. His poetry collection *Echoes of Tattered Tongues* won the 2017 Montaigne Medal of the Eric Hoffer Awards as one of the most thought-provoking books of the year.

Guzlowski received his BA in English Literature from the University of Illinois, Chicago, and his MA and PhD in English from Purdue University. He is a Professor Emeritus of English Literature at Eastern Illinois University, and currently lives in Lynchburg, Virginia.

His previous novel is *Suitcase Charlie*, Hank and Marvin's first adventure on the streets of Chicago.